treacherous

shadows

An Avalon Valley Novel, Book One

JENNIFER PARR

Treacherous Shadows
Copyright © 2016 by Jennifer Parr
Published by Jennifer Parr

This is a work of fiction. Names, characters, places, and incidents either are the product of the author's imagination or are used fictitiously. Any resemblance to actual persons, living or dead, events, or locales is entirely coincidental.

ISBN: 978-0-692-63697-8

Cover by ◈ *JD Netto Designs*

Dedicated to those who feel so deeply that fiction becomes *alive*.

prologue

Stillness surrounds me. It blankets me in a new kind of security I have never felt before. Father and Mother are asleep. But I am not.

Moonlight steals through my open window and the August air dances in, lithe as a golden leaf fluttering in the breeze. Its sweet voice whispers in my ear, "Come out. Come play."

If I am quiet enough, no one will ever know.

The thrill of recklessness and daring creeps through my bones. I swing my legs over the edge of my bed, feeling braver every second. My pulse quickens in spite of that, and my heart is making a terrible racket in my chest. I have to remind myself it resounds to me alone.

I am as swift and cunning as a mountain cat, moving about the house more silently and gracefully than a copper-winged butterfly; I make not a sound.

A sly smile curls my lips as I reach the back door. It is the only thing that separates me from my moonlit adventure. I must use a precious measure of care in opening it, knowing our history. The treacherous thing once cost me an extra evening of chores, the way it practically screamed on its hinges. I'll not be betrayed again.

With a generous amount of cooking grease on my fingertips, I coax pure silence out of the door and slip through undetected. The air outside, scented with pine and the remembrance of the sun, is still warm. It kisses my cheeks in greeting, as if to say the night stayed warm just for me.

As I inch toward the nearby boundary of the woods, I feel less brave, more daunted with every passing step. The blackness touches everything. The trees reach taller to parade their eminence over me. The same trees I've seen day in and day out take on a new, sinister quality in this darkness. I am just thirteen, and I have never done anything like this. Never stepped foot inside the circle of the woods at this hour, especially not alone. Any degree of security I once felt has forsaken me.

I swallow, and it sounds louder than anything else thus far. I've stepped toe to toe with my own cowardice. It stares down at me with the trees. They challenge me to enter, to leave the safety of my back door. I cast a glance over my shoulder, tempted to return to my bed, where the pitch-colored night and all its dangers cannot touch me.

I turn in surrender, but somewhere in the distance the wind whispers my name. It gently tugs at my nightdress, implores me softly to find my boldness once again.

Before I realize it, my lantern is lit and I'm giving myself to the mysteries the woods hold after the summer sun goes down to sleep. A small flicker of light reveals my path, wards off the all-consuming shadows. My footfalls are cautious, unsure, as if treading on uncharted ground. Creatures of the night call and chant and scurry about. Their sounds will me to leave them in peace and test my fortitude to no end. Still I press on, ever so slowly.

Finally, after thinking these woods will stretch on and on, the trees up ahead part like a curtain, a veil between me and the mysterious new world that awaits. A trace of moonlight shines forth, reminiscent of the promise of a new day's sun. I pass through my curtain, immediately entranced by the silver-white moon and the numberless stars that illuminate the sky. They wink boldly at me, proud of me, I imagine, for having the guts to step outside myself for a change and play in their company. With the foreboding woods at my back and my gaze set on the distant falls, I too am proud.

My feet have grown still since emerging, but unlike in the woods, no effort is required to urge them forward. I bound across the clearing with the erratic pattern of a jackrabbit in chase. Except I am the chaser, chasing down the adventure I have only yet dreamed about.

Already, the water sings to me. I imagine myself leaping into the air, falling, falling, falling, until my entire body is submerged, weightless, wrapped in sparkling bubbles. I'd suck in a triumphant breath and—

Stop dead in my tracks. I'm motionless, save for the blood that surges within my veins. Even my heart has stopped.

I am not alone.

Too far away and too distracted to notice it before, the shadow-laden herd is now all I see. I can make out at least eight. Others in the village warn against horses like these. Feral, territorial, unwilling to be ruled by man. Hot-bloods, driven by protective, defensive instincts that cannot be outrun or outfought.

So backward I pad. Slowly. Back toward the lightless woods, toward my back door, toward my room, my bed. Back to safety and away from what lies in wait.

I only make it a few steps. I hear so many things at once, snorts and screams and stamps, the rustling of brush, and then nothing at all. They've gone.

All but one.

As if frozen in time, I watch the lone herd member come forth from the shadows, with a hide that gleams like obsidian under the moonshine. Our eyes meet. Wonderment fills me. I feel drawn, summoned somehow. The stallion nickers at me. Gives a small shake of the head. Lowers it to the ground. Closes the space between us.

Standing but an arm's length from me, he stares with these big, brown eyes. The kind that are warm and reassuring. They tug at my innermost parts, where I've locked up things like trust and faith and all my secret hopes. The stallion nickers again, softer this time, the way a mare would to her newborn foal. It quells my remaining fears. Be it senseless or spirited, I reach out to him until my palm is filled with his muzzle of velvet.

The stallion pressed his forehead to my chest then, and I could feel the warm rush of air through my nightdress as he let out a gusty breath. It was the kind of breath that revealed something, only I didn't know what that might be at the time.

I circled my arms around the back of his neck and he pressed closer still, as if he couldn't get near enough. As if he was mine from birth and we had been separated for an eternity. That was the kind of breath he released. And that was the moment the black stallion truly stole my heart.

Together, we circled the clearing for hours beneath our glittering, starry host. I hadn't ever ridden a horse before, much less a wild, unsaddled one, but my stallion knew to be careful with me. His gait was slow and gentle, which belied his true potential, for even my untrained eye could tell he was powerful. And very, very fast.

At the first hint of dawn, I knew our time was through. I ran my fingers through his silky mane and kissed his velvety nose—a sweet farewell—and with a swish of his long, black tail, he was gone.

I never did see the wild horses again, but I never forgot my beautiful moonlight companion.

I was a young girl then, and the world as I knew it operated under the tyranny of the Darkness, a long-ruling affliction that had thrust humanity into the hands of darkness for three days and three nights. Its manifestations were fourfold, though it took a good many years before all were realized: The gods fell silent, lifespans were reduced by at least half, only one child could be born to a couple, and those who did not find love and bear a child in time met death while still at a tender age.

It wasn't until I was seventeen that I realized that the Darkness did not rule me in the same way it did everyone else.

Now I am older, my children grown. I bear no resemblance to the young girl I used to be; this new body of mine is foreign and familiar at the same time.

In the cool shade of an oak, in the same clearing where I met the beautiful black stallion all those years ago, my gaze lingers on my beloveds, from my daughter to my son, reflecting on the path each of them walked to get to this point, on their pains, their losses, and on the costs they paid along the way.

But I can't help thinking back to that solitary act of daring so long ago, and how I never would have imagined that night to be the start of something so . . . *magical.*

ONE

pastimes

B eat you there!" I shove past Aeron, gathering up my skirt as I go. The ground is hard beneath the thin soles of my shoes, the air cool under the canopy of trees. The scent of pine is so thick it sticks to the back of my throat.

"Aeria! Not through the woods," he cautions. Always cautioning.

"Don't worry so much," I call back. My voice is heavy, sounding strange in my own ears. But this— ducking under low-hanging branches and jumping over fallen trunks and avoiding lichen-covered rocks that threaten to turn any inept ankle—this is effortless for me. More natural than breathing.

My brother, Aeron, is less agile here, but once he crosses over to the clearing, he's sure to gain on me. He can outrun me any day, soaring as if the wind carries him along. For now, I am solidly in the lead.

Ahead, I can see where the trees give way, parting like a curtain, granting passage to our destination. For beyond the back door of the thatched cedar cottage that Mother, Aeron, and I call home, cupped in the tender-loving hands of these beloved woods, lies a sprawling man-made meadow we call "the clearing." Residing on all sides of the extraordinary expanse are towering trees as diverse as the seasons that change them—birches and pines, oaks and poplars, cedars and firs. In the distance, majestic mountain peaks inspire a jagged western skyline. But most prominent of all is Eliysha Falls, a double waterfall as breathtaking and picturesque as the pool of endlessly blue water beneath her.

This part of the village, the clearing and the surrounding woods, which has been in our family since Avalon Valley was founded, is restricted property. Here we will be alone—we always are.

We've been coming to the clearing since before I can remember, before we were born, for even as we shared our mother's womb, we were here. In fact, this is where Aeron and I were born a little over sixteen years ago. The clearing had been our mother's favorite place, too. It was the setting of most of our bedtime stories growing up.

Aeron inherited his affinity for storytelling from our mother. Seldom was she more animated than when telling of her days spent in the clearing as a child. She would wave her hands, as if painting a picture on the ceiling of the bedroom Aeron and I share, recalling how blue the sky was, or how the wispy clouds sailed high overhead. She'd recount memories as if you were living them right along with her. You could savor the fresh air as it swept through your lungs, feel it brush against your cheeks. Feel the grass between your toes. We didn't protest bedtime, for we loved the stories far too much.

Of course, we have our favorites. Aeron's always cherished the one when Mother was fifteen and her father persuaded her to jump the falls. Mine has always been the one that involved a certain moonlit adventure when she was a few years younger than I am now.

I never told her this, but I used to dream of her black stallion. I would clamber onto his back and he would ask me, "Shall we race against the darkness, you and I?" Then I'd say, "I'll race with you anywhere," and together we would fly through the night, faster than lightning bolts.

I think of Mother's stallion, of her adventurous spirit, as I draw nearer to the wood line, preparing myself for an outright sprint. Though I've never beat Aeron, I pride myself in the fact that I have never failed to try.

Courtesy of the thick cover of trees, my eyes have adjusted to the shade. So when I reach the clearing, the June sun is almost blinding. Still, I keep running, squinting as I go. Lush grass bows beneath my feet. Crisp air brushes smoothly across my face. My long, amber locks bounce gracefully behind me. The air smells so pure, so fresh, almost making me forget the putrid scents of village life . . . almost. For me, this is a great escape. I love it here.

As expected, Aeron shoots past me with more grace than any of the other boys in the village. It's almost poetic, watching him run. He soars, barely disrupting the blades of grass with each weightless footfall. His chin-length hair, slightly darker than mine with looser curls, sways side to side with the motion of each step. He is lean, like me, which disguises his strength, and it wasn't until last summer that he passed me in height. To Aeron, this was an *event*, something that he had been waiting for. Something that could not go uncelebrated.

Setting aside our infinitesimal differences, Aeron and I look alike: our faces are a near-perfect reflection of one another. We even have the same startling green eyes, a rarity in a world dominated by shades of blue and brown.

These are a few of the things that set us apart from the rest of our village, from the rest of the world. The things that make us different. Make us outcasts.

Aeron and I are Dviinu, which is to say that we shared our mother's womb. I assume it is the reason for our striking resemblance. Mother coined the term Dviinu the day we were born, being that there was no other word to describe us.

Before the Darkness, it was possible for parents to have multiple children, siblings, conceived individually, sometimes close together, sometimes years apart. But that all changed two hundred years ago when the Darkness—A plague? A curse? A treacherous shadow that lingers even in daylight?—came and stole a great many things, including the ability to conceive more than one child.

Our mother was the exception to that rule. *We* were the exception to that rule.

There had never been a double birth before. Until us.

And if all that weren't strange enough, the fact that we don't have a father, that we weren't *fathered* at all, doesn't lend to warm opinions of us, either.

I slow my pace the last few yards and reach the northern end of the clearing minutes after Aeron does. Sitting next to the bank, he's lobbing tiny pebbles into the water, making ripples in the relatively smooth surface. He already breathes at a normal rate, while my heart runs its own race inside my chest. My throat burns. Warmth radiates in my cheeks, beads of sweat stream down my temples.

Aeron frees a handful of pebbles, wipes his palm on his pant leg, and says, "What took you so long?" Grinning, he kicks off his shoes, jumps to his feet, and removes his shirt. His next question follows right on the tail of the one before. "You ready for a swim?"

My eyebrows shoot up. "Will you be joining me this time?"

In the summer months, our Rest Days—rarely do we call them Sundays—are spent with me swimming and Aeron playing his flute or sketching, his two cherished pastimes. It is only on rare occasions that he joins me for a swim.

Instead of replying, Aeron jogs toward the center of the clearing to retrieve the honey-colored buckskin satchel he abandoned there during the race. He shoulders the bulging pack and dumps it off again, this time near the bank of the pool.

Then he says, "Absolutely," and rushes at the water, knees high, splashing and hollering, "Beat you to the falls."

I slip out of my shoes and hurry after him, cutting through the icy water quickly and effectively. Aeron may be faster on land, but we are equals here in the water.

I win, but only narrowly.

"And you had a head start," I tease him, raising my voice to be heard over the *Shhhhhh* of the falls.

"I got a cramp," Aeron yells back, but his crooked smile gives him away.

Later, when Aeron decides that he's had enough, we drip ashore, one of us more reluctantly than the other. Tipping his head forward, Aeron rakes his fingers through his hair, but I push him away before it can pepper me in the face with water.

15

"You, Aeron Morgan, are the worst brother in the world!" It's a jest, obviously, but what's more comical is the reply Aeron has at the ready.

"I am," he declares loftily, but his tone falters and he laughs out the rest, "the *only* brother in the world!"

We laugh giddily at our long-running joke as Aeron plucks two towels from his satchel. While I drape mine over my shoulders, Aeron reaches back into his pack and removes our waterskins and his journal. Then he stuffs his shoes inside. I hand him mine and he stuffs them in as well.

Wrestling his shirt back on, he says, "I thought I'd do some sketching along the way."

I shrug. "I don't mind."

We walk barefoot toward the trail that leads into the woods, me clinging to my towel, Aeron clinging to his journal. Where the pool narrows, it forms a tranquil stream, which winds through the woods parallel to our trail, past our vineyard, and on to the south.

I ask, "What'll it be today?"

"Not sure." Aeron stops and thumbs through the first dozen or so pages. Great oaks, big-eyed owls, bored-looking sheep, and tiny field mice stare back at us. Eliysha Falls dominates one page, a beauty even in black-and-white. I have never seen anyone work magic with a stick of graphite the way my brother does.

The journal is Aeron's most prized possession. It is thick and sturdy, bound in dark leather. Mother gifted it to him last year when we turned fifteen. She traded five bottles of wine to Daveed Mercer for it, though she would never let Aeron know that.

Daveed Mercer, the village tanner, is a mountain of a man. He and his son cure animal hides for a living, but Daveed possesses many more talents one would not think likely. It's always amazed me how Daveed's thick, stocky fingers are capable of carving such intricate details into wood and stitching such complex patterns into cloths and leathers. Despite his intimidating size, he is sweet and gentle. But I have never felt comfortable around the Mercer shop. In fact, I do all I can to avoid going near it, though I refuse to make my qualms obvious. Even to Aeron.

TWO

the trail

We follow the familiar dirt trail under the canopy of massive evergreens, oaks, and cedars. The air is chilling here, and my wet dress and hair make it more so, pulling bumps along the length of my arms. I tug at my towel, cinching it at my neck, but it does little in the way of warmth. Aeron, half dry, seems unperturbed by the coolness, his towel slung over his shoulder.

When we were young and our ill-adjusted legs grew weary quickly, this old trail seemed to stretch on forever. Now, start to finish, we could probably get home in a little over half an hour . . . if we didn't tarry so.

Aeron comes to an abrupt stop and points to the other side of the stream. Its current is steady, but the surface is calm and smooth. He's sketched the narrow, winding waterway at least twice, but it isn't what has captured his attention.

"Look there," he says. "I thought I saw something."

I stand at his shoulder and follow his gaze, peering through the trees. I shake my head. "I don't . . ." I start, but Aeron whispers, "Shhh."

Then I spot him. An elk as black as obsidian, his hide gleaming in the dappled sunlight. He stands tall, proud. Watchful. Magnificent black antlers crown his head, glistening like the kiss of sun on metal.

I stay perfectly still, holding my breath as if the sound of air entering and exiting my body will startle him. Even the woods seem to be holding its breath, for it has gone absolutely motionless. It is if the world has been temporarily halted, and I wonder when time will start up again. There is no sound, save for the faint scratching to my left. I know the sound well. Graphite on parchment.

I remain fixed in place; only my eyes search, finding the graphite in Aeron's hand rushing to capture the image of the majestic animal. I can't see his sketch in my periphery, just movements as he strikes the parchment with long, gentle strokes, then some quick, short ones.

The black elk is still, too. He meets our gazes— mine is unerring while Aeron's flits back and forth between the real elk and the graphite version of him—and then to Aeron's dismay, he gracefully bounds out of sight.

Aeron sighs. "I got most of it finished." He turns the page to me, a question between his brows.

My eyes feel as big as an equine's as I study the work of my brother's hand. Huge antlers fork out wildly in different directions. Long, slender limbs hold a perfectly proportioned upper body. Ears alert, it stands just as proud as its living, breathing counterpart.

"It's perfect," I assure him. "Your best piece so far. Mother will love it."

Turning the page back around, Aeron smiles from ear to ear, appraising his masterpiece. "He was a beauty."

"I've never seen a black one before."

Aeron swipes his thumb along the curve of the graphite elk's belly and says, "Mother has." He casts another glance to where the elk stood, but he isn't there.

We continue on toward our destination. Roughly halfway between the falls and our vineyard lies our favorite childhood resting spot. We would stop there at the patch of grass under the oak, granting respite to our jaded legs. When we were thirteen, Aeron carved two big, interlocking A's in the tree's thick trunk. "Our lives are intertwined, linked, like these A's. Nothing can ever separate us," he told me that day, naming the place *our spot*. Suffice it to say, we never pass our spot without paying it a visit. We eat, rest, talk. We've had some good talks here.

Currently, and to my great fortune, the area is dappled with summer's glowing light. I plop down in my usual spot, warming myself under the pleasant beams shining through the boughs. Aeron takes up his spot, journal still in hand. Bringing my knees up to my chest, I fold my towel around myself while Aeron chooses his next artistic subject.

I close my eyes and make nature's lullaby my sole concern. Leaves rustle in the gentle breeze. Birds chitter from perches overhead. A soft buzzing comes from a nearby hive. Water ripples steadily over rocks between the banks of the stream. Everything is so peaceful.

When I open my eyes, I see that Aeron has finished his sketch. He sits quietly with his eyes closed, a mirror of my former state. I wonder how long I'd been lost in daydreaming, and when he'd decided to join me. I laugh, and Aeron's lids fly open. He makes a counter-feit expression of irritation that requires work to be believable.

"I'm hungry," he declares, reaching for his satchel, which is propped against the base of the old oak.

"Me, too. What did you bring? I wish we had some of Mother's onion rolls. I smelled them baking this morning, and they were just—"

Aeron produces a lumpy bundle that catches my attention. He unties the knot, revealing two perfectly browned rolls. He beams, likely proud he's read my mind. Again. I inhale the aroma, mouth watering.

The rest of our meal includes lanky carrot sticks, a small cluster of green grapes, a wedge of yellow-orange cheese, and several strips of Mother's sun-dried, peppered beef.

Aeron tosses a grape into the air and catches it be-tween his teeth. "So," he says, chewing, "did you hear about the new guy?" I shake my head, so he continues, "I overheard a group of people talking to him last night. He walked all the way from Garrison, one of the villages down south. The one on the shore of the Aandorn River." Aeron pauses, and I nod in under-standing, pretending to be interested.

He goes on. "Took him a full day to get here. And in this heat! Poor guy looked exhausted. From what I could gather, he had some kind of falling-out with his parents and that's why he came. For a fresh start. I didn't catch his name but he's a big guy. His forearm is thicker than my neck! Looks like he's about our age, too."

At that my interest is piqued, if only for a fraction of a second. Then I remember who I am, a girl with too strange a past to overcome. An outcast with no hope of finding love.

Because once this newcomer hears of my family's sordid history, he'll be like all the others in Avalon Valley. Aeron, of all people, should know that, so it perturbs me that he acts as though somehow this newcomer joining our village will be the start of something different.

I tear into a beef strip. "Can we talk about something else?"

Aeron eyes me cautiously, but he doesn't say anything. We finish our meal in silence, and even as Aeron packs the leftover portions into his satchel, he remains quiet.

Finally he says, "There is something I've been meaning to tell you." He scratches his neck, tucks his hair behind his ears, stares off into the woods, eyes glazed.

When he turns his gaze back on me, the weight of his expression makes my stomach recoil. He says, "I'm leaving for Jesyel Grove. Tomorrow."

His words feel like a white-knuckled fist to my chest. I struggle to catch my breath. "What? Why? I'm coming . . . right?"

"Aeria," he says slowly, "you're not coming. I wasn't even supposed to go. Jas was supposed to handle the summer trades, but Mother overheard that he rolled his ankle yesterday. Reed would go, but he's had this fishing trip planned for weeks and his group leaves tomorrow for that and, well, Mother thought the trip would be good for me."

My voice is small and my vision is blurry. "But . . . we've never been apart."

Aeron detaches himself from the base of the oak and sits beside me. He wraps his arm around me, and I lean my head against his shoulder.

"It's only two days," he says. But it's funny how a statement can say one thing while a tone says another. It may be only two days, but I know he hates the thought of us being apart as much as I do. "Everyone is counting on me. I have to go."

Several long moments of silence pass.

"Two days?" I say. "Promise?"

When I lift my head, Aeron's expression is heart-wrenching. He blinks back the moisture in his eyes and says, "I promise."

It's too late and this trip is too important for Aeron to try and talk himself out of it. I understand that, so my only hope is that he can convince Mother to let me go.

I should have known he couldn't.

Mother's "No" is an indisputable force that is as crushing as it is resolute. I rush to my room, curl up on my bed, and try to listen in as Aeron and Mother talk in the front room, but they keep their voices hushed. Between that and the distance, I can't make out what they're saying. Occasionally, I hear my name. I know Aeron fights in my defense, but that proves futile.

Aeron is going to Jesyel Grove. Without me.

THREE

alone

A hand coaxes me from my restless sleep.

Aeron stares down at me, his features barely visible in the scant pre-dawn light. He's already dressed for the day, and something that looks a lot like anxiety has settled between his brows. He sits on the edge of my bed.

"Didn't sleep well, did you?" he asks, but amply supplies his own answer. "You were tossing and turning all night. I even heard you talking in your sleep. Something about eyes? And possibly a bear?"

I rub the slumber out of my own eyes. "I don't remember."

What I do remember is this: Aeron is still leaving for Jesyel Grove. And I still hate the idea.

"Come on," he says with a wave of his hand. "Breakfast isn't going to eat itself."

I can already smell the bacon. My stomach grumbles, protesting my paltry appetite from the night before, when eating was the least of my concerns.

ALONE

Once Aeron is gone and our bedroom door is closed, I trade my nightdress for an ivory top and a plum-colored skirt. I twist my hair into a quick braid and tie it off with ribbon, but all the while I'm eyeing Aeron's empty bed in the corner of the room, utterly unprepared for us to be separated.

My mother greets me with a kiss when I enter the front room. "Good morning, dear." She wears a very brown skirt, nearly the color of the bacon strips still sizzling on the plate in her hand. Her hair is also very brown with a hint of red, like mine, and her warm smile travels from the corners of her eyes like roadways to happier places.

I don't want to return her smile, but it is infectious.

Aeron is jittery at breakfast. His knee bobs and his fingers drum and he speaks as if he'll soon run out of words. He finishes eating well before Mother and I do.

We leave our dishes at the table—I'll deal with them later—and head outside just as the sun breaches the horizon. It is unspectacular as far as sunrises go, a muted blue and yellow blush and nothing more. Blanketing the sky, the clouds are lazy, indefinite things that haven't taken the time to properly form.

After fetching Sebaan, our donkey, from the paddock, Aeron hitches him to a lightweight cart weighed down with goods for trading. The cart, loaded last night before supper, is covered with a cloth now, under which exists a complicated yet organized patchwork of Avalon Valley wares. Not a single inch of cart was left wanting. Woven baskets overflow with brightly-colored fabrics and tapestries. Long, wooden crates teem with fruits and vegetables. Animal pelts, wools, and leather hides are piled at the front, along with a stack of Daveed Mercer's leather-bound journals, bundled together with black cord. Wine bottles, nestled in straw, are packed carefully into four more crates beside the ones that hold the crops. Also making the journey is a long-eared hare, eerily similar to an injured one Aeron and I found in the clearing a few weeks ago, housed in a small, round cage made from twigs.

Everyone was so eager to load up their goods, but now that it's time for Aeron to leave, not one of them is here to see him off. It's just Mother and me. I think that Aeron will notice, but he doesn't seem to.

Rubbing his palms as if cold, Aeron says, "Well." His eyes cut from me to Mother. "Well," he says again.

Mother claps him on the shoulder and unleashes her wonderful smile. "You're going to do great."

Aeron grins, whether he wants to or not. He kisses her cheek, tells her he loves her, that he'll miss her, promises he'll stay safe.

Then it's my turn.

I look him squarely in the face. "Be careful. Tell me you'll be careful. Did you remember everything? It'll be hot. Do you have enough water? And food? You mustn't let Sebaan get too tired. Make sure you stop to rest along the way."

I'm talking much too quickly, my sentences melting together so it's impossible to distinguish where one ends and the next begins. My head's so full of concern that it must show on my face, for Aeron pulls me into a hug and whispers, "I'll be fine, but I need to know that you'll be all right."

Tears sting behind my eyes, building but not falling. "I don't know how to be without you."

Drawing back, Aeron takes hold of my shoulders. "I'll be back tomorrow," he reminds me. "I promise."

Feigning relief, I attempt a grin. But all I can manage is a ghost of a smile, and my lips feel betrayed by the small gesture.

"I love you, Aeria."

"I love you more."

"I doubt that," comes his retort. Then he shoulders his satchel, pats the scruffy tuft of mane between Sebaan's ears, and turns toward the dirt road that will take him far away from Avalon Valley. Far away from me.

Mother circles her arm around me and we watch in silence as Aeron leads Sebaan down that long stretch of road.

Will he have to go to Jesyel Grove again next year? I wonder. *And the year after that?* Because if Aeron's trip proves successful, he may find himself assigned as emissary between the two villages, and I don't know which would be worse, his failure or his success.

Mother squeezes my hand. "I'll give you a minute." Then she leaves to start her work in the vineyard.

I stand alone, eyes never leaving Aeron's gradually ebbing figure. Occasionally he brings his hand to his face. Wiping away tears? Just the thought calls tears to my own eyes. My heart aches. I draw in a fortifying breath and sigh, though it offers no consolation. In a voice so small that I can hardly hear it myself, I confess, "I don't know how to be alone."

When they're out of sight, I join Mother in the vineyard. Running parallel to the stream, the vineyard is twenty rows wide, thirty vines deep, and in most rows the leafy canopy reaches well above our shoulders.

Mother pulls a pair of soft, cotton gloves from her apron pocket. She smiles at me. Her expression is kind, understanding. "You will find," she says, "that time moves quicker than you'd like. Do not be its victim. Embrace the time apart. I think it will do you some good. Discover what life outside of being Dviinu holds for you. Maybe try to make a new friend."

Fighting back the urge to laugh aloud, I flash a smile, putting on a façade. Mother has enough to do without fretting over my emotional state.

I get to work, plucking excess leaves around the grape clusters, hoping that busy hands will, in turn, keep my mind preoccupied on something else. Anything else. Anything but this missing Aeron and feeling like part of me is half a world away.

At lunchtime, we sit at our normal spots at the table. The two of us, where there should be three. We utter not a word as we eat, and all the while I'm eyeing Aeron's empty chair.

"It's quiet with him gone," I finally announce, pushing my empty plate toward the center of the table and covering a gouge in the wood there. The result of a supposed roast-carving mishap back before I was born. Fortunately, no limbs were lost in the incident, albeit the table's seen better days.

"Yes, let's enjoy it while it lasts, shall we?" Mother teases, winking at me as she pushes out of her chair. "And let's keep you busy. Idle hands mark time in reverse." She ticks off a list of chores, plants a departing kiss on my forehead, and then she leaves.

The house is so full of emptiness that I sigh.

With a basket of dirty clothes on my hip, I gather up the soiled dishes that litter the kitchen and trudge outdoors, following the footpath to the stream that flows alongside the vineyard. It crawls past the crop fields, eventually meets up with another stream, and together they form the Aandorn River.

No one's at the stream, and I can't help but think that if Aeron hadn't gone, he would have helped me with all this.

"Alone," I whisper, but I don't know why since the very meaning of *alone* is to be isolated from anyone who could possibly overhear when one decides to talk to oneself.

I consider my mother's advice, about embracing the time apart, and decide to take a rare moment for myself. I dip my feet in the stream, the cool water's fingers around my ankles. The sun bursts through the trees, reflecting the bright, blue sky overhead. The warmth feels nice on my exposed skin. My face and neck and arms, all kissed by the afternoon sun.

Pebbles shift under my feet, making sediment rise as I wade in to my knees. My skirt tries to float away with the delicate current.

I walk out farther, until the water haloes my waist. Cupping the cool liquid in my hands, I splash it on my neck, my chest, slide my wet hands down my bare arms. It's so refreshing, and in this moment I am glad to be alone. I close my eyes, soaking it all in, and like the current, my thoughts keep drifting away.

As startling as lightning striking the earth where you stand, the sound of a horse whinny jerks me back to reality.

Well that was short-lived, I think, searching without success for the source of the whinny. The vineyard blocks much of my view of the village.

Taking to my chore, I wash each dish, then each garment, the process slow and meticulous. Top to bottom. Inch by inch. Seam by seam. I fret over invisible grass stains and already-gone dirt smudges and impossible-to-remove speckles of grease. And despite washing each and every item in this ridiculously fastidious manner, I do not feel at all accomplished as I launder the last article: Aeron's favorite shirt.

Sloshing out of the stream, my skirt clings to every curve of my body. Water trickles down to my feet, leaving a dripping trail all the way home. I continue to move like molasses, changing, hanging the clothes on the line out back, drying and shelving the clean dishes. Still, my thoughts roam to Aeron. I pray he's handling this separation better than I am.

The last of the dried peaches were sent with Aeron for trading, so I'll have to pay the orchard a visit next, though hesitation marks my progress as I wend through the village. The sun beams down on my fair skin, feeling hotter with each passing step.

Several young children play in a stretch of grass between two squat, thatched homes similar to mine. The children laugh and run and taunt, "You can't catch me!" A small group of adults are with them, talking amongst themselves, but I don't look at their faces to attach any names, and they don't look at me, either. Instead, my gaze falls to my feet, watching as I scuff the dirt with every languid footstep.

I pick up my pace as I near the end of Central Plaza, an open square at the heart of the village, used for celebrations and ceremonies and other such events. My heart beats like a warning drum, for the Mercers' workshop is a short twenty yards ahead.

I feel a familiar shudder moving through my bones. The same icy shudder that overtook me the last time I passed this way, and the time before that, and the time before that.

Not that there is anything out of the ordinary about the shop, aside from its set-apart-from-the-rest location. In fact, if you were to put any of the other workshops beside Daveed's, there are few differences. The Mercer family brand, a tall, narrow M, is emblazoned on the door, a long planter of red poppies rests below the always-open, east-facing window. The only real difference is the abounding presence of once-living creatures and lye and leather, exuding the smells of death. Currently, five raccoon pelts hang

31

stiffly on a line, and beside them, the coppery pelt of a fox.

As bad as the smell is, it isn't the true reason I race past the shop. *Maybe he won't see me this time. Maybe he won't see me.*

I rush through the orchard gate, head straight for the lean-to, and grab the stepladder, knocking it around a little in my haste. I've come here often enough, but certainly never alone, and despite being nearly invisible amidst rows and rows of peach trees, I still feel hauntingly exposed.

Back home, I heft the basket of peaches onto the worktable, a thick, rectangular preparation table pushed against the kitchen wall. I'm glad to be back inside, but the immense void left by Aeron's absence echoes all around me.

Later, when the drums sound for everyone to meet at Central Plaza to see off those leaving for the fishing trip, I try to get out of going, but Mother says, "It's good that we show our support," and so we go.

The drum beats quiet well before we arrive, and as much as I try to pretend everything is normal, there's an overwhelming sense of wrongness in Mother and me showing up without Aeron.

We stand at the back of the already-crowded plaza, our arrival seemingly unnoticed, save for Mother's best friend, Tavine Mercer. She smiles in greeting, but it is as if one side of her mouth is weighted. That's when I realize that her son is part of the group leaving today. The thought of him, of Iverett, calls a familiar chill to my bones.

If idle hands mark time in reverse, Iverett's presence halts it.

Finally, after the handshakes and shoulder-claps have been doled out, and "safe travels" and "prosperity" have been wished a thousand times each, Reed

Mason, his fourteen-year-old son Elancian, Saiah Daeston, Zede Cole, and Iverett Mercer strike off toward the Aandorn River for a weeklong fishing excursion. Two horses, backs loaded with gear, trail behind obligingly.

"Can we go now?" I whisper to my mother, lifting my gaze at exactly the wrong moment. For on the other end of my gaze is Iverett Mercer's haunting stare. It divides the distance between us to a thread, and I feel like there's nothing I can do to shake myself free from his hold, until at last he turns back and continues on his way. And I am glad to see him go.

While Mother and I prepare supper I put on a show, telling her how well my chores had gone, that she was right about how quickly time passed; but really I'm thinking, "I cannot wait for this day to end." Because in all honesty and despite my mother's reassurances, the minutes are stubborn things that drag their heels.

I don't eat much, naming exhaustion the culprit. I bid Mother goodnight, change into a nightdress, and sprawl out, rather ungracefully, across my bed. Glancing over at Aeron's empty one, I wonder how I will ever manage to sleep in this lonely room. Beyond my window, I watch as the sun settles and the moon takes its proper place as the shining beacon of the clear, night sky. The air is still so thick and warm, making my walls feel closer than ever. Suffocatingly so. I lie there, unable to find sleep, the emptiness discomforting.

Mother has long since turned in for the night, and I am certain she's fast asleep, as it seldom takes her long. I think back to my favorite of all her stories, when at the tender age of thirteen she stole away for a moonlight swim.

This could be my only chance. The night is perfect. And I am dying for a swim.

I tiptoe a silent path to the kitchen, stuff a little food into a small basket, and retreat to the back door. It lets out a small groan as I squeeze through and hurry outside.

Coming to the fringe of the woods, I light my lantern and step cautiously but eagerly into my own adventure.

FOUR

adventure

It takes longer than I expected to reach the waterfall, but by the soft glow of the lantern I make it unscathed. The milky-white moon fends off the darkness, illuminating the clearing as if dawn will soon arrive. The starry sky reflects off the crystalline water, glittering like thousands of brilliant jewels, the kind that are much too precious for wearing, but even more precious to be seeing. It is the kind of magnificence that belongs to dreams and over-glorified memories. A sight to behold. And it is exactly how I imagined it from Mother's story, sans the herd of beautiful, wild horses.

For only the second time today, I am actually glad to be alone.

Aeron and I always come here together, so I seize the opportunity that's never been afforded to me before. I slip my nightdress over one shoulder, then the other, sliding it past the curve of my hips until it comes to rest at my ankles. Never have I felt so exposed. Or so free.

Water roars over the falls. So inviting, she calls my name: *Aeria. Aeria.*

I unplait my hair. Step toward the bank. Wade in slowly, palms flat atop the surface, fingers splayed. A starry sky yawns above me and below me. The water isn't warm by any means, but I acclimate quickly. Until it haloes my hips, that is. Small bumps sweep over my naked body. Rather than prolong my suffering, I sink down until I'm completely submerged. I pop up, gasping for air, my heart thumping in elation. I feel so utterly not-myself that I am beside myself with pride.

I dunk down once more, then push off, kicking up water behind me. Each stroke of my arms propels me forward as I purpose toward the waterfall in the distance. With foamy bubbles for a bed, I lie weightless, staring into the clear sky above, my hair fanning out around me like a strange crown.

Eventually my hunger catches up with me. My stomach grumbles its disapproval of my inadequate meal. I come to the shore where I entered the pool, my basket, lantern, and nightdress yards away. Twisting my hair so the water *drip-drip-drips* at my feet, I lift my eyes.

The massive form stands several paces before me, blending into the black of the woods. My heart drops to my stomach, searching for a place to hide. All I can do is stand horror-stricken, feet planted, unable to move. I don't bother to scream, for no one will hear me.

I am alone. Except for him. A tall, dark figure that should *not* be here.

I try to veil my nakedness with my arms. "I'll just get my stuff and be on my way." My tone starts out confident, but falters quickly. "If you don't mind." I cannot even fathom what someone would be doing here. These are *our* woods, *our* clearing. *Our* sanctuary.

He wears all black, and on his head is a black stocking cap pulled down to his thick neck, a makeshift mask with holes just big enough to reveal his lips and eyes.

He doesn't speak. He only glowers from under his dark mask, the white of his eyes glowing eerily in the moonlight, casting a deeper spell of fear over me. I let out a held-in breath, the sound even more haunting under the weight of his unforgiving gaze.

That's when he launches himself at me, hitting with such brute force that it knocks the wind out of me. I'm on the ground, burdened by this immovable heaviness. He straddles my waist, pinning me between his great thighs. I make a feeble attempt at screaming, but his big hand spreads over my mouth, covering it fully, including part of my nose so that I'm starved for air. The taste of his clammy palm seeps past my lips.

I struggle for each breath, squirming and kicking and thrashing my legs as much as his bulk will allow. I pound at his chest with clenched fists, dig my heels into the ground in hopes of arching my body out from under his crushing weight. But it's to no avail. Same for my useless shrills, which are just powerless bursts of sound trapped in my throat.

He throws his upper body forward so that he hovers more, allowing his enormous hands to push my wrists to the ground above my head. A tear rolls past my cheekbone as he leans nearer to my face. I can feel his hot, heavy breath in my ear as he draws in the scent of my hair. I cringe. His grip tightens in response and he pounds my wrists to the ground, again and again and again.

Closing my eyes inadvertently issues another wave of tears. "*Please*. Let me go." My plea is broken, muffled by sobs. Why is he doing this to me? What have I done to deserve this? It makes no sense. Things like this just don't happen.

Holding both of my wrists with one hand now, he begins to run the other hand over my wet hair. Strokes my cheek, far too tenderly. Traces my jaw line with deliberate slowness. Follows the curve of my neck to my collarbone. I hold my breath, attempting to evade thoughts of what this stranger might explore next.

In a split second, my body is free of his oppressive weight. But I'm too terrified to move, to see what's happened. I hear the rustling, but I still can't move. Tussling. Grunting. Then *thunk*.

Another *thunk* immediately produces a sickening *crunch*. Someone groans.

The rustling ends with weighty footsteps that fade quickly. I turn in that direction to find a dark figure retreating toward the western tree line. Another figure is hunched over on his hands and knees, his breathing hard and laborious.

"Are . . . you . . . all right?" Strenuous breaths separate each word.

I make myself as small as possible as he struggles to his feet. He extends one hand to me, covering his averted eyes with the other. "Here, let me help you." When I don't take his hand, he turns his back to me and says, "Do you have something to, uh, wear?" His voice wavers some, but it is more controlled now.

Unlike mine. I stammer faintly, "A d-dress, n-near my basket." I'm unsure that he's heard me until he walks over to my things.

After a moment he calls back, "There's a basket, but no dress. He must've taken it."

Incredulous, I spring to my feet before properly assessing the consequences of rushing headlong toward a complete stranger wearing nothing but grass stains and disbelief. When I gasp, because sure enough, my nightdress is gone, he turns in my direction. My face feels hot, hot, hot as I screech, "Don't look! Don't look!" He whips back around, throws his hands in the air, and says, "I'm sorry! I didn't see anything. I swear," and I'm left gasping for breath, my heart pumping with equal parts embarrassment and relief.

Then I watch in shock as, still facing away from me, he begins tugging at folds of his shirt, pulling it in different places until it's completely untucked. His hands move to the front, unfastening the buttons top to bottom. He pauses. Then pulls the sleeve at his wrist. The fabric brushes along his skin as he removes it from his left arm, revealing the muscular shoulder and bulging bicep that were hidden beneath it.

My throat closes shut, my heart's about to burst. I attempt to swallow, find no success, and settle for a deep breath. Then another.

My rescuer continues removing his shirt until his upper body is completely exposed, and I can't help but drink in the shape of his body, from his jagged, V-shaped hairline to his broad shoulders and the incredible muscle definition in his arms, trailing slowly down the curve of his spine to the two tiny dimples just above the waistband of his pants, which sit breathtakingly low on his hips. *No*, I decide, *dangerously low*. His back is an agreement of muscles and smooth, sun-tanned skin. He holds out the shirt behind himself. "Here, put this on."

Small steps bring me to him. *Not too close*, I think, lengthening my arm as far as I can. Shirt in hand, I pad backward a few paces, insisting on putting more distance between his nakedness and mine.

"Thank you," I say, louder this time. I throw the shirt around my back. Not only is it warm, but it smells woodsy, too, of fresh pine. I shove my arms through the holes of each sleeve. My fingers fumble a bit as I try to push each button through its too-tiny slot. When I finish struggling with the uncooperative buttons, I frantically smooth my hands over my wet tangle of hair. Then I just stand there, not really sure what to do next.

"I'm done," I finally announce. I sound as nervous as I feel.

Looking to the ground, he pivots, very slowly, and faces me. I can't help but notice his stomach, firm and taut, the muscles like rolling hills and valleys. He doesn't raise his eyes, and I suspect his cautiousness is to avoid frightening me. His muscular chest expands as he draws in a shaky breath. It occurs to me then that maybe, just maybe, he's a little nervous, too.

My face feels flushed—on fire, really—as I study his features. Taller than me. Dark, brown hair, long, and tousled from his recent wrestling match. Looks like he hasn't shaved in days, which does little to weaken the curve of his masculine jawline. His unfamiliar face is strained with concern. I wonder if this is the newcomer Aeron was telling me about.

"So, are you all right?" he asks. "Are you hurt anywhere?"

"I'm not hurt." My head is spinning, though no longer on account of being knocked to the ground. "You?"

"Me? I'm fine. My hand stings a little." He holds it out, examining it. "I think I broke his nose," he proclaims proudly, meeting my eyes for the first time.

That's when my stomach ties up in terrible knots, and suddenly I can't breathe again with this invisible weight on my chest. Time stands perfectly still, and I see a glimpse of something, something amazing. Something that could be. . . . If only my name weren't Aeria Morgan.

"Do you know who that was?" he asks. I think he's working to stifle a smile.

I shake my head, sure that speaking one word will reveal the thousands of things I'm thinking.

His eyes tighten. "What were you doing here alone?"

Something dawns on me. My voice is small, sheepish. "Did you . . . follow me? How did you know . . .?"

I've already taken several steps back when his arm stretches into the void between us. "No, it's nothing like that. I swear it. Please, don't go."

He says it with such conviction that I stop.

I wait, not entirely convinced.

"It's kind of a long story." He purses his lips, as if deciding whether or not to elaborate. "I saw you earlier today, at the stream. Then, while I was talking to a few of your neighbors, you walked past us, kicking up dirt as you went on your way. I just kept seeing you everywhere. At the well, the plaza. And then sneaking out." He looks at me expectantly, waiting for some kind of explanation perhaps.

I give none.

"I didn't follow you at first, you have to believe me. Then I saw a very insidious-looking individual go into the woods after you, so I decided to make sure you were safe, that's all." He blushes and his mouth works a little. Definitely holding back a smile, but I can't figure why. "I didn't know if you were expecting him, or if he had some *ulterior* motive," he adds, a suggestive arch to his brows. "I ran as fast as I could when he came at you."

There is a long span where I simply digest his story. What would have happened if he hadn't come? I can only imagine, except I don't want to.

"I'm Lyam, by the way. Lyam Trey." He offers his hand.

I come closer to put my hand in his—it's rough, but warm—and I am instantly intrigued by his unusual eye coloring. They're a sort of golden ochre, haloed by a rim of rich brown. I think at first, *I have never seen such eyes*, and then I realize with a bit of a start that that isn't true. *My dream last night. I remember now. He saved me from a bear. They were* his *eyes. Lyam's eyes.*

I don't offer my name. "Thank you again. I'm truly grateful." My lips curve into a bashful smile, and now I'm the one working to hold it in.

Lyam gestures for me to sit, lowering himself to the thick grass. I follow, sitting on my knees, tugging at his shirt to cover as much exposed skin as possible.

A stillness sits between us. There's something comforting about being in his presence. I feel drawn to him, as if some uncontrollable force connects us. That somehow it brought us to this very place in time. In all actuality, I owe him my life.

He's close enough so I could place my palm on his toned chest, or trace the waves of his abs with the tip of my finger. Admittedly, part of me wants to. And is it only my imagination, or is the warmth that surrounds me an indulgence of his body and not the warm night air? The only sound I hear is that of my heart, thundering like hooves with each passing moment of silence. I wonder if it is as resonant to him as it is to me.

Beyond Lyam, the shimmering pool looks like an extension of the vast sky, the way it glitters with stars. I force my eyes there, but struggle to govern them wholly. When my resolve does falter, I find him gazing hypnotically at me from under long, black lashes. My eyes shy away every time, but I am powerless to keep them away long. I have never, ever felt so captivated.

It's Lyam who breaks the silence. "You're Aeria, right?"

So he knows who I am.

My heart sinks a little. Especially because my name sounds so heavenly on his lips. I can tell he doesn't know much yet, but soon he will, so I am certain this will be both our first and last conversation.

"So, what brings you to Avalon Valley?" I'm buying seconds, minutes, whatever I can, but I'm also genuinely curious.

He chuckles. "Another long story."

"I don't mind." My focus shifts to my lap, afraid I'm being too forward.

I hear the smile in his voice. "All right," he concedes. "I came from Garrison, as you may have heard. My mother does odd jobs around the village and my father's a carpenter. He taught me everything I know. I always worked hard for them, but the older I got, the more they began pressuring me."

"Pressuring you how?"

"They could see that I had plenty of friends, but I just wasn't . . ." His eyes dart around, searching for the right words. Beginning again, he says, "I just wasn't *connecting*."

My breath catches. "Oh."

"They were concerned," he goes on, "that I was already seventeen and still hadn't found someone. As much as I tried to explain it, they just couldn't understand, but Darkness be damned, I would rather risk my life than marry someone I do not love." A blush tints his cheeks as the last word rolls off his tongue.

"All they could talk about was finding me a wife. They would arrange for these visits, you see, hoping to *persuade* me." He smiles widely, his eyebrows rising in a suggestive manner that is positively charming.

"Sounds terrible," I say.

"Yes, well, it was, actually."

"Then what happened?" I'm becoming more and more comfortable being myself with him. Perhaps it's the kindness in his eyes when they look into mine.

"Then the requests became demands and I decided I couldn't take it anymore. I packed up some food and clothes and left. I knew it would be too easy to find me if I went to Falcon Crest or Crowellhaven, so I came here. And everyone was so welcoming, right from the beginning. I knew I'd be able to start a new life here."

I think of my mother and how she would feel if she woke one morning and either Aeron or I had vanished. "Don't you think they deserve to know where you are? That you're safe? Why you left?" It's not really my business, but I continue anyway. "They must be terrified. Not to mention the fact that they're probably wasting time and energy looking for you."

Lyam's forehead furrows, thoughtful.

I try feigning enthusiasm and change the subject. "Maybe you will find what you're looking for here, and they'll be happy, too. There are a few girls who aren't Promised yet. Not Sama, she's Promised to Alahn. I take that back, it's not official yet, but it will be soon. But give it some time and I'm sure you'll have a connection with someone. Have you met Satr—"

Pressing a finger to my lips, Lyam draws nearer. He stares into my eyes and whispers, "What if I've already found it?"

I can't help biting my lip. My heart goes still. So does the rest of me. I can feel my blood heating and burning and surging through every inch of my body.

We sit in silence, only this time my gaze doesn't avoid meeting his. His warm hand reaches out for mine, interlocking our fingers so that our two hands become one. Our eyes never part.

Until Lyam forces himself to his feet, brows scrunched. An air of disappointment hangs around him. I can see it in the set of his eyes, his lips, like he can't bring himself to say, "I should get you home." But he does.

"All right," I breathe, unsatisfied.

Lyam retrieves my basket and my still-lit lantern, my hand firmly in his. We don't say a word the entire way back, and all the while I'm recounting in my head the decisions I had made and the events that brought me to this very moment, and I do not regret a thing.

When we reach the edge of the woods behind my home, Lyam stops, unwilling to leave the dark cover of the boughs. He snuffs out the light of the lantern and faces me, holding my hands to his solid chest.

"Your brother, Aeron, he'll be back tomorrow?"

I nod.

"I need you to do something for me. Promise you won't come here again after dark. In fact, don't come here at all. Stay with Aeron. Can you do that?" His whispered request is heartbreaking.

All I can manage is another small nod.

Lyam takes one of my hands and closes his around it. "Goodnight, Aeria. Sleep well." Then he lifts my hand to his mouth with calculated slowness . . . and bestows upon it a kiss.

The world sways a little and I can scarcely think clearly. Somehow, I muster up enough clarity of mind to say, "Goodnight."

My fingers leave his grasp slowly as I turn toward home. Returning as cautiously as I had left, I lie in my bed, still wearing his too-big shirt, but my heart refuses to settle. I'm torn between the events of the night, confused and terrified by the attack, but overwhelmingly consumed with thoughts of my strong and breathtakingly handsome rescuer.

I relive our moments together. The way he undressed before me. His strange eyes burning into mine. Soft, sweet lips pressed against my hand.

I can't get him out of my head. All day I had loathed being by myself. Then this perfect stranger enters my life, my mind, and now . . .

Now, I can't get a moment alone.

FIVE

longing

Under lofty peaks of thick, forest pines, alive with the echoes of a multitude of squirrels barking and birds chattering, we walk hand-in-hand. Sapphire-crested butterflies flutter gracefully around us, carefree, dancing in the pleasant breeze. The soft earth squishes beneath our bare feet as we approach our destination, a lush meadow that is ours alone. His strange, ochre eyes gaze longingly into mine, wanting. My heart pounds with anticipation, my hand trembles in his. This feeling is new, exciting. Unlike anything I've ever felt before. I feel loved in a way that keeps my blood boiling through my veins.

Soon, storm clouds roll in, darkening the already-shadowy woods. The sun has vanished. Lightning blazes across the sky. Thunderous rumbles sound in the distance. Rain begins to fall past the treetops, and we're drenched in no time. My hair mats to my forehead, my neck, my clothes pasted to my body. Rainwater runs down my face, gets in my eyes and mouth, drips off the tip of my nose.

He turns to me. Inches closer, closer, closer to my lips. My eyes shut. My breath stills.

But the moment is stolen by rustling in the brush. My eyes jerk open at a sound, a low growl that summons chills from my very core.

The creature rises slowly, as if unfurling itself inch by inch, joint by joint. The monstrous black bear glares at us, his enormous eyes wild with fury. He growls again, his ravenous teeth bleeding saliva.

In a flash, we're dashing through the dense forest, forcing branches out of our way, and I ignore the ones that drive up into the soles of my feet.

The once-peaceful scenery blurs with each fleeting stride, strides that profit us little advantage against our four-legged pursuer. When we reach a jagged cliff overlooking a treacherously foaming river, we do not hesitate. Still hand-in-hand, we make the leap. I brace myself for impact, wondering if an icy death is preferred over the mangled one we just escaped.

The frigid water swallows us whole, tries to drag us to its depths. We gasp when we finally break the surface, drawing oxygen deep into our lungs, loud and long.

I gasp, searching for his hand. It isn't there.

He isn't there.

Soft, dry fabric fills my fists. *A . . . blanket?* I suck in a deep breath. *Bacon?*

My eyelids part slowly, batting back the sudden brightness. Sunlight spills past the window, bold and purposeful, despite the curtains that try to hold it back. I find myself staring at the ceiling of my once-dark bedroom, clutching my blanket in trembling hands.

A dream? Was it all a dream? I sigh, a pitiful little sound. My Lyam wasn't real. I had dreamed the whole thing. Sadness washes over me like the downpour of my nighttime fantasy.

I raise my hand to wipe stray hairs from my face. Then I see it.

Lyam's white shirt sleeve hangs loosely on my wrist.

No, it *was* real—save for the surging mass of black bear.

Images of last night flash through my mind. My naked moonlit swim; the dark figure that hurled himself at me; the handsome stranger rushing to my rescue, giving me the shirt off his back; the mesmerizing glances we exchanged.

The cadence of my heart is as rapid as it had been last night.

Two things strike my memory. One, this dream was the same dream I had two nights ago, only I couldn't remember it until I looked into Lyam's eyes. The second is that Lyam had mentioned Aeron by name, knew that he was my brother. Could he know all there is to know about me and be undaunted by it nonetheless? And further, was it possible that Lyam had felt that same connection I had?

What if I've already found it?

His words cause a flurry within me. I'm not absolutely sure of their meaning, but I long to find out.

The savory scent of bacon begins to pour into my room. I'm starving. My stomach roars in agreement.

I unbutton Lyam's still woodsy-smelling shirt, picturing him—his back, his arms, the shape of his shoulders—as he undressed. I drink in the shirt's powerful aroma, deeply. *He's not getting this back*, I decide unequivocally, indulging in his scent again. I pull it close once more, then tuck it under my pillow. It leaves a conspicuous lump, which I pat flat.

I am purposeful in choosing my wardrobe, lifting a pale, blue cotton dress from the cedar chest at the foot of my bed. Its braided shoulder straps are feminine and alluring. The embroidered bodice hugs my torso, highlighting my shapeliness. The hem falls gracefully below my ankles.

This is my favorite dress. I rarely have an opportunity to wear it. Aeron's return home will serve as the perfect guise.

Next, I work through the tangled mess that is my hair and chuckle, imagining what Lyam would think if he saw me like this.

"Oh good, you're up," Mother says when I reach the kitchen. "Well don't you look lovely! Anyway, I was just about to come get you. I'm not used to Aeron being gone." She says this because Aeron usually wakes me. "It seems we're both a little lost without him."

I eat too fast as Mother tells me of her plan to welcome Aeron home with his favorite supper. As she ticks off the resulting chores, in addition to my other duties, I'm still inhaling my food as though it can't possibly reach my stomach fast enough. My chest burns like I've swallowed embers and I give pause, a strip of bacon pressed between my teeth.

I nearly jump out of my chair when someone knocks on our door. My bacon rattles against my plate as an ominous realization, one that I had previously overlooked, thunders inside my chest like a brewing storm. Could it be possible that my attacker lives here in Avalon Valley?

Heart pounding in my ears, I can barely make out Tavine's voice at the door. My vision floods with familiar faces of men I've known my whole life as I work to reconcile them to what I know of my attacker, but I don't have much to go on.

He towered at least a full head above me, instantly eliminating those vertically ill-endowed. I rule out many based on body mass alone, or lack thereof, really; I specifically remember the way his heaviness crushed me to the ground, knocked the breath out of me.

That leaves the tall, strong men of the village as potential suspects. Save for one last thing. My entire body quakes as I recall those dark, dark eyes boring into me from behind that black mask.

I have to find out who did this to me.

My head's in a whirlwind as I try to sort the safe and innocent from those who could be at fault. But that isn't enough. Whoever did this to me has to be wearing some sort of physical evidence of his confrontation with Lyam. Swelling, bruising, a cut along the bridge of his nose, something. And those are not things that can be easily hidden.

The front door closes and Mother returns to the table. "Daveed's gone trapping for the day," she tells me, "so Tavine will be joining us for lunch."

I nod, smile, tone down my smile, tuck my shaky hands beneath the table, and rearrange my features, but the ability to summon "normal" has evaded me.

Mother raises a single brow. "Are you all right?"

"Ate too fast," I choke out, placing a hand over my runaway heart.

I hate that I can't tell her, but I have to keep my mouth shut. One of Avalon Valley's oldest laws states that if a newcomer is involved in an act of violence, whether the act was instigated by the newcomer or not, he—or she—will be banned from Avalon Valley. Forcibly removed, if necessary.

The story goes that there was once a great divide that broke the heart of Avalon Valley. Time eased the pain, but it was replaced with distrust. For two years later, a newcomer arrived to call Avalon Valley home, and when a stallion went missing some weeks later, followed by three more, the newcomer was confronted. A bloody fight ensued.

As painful as the loss was, no one could prove the newcomer's involvement, so there was nothing to be done. But a scout was sent to Jesyel Grove in secret, in search of the missing horses. Under the cover of night, he discovered a questionable-looking structure, recently and hastily constructed, just beyond the fringe of the woods there. Inside were four stallions. All bore Avalon Valley family brands. The newcomer was never seen again.

There are a handful of similar stories, each with its own unique circumstances, each with a similar ending.

I have to find Lyam. I have to warn him. He can't tell anyone.

The thought that follows makes my pulse trip. *What if he already has?*

Outside, the sun smiles on me, bright and pleasant. The daylight is comforting in a way I've never experienced before. A promise of safety. A promise that the truth cannot hide for long.

Driven by a sense of purpose, I move throughout the village, eyes alert rather than planted to the worn, dirt path beneath my feet. I head for Saeth Brown's workshop, hoping to find Lyam there, being that he and Saeth are both carpenters.

I've scratched Saeth from my mental list of suspects, owing to the fact that his blue-gray eyes are too unlike the dark ones from last night to author any mistrust. Which is a good thing, because he certainly has the height and strength working against him.

The door to the shop is open, as are the two shutters opposite. Saeth stands at his workbench, his broad back to me. I see his elbow glide from side to side. Sanding, perhaps.

To my dismay, Saeth is alone.

My attention after that is divided into three parts: looking for my attacker, looking for Lyam, and looking like I'm doing chores.

Making my way to the community crop field, I see Isa Lofton, the final authority on all things farming, handily negotiating a wheelbarrow full of cucumbers. I've ruled him out based on pole-like leanness alone. Slowing the barrow to a stop, he tips the brim of his big, straw hat at his wife Shara. She curtsies to him, flashing her bright smile, and as Isa continues on his way, Shara returns her attention to Tavine Mercer and Hinna Solmon.

I pass a group of children playing catch while the doctor tends to one that cries out in pain. Even if he fit each and every description of my attacker, I would still have no misgivings about Doctor Solmon because he's been such a godsend to my family. As it is, being I can stand toe-to-toe with him and nothing in my line of sight is obstructed, uncertainty about his character flies right over his strikingly low shoulders.

His daughter, Satrie, helps Isa's daughter, Eleaz, carry a heavy bucket of water, which sloshes around, dappling both of their dresses with dark water spots. They're giggling about it, and I can't help but feel a pang of jealousy at how easy they make friendship look.

The Drake men are headed to the barn, I assume, with a buckskin foal that looks more interested in the grass than the destination. Lotz and his son, Turstan, though bestowed with heft and brawn and lofty stature, have also been blessed with the bluest of eyes, sparing them from suspicion as well.

Lotz clucks his tongue at the foal, once, twice, and I'm thinking the youngster ought to mind his master when all at once he stops clipping the grass, lifts his head, casts a curious gaze my way, and on the third cluck, the foal moves on obediently.

I'm returning from the stream when I see a circle of men gathered up ahead. Their conversation booms mirth and camaraderie but still my stomach twists, warning that my attacker could be among them.

Jas Eland, who was supposed to leave for Jesyel Grove yesterday, faces my direction, as does Owan Harris. What Owan lacks in brawn he makes up for in height. And Jas? Jas has enough heft for the both of them, all of which he struggles to keep off his injured ankle, a set of crutches tucked in the crook of his arms.

The three remaining men have their backs to me. Arms crossed, I recognize Saeth's father, Thellan, by his mop of dark hair and rigid posture. I call up the image of his serious, brown eyes and cringe. Beside him is our leader, Chief Cole, his slick, black hair gathered at the nape of his neck. I imagine his tiny eyes set in his leathery face and almost laugh at myself for considering him for even a second. At his flank is our lawkeeper, Liet Els, a man as stern as they come, with a penetrating gaze to boot.

So much of me wants to turn around and go another way, but I have to know. I have to get a look at Thellan's face. At Liet's.

It's been two hundred years since the gods, brothers Autors and Zveers, creators of man and beast respectively, fell silent, and though I do not know if they can still hear us, I send up a petition nonetheless, asking—no pleading—that neither of these men is responsible for what happened to me.

I skirt around the group, heart about to burst, knees fluid as water, and throw a backward glance over my shoulder. Thellan's face is clearly unmarred, and I let out a tiny breath. But my view of Leit is obstructed by Jas, and soon my quick glance becomes lingering. The last thing I want to do is draw attention to myself, but leaving without seeing him will positively ruin me. The lingering borders on staring and then finally, finally Jas shifts his weight and Liet's face comes into view. The rush of relief is so sweet and so sudden that I have to hide my smile with my shoulder and speed away.

As the morning continues to wear on and my list of suspects grows shorter, I've halfway convinced myself that I was wrong to think someone here could be involved in something so atrocious. Aside from a general distaste for my family, these really are good people. Hard working and honest. Violence is just not in their nature.

By lunchtime I've searched nearly every face in Avalon Valley, but I still haven't seen Lyam. Yesterday he said he had seen me all over the village and I'd been none the wiser. So where is he now when I am so desperate to find him?

Oh, how I wish we were in the clearing again, just he and me. My cheeks feel warm, remembering back to my dream, how he turned to kiss me. And how my lips longed for his. Though it was only a dream, it felt so real.

Before I know it, I've daydreamed myself home. Mother's in the kitchen slicing peaches. "For cobbler," she tells me, though I haven't asked.

Onion rolls are already rising on the prep table for Aeron's welcome-home supper—they're his favorite, too. Beside them is the basket of carrots, peppers, red potatoes, and string beans I picked earlier.

Without looking up, Mother says, "How was your morning, sweetheart?"

I lie, "It was fine."

"Don't worry, Aeron will be home soon. Then everything will go back to normal."

It's a kind sentiment, but she has no idea how wrong she is. My life will never return to normal, and there's a part of me that's glad. For a girl who's going to die if she doesn't find love, living through the pain of my attack seems like a small price to pay for the chance at a relationship.

I play along though. "I know."

I grab a knife and a peach, and Mother and I slice in silence for a while. Aeron's always been the chatty one, and without him there seems to be less to talk about. When we finish I excuse myself, using fetching a bottle of wine from the shed as my ruse. *Lyam has to be somewhere!*

Once again my eyes dance around, searching but not finding. I slow my pace to a snail-like one, seeing many of the same faces as earlier, accompanied now by some I had not seen. But never my attacker's. And never Lyam's.

Tavine comes over. We eat lunch. I wash the dishes in the stream.

I continue my search, but my heart grows more and more leaden as time slips by. For still, there is no sign of Lyam anywhere.

SIX

deliveries

Supper preparations are nearly complete when we hear a small commotion. Optimistic at heart, Mother sings Aeron's name.

We rush outside and find that a semicircle has formed, all gazes set on the two figures in the distance: Aeron and Sebaan, side by side, the wooden cart in tow. Even from afar, they look weary from their travels and the heat.

Being the patient soul that I am, I run down the path to greet him.

I throw my arms around his neck, never mind how tired he may be. "You look good, baby brother."

Aeron gives me a wry smile, and I think he's going to comment about my dress, but instead he says, "I'm only younger by twenty minutes."

I give him a tiny shove. "I'm glad you're home."

We walk back together to where the small semicircle has formed. Now it has grown into something louder, larger, and much more animated. And still more come. This peeves me because they're more concerned with the status of the things traded for than the one who did all the legwork of the trading. If it were anyone else standing beside that cart, this would only be partly true.

I am doubly peeved because I keep coming up with the same results as before, unable to find the one face I hope to see.

"Please, let my son come home and rest a bit," Mother says, trying to gently disperse the crowd to give Aeron some space. "He is weary and hungry from his travels. We will deliver your goods to each of you personally. Thank you for your patience." Her method is effective, though some grumble in hushed tones.

It's not the usual way of doing things, but I suspect there's a reason behind Mother wanting him to hand deliver the goods. An image-boost, of sorts. It reminds me of two springs ago when Aeron and I had the grand idea to spend an entire Rest Day making date loaves for the entire village. Unfortunately, the effect was short-lived.

"Welcome home," Mother says, planting a kiss on his cheek. She hooks her arm around his shoulder. "Let's get you inside. I can't wait to hear about your journey."

She doesn't have to, for no measure of time away, no degree of heat, no length of travel or absence of a meal could knock the wind out of my brother.

"It was hot," he starts, "but that's to be expected. Jesyel Grove was beautiful, more beautiful than I ever imagined. And everyone was so friendly and welcoming. Their chief offered me a place to sleep, and they took good care of Sebaan, too. I missed you both terribly. It's a long way with no one to talk to but a donkey." Aeron turns to Sebaan and scratches behind his ear. "No offense, old boy."

I'm sure none was taken, seeing as Sebaan drives his head into Aeron's side, hoping for another scratch or two.

We walk Sebaan to the paddock and Aeron un-hitches him, but Sebaan will need food and water and I know it's a chore Aeron would rather not fuss with right now, so I offer to do it. Aeron's eyes thin questioningly, long enough that my pulse skips under his scrutiny, but in the end he raises no protest. The trip must have been more taxing than I'd guessed. After a grateful nod from Aeron, blithe conversation carries Mother and him toward home.

While it's good to have Aeron's smiling face back in Avalon Valley where it belongs, I hate that I now have something to hide from him. The thought of things changing between us is about as palpable as bark, but telling him what happened is out of the question on so many levels. I wonder how long I can go on as if everything's normal. Already, he senses something is off, I could see it in his eyes. How long can my resolve stand up against that kind of pressure?

I resume my search as I lead Sebaan down to the creek, let him munch at a patch of clover until it no longer interests him, and give him a few departing scratches at the paddock.

Still Lyam is nowhere to be seen.

I rejoin Mother and Aeron. We sit around the table while he talks about his trip and the villagers of Jesy-el Grove. I nod my head now and again, laugh when Mother does, but my mind is elsewhere. After I don't know how long, Mother returns to the kitchen to finish last-minute preparations for Aeron's favorite meal.

I set the plates, pour the wine. Mother centers a big pot on the table, made heavy with a roasted chicken and colorful vegetables, all divinely seasoned with her blend of herbs and spices.

"It smells wonderful, but you didn't have to go through all this trouble just for me," Aeron says.

"That's absurd. How often does your mother get to make you a proper homecoming meal? Besides, I'd pay a world of trouble for you. For both of you."

She's not wrong; she has paid dearly for having us.

Mother smiles, the expression so full of tenderness and honesty that even a person without a heart wouldn't dare doubt hers.

I dish out heaping portions onto Aeron's plate, followed by more appropriately sized servings for Mother and myself. Aeron goes on with his story, telling us about the celebration that was thrown in his honor, about the fire as big as the sun, and the desserts so sweet they were positively criminal, and the music more clamorous than a storm. I can't help smiling back at his beaming face and wild exaggerations.

"I really missed you," he says, serious now, "but it was nice to get out of here. To be in a place where no one knows who you are, apart from who you present yourself to be. Where the past doesn't sit so squarely on your shoulders. Hell, I could've said I was the best hunter in Avalon Valley and they'd never think to question it." He shovels in a big chunk of potato, then adds, mouth full, "There was even this girl." He blushes and swallows, loudly, as if he hadn't meant to be so candid.

When he doesn't go on, Mother leans forward, her elbows on the table, and waving a hand, she prompts, "The girl."

Aeron shrinks back in his chair a little. Rubs the back of his neck. Clears his throat. "Uh, well, it was just nice to have someone notice me for a change. That's all."

"Does this girl have a name?" Mother presses.

"Mahdii. Mahdii Hart."

It's funny because, when Aeron and I were younger, we used to dream up stories about the two of us running away to Jesyel Grove, though we'd never actually do it; we just couldn't leave Mother behind, and she'd never leave our home and the vineyard behind. But as the years wore on, the stories began to change. For no matter how we intended to finish them, they always ended with us being too different, even someplace far from home, and our make-believe selves never could find love.

This was because the journeys always began with Aeria and Aeron Morgan. Siblings. Dviinu. Had they been solo trips, just Aeria, or just Aeron, perhaps our make-believe selves would have found what we were looking for. Our real selves had decided long ago that him staying and me going, or him going and me staying, was a price neither of us could bear to pay.

"I'm stuffed," Aeron concludes, and so ends the conversation about Mahdii Hart. A few potatoes sit uneaten on his plate. He sips the last of his wine, then rocks his chair on its back legs.

"Are you ready for those deliveries now?" I ask. Despite being at a loss for explaining to Aeron how I've come to know Lyam, I am unwilling to put my search to rest.

Aeron stifles a yawn, lets down his chair, and comes to his feet. He's weary, his eyes wandering to the hall that leads to our room. "Sure, let's get this over with. I'd like to turn in early." He stacks our plates, thanks Mother for the meal.

"There's peach cobbler when you're finished." Mother's smile is so, so beautiful.

Aeron grins. "My favorite. Hurry up, Aeria. Deliveries, cobbler, sleep, in that exact order."

The cart stands alongside the paddock fence where we left it. I step onto the lowest rail and rest my arms over the top one, stretching to meet Sebaan halfway. He's friendly enough to come say hello, but donkey enough that you have to work at returning the sentiment. Aeron gives me a look that says I'm wasting time. I give him one that says I can leave the deliveries to him while I go in and have cobbler. He laughs.

We untie the load, and with a flourish Aeron uncovers the hoard of valuable cargo concealed beneath. The trip was unmistakably a success. The pride I have for my brother in that moment eclipses the worry that he'll have to go away again next summer.

"Everyone was so generous," he explains, without really needing to. I have never seen a trade cart so full. It's a wonder Sebaan isn't shunning the two of us. Aeron for making him pull it back, and me for mere association. "They loved Mother's dried beef and peaches, not to mention the wine. Oh, how they loved the wine!"

According to Aeron's tale, the villagers lit a bonfire and emptied the majority of the bottles that very night. It was a rowdy gathering that apparently emptied the majority of their reason at the same time. I amend my earlier assumption that Aeron was just exaggerating again. "Generous," I say mockingly. "More like drunk dumb."

He laughs again, then pokes me in the arm. "So tell me about you. Was it as bad as you thought it was going to be? Me being gone? You look like you survived."

If you only knew, I reply internally.

"You look beautiful, by the way," he tacks on a short second later.

My cheeks flush. I feel rueful that he thinks my attire was to celebrate his homecoming when it was actually just a front. "I did all right, I guess. Where to first?" I say.

"The Solmons'."

We tow the cart along the footpath, which is lit every ten feet by torchlight, though there's still a trace of daylight to see by.

When we reach the Solmons' house, we let down the cart and Aeron removes a small crate full of tiny, earth-colored vials and containers. Medicines, I presume.

I knock on the door and it yawns open a minute later, revealing the doctor's sixteen-year-old daughter, Satrie. Her face blushes red the instant she sees us, and curling inward like a petal, she hides her face behind her sheet of long, flaxen hair and rushes off to fetch her father.

I throw a questioning glance at Aeron, who only shrugs. Then Doctor Solmon stands in the doorway. He accepts the crate with a grand, mustached smile and thanks Aeron heartily. Inside, I catch a glimpse of Satrie peeking around the corner, but she shrinks back when my eyes fall on her.

When we get back to the cart, Aeron keeps his voice low and says, "Doctor Solmon once told me that Jesyel Grove is known for its grove of barvju trees. They have these huge, sprawling branches, and the leaves are quite beautiful—they remind me of butterfly wings—but it's the roots that make them so extraordinary. They snake in and out of the ground and reach from tree to tree so that they're all connected." Aeron laces his fingers together to demonstrate. "It's as if they're one. But what outsiders don't know is that the roots have magical qualities. They're grinded down to a paste that can be used medicinally, and they've only ever traded them to Doctor Solmon. We just made him a very happy man."

SEVEN

Secrets

The next delivery is for Saeth Brown. Two crates of tools, most of which I've never seen before, but the weight of them is now forever burned into my mind, causing me to question what sorts of libations Sebaan was served in exchange for not shunning the whole lot of us.

Saeth and his wife Emay are only three years older than Aeron and me. They were Promised at fifteen, married at sixteen, the youngest age anyone is permitted to marry, and had their daughter, Ilora, shortly thereafter. It's Emay who opens the door, their two-year-old situated comfortably on her hip. They're both crowned with golden tresses that gleam, and bright, blue eyes that are like the sky when the sun's out in full force and clouds are nowhere in sight. I have to work to swallow my envy.

Emay's greeting isn't warm, but it isn't cold, either. It is the tepid acknowledgement Aeron and I have grown accustomed to, and it is preferred over being ignored completely, which we have also grown accustomed to.

She calls Saeth and exits the doorway, which Saeth more than fills a moment later, his blue eyes fixed on the goods. I offer the first crate, the lighter of the two, and when Saeth returns empty-handed, Aeron passes off the second.

A beautiful, mulberry-colored dress has Chief Cole's wife's name all over it. She beams when she sees it, and kisses her husband's long, leathery face.

Isa Lofton sees us coming from the front window, opens the door, and steps outside to meet us at the cart. His daughter follows him out. Eleaz is fourteen, petite despite her father's height, and she is known to be a giggler.

"Hi." She's bubbling like water over fire, her sandy hair shimmering in the waning sunlight.

I reply with a smile, nudging Aeron's arm when he doesn't respond. "Oh, hi," he says shyly.

Isa is still wearing his big, straw hat. His blue eyes sparkle with pride from under the brim. "You did good, Aeron," he says, surveying the cornucopia of produce before him: eggplants and sweet potatoes, cantaloupes and watermelons, apples and plums. He puts an arm around Aeron, who continues to look bashful. "My faith in you was well-placed. Looks like we may have to add you to the trade schedule from now on."

We make a few more deliveries after that, including to the Daestons, the Masons, and the Elands.

The last home is that of the Mercers, the largest delivery of all. Several small animal furs, a black bear skin, a few articles of clothing, a colorful patchwork quilt, and more tools, their functions and weightiness also beyond my grasp. I tuck the quilt under my arm and balance the basket of clothing on my hip, making it appear to be more of a chore than it is.

"Go on ahead," I tell Aeron, who carries two armsful of furs. I watch from the path as Aeron uses the toe of his boot to knock as respectfully as possible, bracing myself for the moment I see Daveed. With him having gone trapping all day, he is the one person I haven't been able to strike off my list. I pray with every fiber of my being that I can.

Daveed is a married man. The thought carries less weight than I had hoped.

It's Tavine who greets Aeron at the door. "Daveed," she calls. "Come, come." Then she helps Aeron with the furs and I see a glimpse of Daveed as he rushes by the window and accepts them into his arms.

When Daveed steps into the doorway several heartbeats later, there is so much Daveed and so little doorway that it's a wonder he can make it through.

"There's more in the cart," Aeron explains, gesturing to where I stand.

Daveed's strides are long, closing our distance in half the time that it takes Aeron. Torchlight dances across his features, illuminating his too big nose, his unruly brows, his thin smile, and the fact that there's not a single mark or imperfection on his kind face.

Thank the gods!

"Good evening," he says to me, then he whisks away with the crate of tools as if it's a bundle of straw.

Back at the cart, Aeron narrows his eyes and throws his hands up in question. The gesture says, *Why aren't you helping?*

"I'm coming," I grumble, shifting the load on my hip.

Aeron carries another bundle to the door and I follow.

"Where's Iverett?" Aeron inquires, handing Daveed the skins while peering inside the house.

Even though he's several hours away, my stomach still recoils at the mention of his name.

"He's gone on that fishing trip," Daveed answers absently, his attention on his new skins. "These are real nice, boy. Real nice."

I hand Tavine the basket but she's more interested in the multi-colored quilt. "This is just *lovely*." There's a song in her voice, admiration in her fingertips as she appraises the elaborate stitching. "This will look wonderful in the bedroom."

She gives Daveed a one-armed hug, unable to completely wrap her thin arm around his robust frame.

Pulling the empty cart back to the village's storage shed, Aeron says to me, "People were really friendly tonight. You think this will change things? Change the way people view us?"

His hopeful tone makes me hopeful, too. "Maybe."

Though we've made all the deliveries, I still haven't seen Lyam anywhere. A bad feeling has moved in, taking residence mostly in the pit of my stomach.

Aeron eyes me suspiciously. "What's wrong?"

"Oh, I'm fine. It's . . . it's been a long day." I've been lying so much lately that I'm starting to sound convincing, even to myself.

"If you say so. But something seems off with you."

Maybe I'm not as convincing as I'd thought. I concede that I'll have to tell him. Eventually. I vow to put it off as long as possible.

We go home, where piping-hot cobbler awaits us. Taking a bite from his second serving, Aeron mumbles, "You are the best mother—"

"*Ever*," I finish his sentiment.

Aeron bids Mother good night. To avoid more questions, I give him ample time to settle into bed, with the hope that he'll fall asleep quickly.

The aged door moans in protest as I inch it open. I peek in. The curtains are drawn, save for a vertical gap where they don't quite meet.

I pad toward my bed, my footfalls silent as a forgotten secret.

"Aeria," comes a small whisper from the darkness.

"I didn't mean to wake you."

"Actually, I've been waiting for you," he says, voice pitched low.

My voice is quiet, too. "You have?" I am thoroughly and utterly unprepared to have this conversation.

Aeron lights his lantern, comes toward me. He's cupping his hands, as if sheltering some precious thing. "I have a surprise for you. Sit down."

I sit on my bed, crossing my legs. He places the bundle in my open palms. It's a deep-purple, velvety swatch folded around something hard. Really hard.

"What is it?" I wonder aloud, keeping my eyes on the secret in my hands.

"Open it already."

I'm cautious as I peel back a tiny corner with the tips of my thumb and index finger.

"It's not going to jump out and bite you. Come on, open it," he urges, taking on a bit of my impatient spirit.

"All right, all right." I unfold the rest of the corners and discover a stunning necklace, fashioned from threefold cords as soft as silk, with subtle silver, white, and blue hues. From them hangs a shimmering gem, which bears a distinct resemblance to a heart. Bigger than a walnut, harder than a stone, it is more brilliant than any other blue my eyes have ever beheld.

"They call it a *dimanta*. Someone found them a few years back, growing in this cave on the outskirts of Jesyel Grove. Mahdii said they've never given one to an outsider before." His brows arch boastfully.

I smooth my finger over the natural facets of the gem, awestruck by its intensity. It throws flecks of light on the walls with each twist and turn, blue fireflies against the darkness. "Oh, Aeron, it's beautiful. How did you get it?"

"A magician never reveals his secrets," he jokes. My forehead scrunches. I glower at him. Aeron throws his hands in the air and groans. "Fine! I made a bunny disappear and this," he gestures at the necklace, "appeared in its place."

"The rabbit on the cart? Was that the one we found in the clearing?"

He nods. "The very same. Doctor Solmon and I nursed it back to health. Said I could have whatever I traded it for, since we were the ones who rescued it." He smiles, proud.

"*Generous*," we say in unison, causing echoes of laughter to bound around the room.

Serious now, he says, "Now you'll always have my heart with you when we can't be together."

I throw my arms around him. "It's amazing, Aeron. Thank you." But a tinge of guilt wells within me, for I don't deserve a pinch of generosity after how deceitful I've been.

I don't sleep well that night.

Morning comes, same as the last, and my agenda is also the same. Unfortunately, so are my results.

No Lyam.

I'm washing supper dishes when a new storm of worry cripples my already weakened posturing. *What if something's happened to him? What if he went out in search of my attacker and things went horribly wrong?*

My legs have the strength of a newborn foal and I nearly drop a plate.

I dream of Lyam again that night. It begins like the bear dream, with us walking hand-in-hand. Only this time two tiny, brown mice approach us, twitching their whiskers in keen interest upon seeing me. We kneel before them, and in their wonderment they lead us to a golden rock so heavy that Lyam cannot lift it, try as he might. The smaller of the mice gestures to me with its tiny paw. I pick up the golden rock as though it weighs nothing and put it in my mouth.

When I wake, hair pasted to my face from silent tears, my thoughts are far from my odd dream. Instead I am filled with the same sense of desperation and longing as yesterday. Much to my dismay, despite three full days of searching, I still do not find him.

EIGHT

distractions

I'm going to get some fresh air," I announce Thursday after supper.

"Are you not feeling well?" Aeron is visibly troubled. He offers, "I'll come with you."

"No, no. I'm all right. I thought I'd get us some wine to go with dessert. I won't take long." But really, I am not all right. I'm strained with worry, dread . . .

Mother presses, "Are you sure Aeron can't go with you?"

I force a laugh. "I'm just going to the shed." I don't care that it's nearly sunset. I have to keep searching, though it seems to be in vain. I'm starting to believe I will never see Lyam again, but my foolish heart won't give up hope.

It's nearly a three-minute walk from my house to the shed, but I could make it in two if I were in a hurry. Which I am not. I see Sama Ferry, Hinna Solmon, and Turstan Drake in passing, and by the time I reach the shed my feet feel heavier than when I left.

The shed door is gray with age, thin, and rickety, and when it swings open it feels as if it will fall from its hinges at any moment. I leave the door hanging open and step inside. The walls are lined with rows and rows of shelves, some higher than I can reach, most stocked full with goods to share. On the back wall I search for a suitable bottle of wine. Not a full one, being there are only three of us. It's doubly fitting because I'm not in the mood for wine and dessert anyway. Maybe I'll excuse myself and go to bed early, granting temporary escape from all this.

Wine in hand, I latch the door behind me. Someone will have to talk to Saeth Brown about the much-needed repair work, and soon. I consider mentioning it to Aeron, although attitudes toward us returned to normal the day after the deliveries. It's as if nothing has changed, except that Aeron now has this budding confidence after his solo journey to Jesyel Grove. The trip's done him some good. Me? Not so much.

Fighting that old tendency to keep my eyes fixed on my feet, I turn around, chin aloft, and gasp aloud, startled into stillness.

A good thirty feet divides us but his attention is trained on me, and I wonder how long he's been watching. If he saw me leave my house and followed me here in secret. His burning expression brings me back to that night in the clearing: his intensity, my name on his lips, the way my hand felt in his.

His presence alone brings surrender to the tension within my body. Relief replaces the anxiety that's been building in me. He shortens the distance between us with long, hurried strides, smiling a smile that makes my heart trip over itself.

To avoid putting our reunion on public display, I sink back into the shade at the side of the shed and wait. A host of warring emotions complicates my thoughts, and I work feverishly to organize them. *What do I say to him? Should I tell him how worried I've been, or how I couldn't stop thinking about him? That I feared he might be dead?* My heart is an uncontrollable force of nature bottled up inside a fragile shell.

There in the relative darkness we stand, boy and girl, face-to-face. It's all I can do to keep my arms from flying around him just to know this isn't a dream. I'm so unsure of things—why he was gone, what he meant by what he said in the clearing, if he could possibly feel something toward me—that I bite my lip to buy its silence.

He raises his hand, and I think he's going to touch me, but he hesitates . . . and lets it fall. Then I hear my name on the wind of a whisper. It comes like the coo of a dove, soft and lamenting. It tells me everything I need to hear. *Almost* everything.

I meet his eyes. I'm afraid I might cry. "Where have you been?"

"Garrison," he says, his voice colored with remorse. Then he cups my cheek, and I feel like I'll melt. And possibly still cry. We're gazing at one another, and I wish I could read his mind so that words won't tarnish this moment, or that he will just come out and declare that he has feelings for me. But even more so is this foolish hope deep within that he will kiss me and everything will be right with the world.

None of that happens.

Instead he says, "I thought about what you said, about my parents deserving to know where I am and that I'm safe. It ate at me all night. Finally I decided you were right, but I couldn't bear to say goodbye to you."

"I wish you'd told me."

Lyam drops his head. "I couldn't. And I am so sorry for that." He pauses. Raises his gaze. Smooths his thumb over my cheek. "I knew that if I stood before you, staring into your eyes as I am now, that I'd change my mind. I'd stay, and my parents would never know what had happened." A crooked smile turns up his lips. He touches his forehead to mine. "I never want to leave you again. I couldn't think of anything but you. I missed you insanely." His breath is heavy against my skin, and so, so sweet.

"I thought something had happened to you," I say in a small voice. That's when I realize what I truly feared the most. "Or that you decided Avalon Valley wasn't the right place for you."

Taking my chin in his hand, he forces me to meet his eyes. I can't get over the color of them, like molten honey cupped in the palms of newly turned soil.

"Everything is going to be all right now," he tells me. "I'm here, and I'm not going anywhere. This is where I want to be. With you."

Stinging starts behind my nose, a warning that tears are on their way. No words have ever brought me such comfort and happiness than those. To distract myself, I ask, "When did you leave?"

"The morning after we met, before the sun rose. I borrowed one of Saeth's horses and went as quickly as I could. My parents were so grateful I came back. I had so much to say to them. I can never thank you enough for that. They tried to convince me to stay, but I told them that Garrison offered nothing for me. Then I told them about you, that I hoped you'd be waiting for me when I returned. I can't even tell you how thrilled they were."

I try not to grin. But it's useless.

"Did anything happen while I was gone?" There's an edge of vulnerability in his voice that I find severely attractive.

I shake my head, and Lyam lets out a relieved sigh. He rakes his fingers through his dark hair, giving it that I-just-saved-your-life look from the night we met, so breathtakingly handsome.

I need another distraction. "I checked everyone. No cuts, no bruises, no black eyes. No one here could have done it. It must have been someone passing through."

Lyam nods, relieved again. "Good. Good. I talked with Reed on my way back here. That group that went out fishing was halfway to Garrison when I ran into them. I tried not to be too obvious, but I mentioned spotting a stranger near the road. Told him they may want to be on the lookout, just in case."

I hadn't thought about that, the possibility that our fishermen could have a run-in with my attacker. *At least now they've been warned.*

"And Aeron," Liam says. "He came back all right?"

"Yes. Two days ago. The trades went well. I didn't say anything to him, but he's concerned. He can tell something's different. You can't say anything, either. About the attack, about us meeting that night. No one can know," I insist, still speaking in a whisper.

"I know. Chief Cole sat down with me when I arrived. Village expectations and all that. But Aeria, you don't have to worry anymore. I'll keep you safe, no matter what." His vow is firm but gentle.

"Just swear you won't leave like that again." Inside, my heart is begging *Please.*

He stares at me with an intensity that I think must belong only to him. "I swear." He strokes the newly acquired necklace hanging at my chest, his finger—unintentionally?—grazing my skin. "This is beautiful." Into my ear he whispers, "But it doesn't hold a tenth of your beauty."

Every inch of me prickles. I press my back to the wall of the shed, knowing I can no longer rely on the strength of my legs to hold my trembling body.

As he peers back at me, I wonder if he can read the longing in my eyes. He braces his hands against the wall on either side of my head. Leans in close. So near to my lips.

I hold my breath.

Waiting.

Waiting.

Waiting.

He stops.

I never grew up imagining how my first kiss would be. I never thought I would have one. And now I worry I've done something wrong. Did I mess up somehow?

"Not here," he says sternly, through his teeth. It's more like he's talking to himself rather than to me. He steps back, brows furrowed. After what seems like an eternity, he tells me, "You should go back to your family. They'll wonder about you."

I imagine myself watching as he walks away. For good.

Making up half the distance he'd put between us, Lyam says, "Do me a favor?" When I don't say anything, he goes on. "Would you mind," he clears his throat, "would you mind telling them about me?" There's a hint of uncertainty in his tone.

I smile by way of reply.

"Tell them we're friends for now. Let them warm up to the idea."

"Come meet them," I suggest, sounding more keyed up than I mean to. "Have dessert with us."

"Not yet, but soon." He presses a quick kiss to my hand, then leaves even more quickly, disappearing into the darkness without a backward glance.

I'm puzzling over what I'll say to Mother and Aeron, and also anxious to hurry home because Lyam's right, they will be wondering about me. As I leave the dark side of the shed, right when I round the corner, Aeron and I collide.

He peers around, though I don't know that he knows what he's looking for. "What's going on?" Then, in an attempt to hide his concern, he pokes, "Did you get lost?"

"Sorry I took so long," I say, scrambling to come up with something because I hate to keep lying. "I, uh, just ran into a friend, that's all." History's been made, as those words have never been uttered by my mouth before. "We got to talking. I didn't mean to worry you."

Aeron's eyes are slits. "Friend? What friend?"

"Uh, remember that newcomer you were talking about the other day? His name's Lyam." It's the first time I've spoken his name aloud. It feels exotic, the way it rolls off my tongue.

"How did you meet *him*?" asks Aeron anxiously. The last word is spoken with pure contempt, as if I've befriended a plague rather than a boy.

I lay out my story as Aeron tows me home. "We met the day you left, when I was doing chores. But then he went back to Garrison for a couple days. He just got back tonight, and we sort of ran into each other at the shed." I give a dismissive shrug.

He relays my story to Mother. She doesn't say a thing, merely sits observing. She and I make small talk over warm turnovers, but Aeron's not so inclined to join. Arms crossed, his shoulders remain rigid fixtures that hold up his ears.

Again, he retires early. I don't follow. Instead, Mother and I take to the stream with the evening's dishes. The sun is sliding past the horizon. A reddish-orange glow paints the cloudless sky.

"How long do you think Aeron will be mad?" I ask her.

"This is new for him. His best friend in the world suddenly has a love interest. He's afraid he'll lose you, that you won't need him anymore. Give him some time to adjust."

"*Love interest?*" My voice cracks. "I said he's a friend."

"Aeria, please do not think your mother a fool. I was young once, too, you know. Did I ever tell you who I had a secret eye for?"

I shake my head. "Who?"

"You can never tell anyone, understand?"

I nod.

Mother shields her mouth with her hand as if to shroud the identity of her mysterious childhood infatuation from the nonexistent masses. "Lotz Drake." A soft giggle slips past her lips. Laugh lines bracket her mouth and eyes. Her cheeks burn with a subtle, rosy color. She brushes her wavy, amber hair from her face. "He was very handsome back then. Much thinner, and he had more hair then, too. But his eyes . . . his eyes were just as blue as they are today."

"When was this?" I ask, disregarding her unnecessary concealment.

There's a curious pause. Then she replies, "Before my accident. We were friends, but I hoped for us to be more than that. A few months after I found out I was pregnant, he and Rebeyah were Promised. Lotz never knew how I felt about him." Flecks of sadness glint in her eyes.

"I never knew any of that," I say solemnly.

"None of it matters anymore. Having you and Aeron was the best thing that ever happened to me. I wouldn't change a single thing." She pinches my cheek.

"But I feel terrible. We stole your childhood. And your future. You never had a chance at a normal life."

"You mustn't allow yourself to think like that, Aeria. You and Aeron are gifts. I always knew you were special, and in a way that made me special, too. I have no regrets."

We continue our chore in pensive silence.

"So, tell me about this friend. *Lyam*, did you say?" His name comes playfully from Mother's lips.

I blush, unable to hide my embarrassment. "Yes, Lyam."

Now I've said his name twice. I feel a tickle in my core that makes my entire body blush. Distraction time. "He lived in Garrison, but he and his parents didn't agree on certain matters, so he came here. He's a carpenter, so I imagine he'll be helping out Saeth."

He's certainly suited for it, I think, with those well-defined arms, those strong, broad shoulders. I could go on and on, about his eyes, his wild hair, how beautiful he makes me feel, but to do so would swiftly negate the whole "friend" claim.

I shake my head. Daydreaming again.

Mother is regarding me, wearing a look I have never seen on her.

"Oh, Aeria, this isn't serious, is it?" She's incredibly flustered. Something in her voice tells me she's referring to Lyam and me being intimate.

What I want to say is, "*I like a boy, I'm not stupid.*" Instead, I work to ease her fears. "Nothing's happened, if that's what you're asking. We've just talked a few times."

By the way Mother releases her breath, the way her shoulders relax at her sides, I'm sure that's exactly what she was thinking.

"Aeria, I know you like him, I can see it in your face. I want you to be mindful that you have a purpose in this life. There is something great in store for you, and though I do not know what that is yet, I know it exists. Does he know everything yet? Did you tell him about us?"

When I say nothing, which is an answer in itself, Mother takes my face in her wet hands and goes on. "I don't want you to be heartbroken like I was, Aeria. There are special plans for special people. The true question is, are you willing to make the hard choice? To choose your purpose, whatever that may be, over him when the time comes?"

I turn my head, unwilling to look into her pleading eyes. I cannot believe I'm hearing this. After years of viewing love as a too-high pedestal, it's finally been brought to my level, and now she's wants me to refuse it for the sake of . . . what? The idea that somehow I've shifted from outcast to too-special-to-love?

Sounding cross, I say, "I'll be fine, Mother. Even if there is some *special purpose* for my life, I'm sure Lyam won't be an interruption. Maybe because of him I'll actually live to see that day come." I free myself from her grasp and hastily gather up the clean dishes. I hear her doing the same as I put distance between me and her so-called *purpose*.

"Aeria, wait."

I pause.

When her soft footsteps catch up to me, she says, "I'm sorry. I just don't want to see you hurt." Her smile is deeply contagious.

I smile back despite myself. "I know, but I need you to trust me. If there's a chance Lyam could love me, I am not going to jeopardize that. Being hurt is a risk I'm willing to take. Please, can you be happy for me? I still have Aeron to deal with. Maybe if he knows you support me, he can, too."

Mother remains quiet. Her eyes flit back and forth between mine. "I will support you so long as I don't feel *you're* the one being jeopardized in any way."

I'm not sure what that entails but I've made ground, at least with one family member, and that's half the battle. I gladly count this as one small victory.

Mother teases, "So, Lyam, huh?"

"Yes," I breathe. That tickling sensation returns, and I'm lost in imagining how near his lips were to mine.

"Bring him by tomorrow."

I frown. "I think Aeron's going to need more time than that."

"Then I suppose you two need to talk." She ponders on this a moment. "How about this, I'll make a lunch for you. You can go to that tree you both love so much."

Already I'm dreading it, but it's a necessary evil that can't be avoided. "All right." We start toward home. "So, Lotz Drake, huh?" I tease back.

Mother shoves me in playful retribution. "You can't help who you love."

Aeron's fast asleep when I climb into bed. The sun has finally set, coloring the room with harmless shadows. A new sense of relief comes over me as I rest my head on my pillow, clutching Lyam's shirt, which hides under it. I've done this every night since we met, only tonight is different. It brings me comfort, knowing that he's here, that he's safe. Knowing he *does* have feelings for me.

I smile, completely at peace with the world.

Well, most of the world. I'll have to deal with Aeron tomorrow.

The mystery of my attacker is another story I've tucked away in the furthest, darkest, untouched corner of my mind. But for now I am at peace.

My eyes close. I fall asleep, where peaceful dreams embrace me.

NINE

the nature of brothers

The morning sun peers through the curtains, waking me. But the joy of Lyam's return is overshadowed by the new day's agenda. Already I feel it tangling up inside me, this dread that seizes every good and wonderful thing and chokes the life out of it.

Aeron's bed is empty, his blanket pulled up and tucked in nice and proper. He's likely helping Mother in the kitchen, but owing to the fact that he didn't wake me, I doubt his mood has improved.

I slip into a comfortable, ankle-length dress. Its subtle lavender shade is soothing to me. I hope it has the same effect on Aeron.

I find Mother preparing breakfast, Aeron at her side. I approach cautiously, unable to read the mood in the room at first. They don't speak to one another, which I take to mean that Aeron is still agitated. I wait until my presence is noticed.

"Oh, good morning, Aeria," Mother says.

Aeron turns, forces a smile, retains his silence.

Again, he doesn't engage in conversation over breakfast, which is so out of character for him that it calls to memory the quiet breakfast Mother and I shared the morning he left for Jesyel Grove. I hadn't felt right then. Don't feel right now. Could it really be so difficult for him to be happy for me? I certainly hadn't harbored animosity when he spoke of Mahdii Hart.

I offer to clean the bowls immediately after our meal, lest the oats harden and form a thick layer of crust that's too much for the stream's cold water. It's also a good excuse to give my brother some room to think.

I round the corner at the edge of the vineyard and give a start. Instantly I realize, *He's been waiting for me!* Leaning against the boulder on the bank of the stream, Lyam has his arms folded casually across his chest. A wide smile parts his lips when our eyes meet. I answer with a giddy smile that warns I've already fallen deep.

My pace increases, longing and needing to be in his presence once again. "Hi," I say in a timid but cheery voice. "How'd you know . . .?"

Lyam shrugs his broad shoulders. "I figured you'd come eventually. I haven't been waiting too long, just an hour or so," he taunts mischievously. "Did you talk to them last night?"

"Aeron wasn't too happy." I recall Aeron's forced smile, his wordlessness. "*Isn't*, I should say, but he'll come around. My mother wants to meet you." I don't tell him what an undertaking it was to reach that conclusion.

"That would be great," Lyam says, though his tone confuses me. He takes our morning bowls and dips them into the water, letting them soak. This soaks the hem of his pants in the process. "But I am worried about you and Aeron. I've heard about how close you are, and I hate the idea of causing a divide between you two."

I can't help but think that nothing, not even death, could ever cause a divide between Aeron and me, least of all Lyam. As I said, he'll come around. Though it may be later rather than sooner.

"Aeron and I have learned to be resilient over the years, so don't worry about him. He's just overprotective."

"I don't know much about brothers, but I do believe they come from the same species as mothers and fathers." Lyam massages my cloth with a bar of soap. "Which means there's no such thing as being *over*protective."

I stare for two reasons. First, because Lyam is washing my dishes. Somehow, this changes the way I see him, stirs up stronger emotions, which I wouldn't have thought possible. Second, because he really does know nothing of the nature of brothers.

I follow him into the water. I hadn't planned on wading in, but I decide being nearer to this strangely more attractive Lyam is worth a bit of water on my dress.

"You're wrong," I say, serious but not condemning.

"Am I?" It sounds like a challenge. Whether by design, I don't know. I take it anyway. "He thinks he has to protect me from every little thing. It's always been that way. One time he carted me off in his arms to save me from a swarm of bees."

Lyam gives me a look that says he's not convinced. Doubly serious, he counters, "I would do the same."

I go on. "Perhaps, except this wasn't exactly a swarm. It wasn't even close. It was only *three* bees. He didn't care, so long as I was safe. He gets a little crazy sometimes.

"There was another time when we were walking through the woods. He thought he heard some growling behind us. It took nearly ten minutes to convince him it was my stomach."

Handing over a clean dish, Lyam concedes with a chuckle. "All right, overprotective. I get it."

"My mother's going to make lunch for us to bring to this special place that Aeron and I have been going to since, well, since we could walk, really. It's right up the stream a little way. I think if I sit down with him and explain everything— What's so funny?"

The laugh that bursts forth is clearly unintentional. "Nothing," Lyam says, wearing a grin that was born of the laugh.

"What?"

He shrugs. "I don't know if that's a good idea, this *explaining everything*. I mean, does he really need to know about," he scans for witnesses, lowers his voice, "the *nude* swimming?" He laughs again, intentional this time, splashing a little water at me.

At once I am embarrassed because I think he's referring to *seeing* me swimming naked rather than *knowing* I was swimming naked. He couldn't have actually seen me. Maybe the slightest of glimpses that couldn't properly stick to memory because of the violent fray that ensued with my attacker. Even when he'd turned around, he'd sworn he didn't see anything.

I splash back. "Besides," I say, coming closer, "you probably don't want me to mention your . . . *stripping scene*." My words are low, dripping with seduction. I'm tracing my index finger down the buttons of his shirt, unsure of the girl that's taken over my body at the moment. She's sultry and confident, impossible to ignore, and so unlike the me I've grown up with all these years.

Judging from Lyam's reaction, this new girl's a good fit. His chest rises and falls as if his heart is trying to settle after a run, but it won't. There's an ever-so-faint tremble in his lower lip that I would have missed if I weren't studying them so intently. Red-hot emotions swirl within me, swelling, surging, sparking my heart to soar to breathtaking heights.

I see him swallow. In my mind we're at the shed again, and I'm waiting, waiting, waiting . . .

Only to have my words thrown back at me, an echo of my seductive tone. It's a good fit for him as well. "Besides, I was only trying to be a gentleman. Kind of like this . . ."

And he drenches the front of me.

I gasp. Separating the words nice and slow, I warn, "You're in trouble now." I cup my hands and toss over as much water as they'll hold. The front of his shirt is doused, clinging ever so wonderfully to his chest.

Lyam dumps a bowlful over my head despite my attempt to shield myself. He swiftly turns so that my next toss misses his face. It wets his back instead. He roars in victory. I send a few handfuls in his direction, but there's more water in my eyes than my hands, so my aim is ineffectual, and the moving target does little to help my cause.

Resolved to do more damage to him than he's done to me, I wipe my vision clear and slosh forward, pounce onto his back, and lock my legs around his waist. I feel relatively satisfied that I've accomplished my purpose. But then we spin full circle, Lyam trying to loosen my grip and me tightening my arms around his neck, fully aware of how much of my body comes in contact with his.

All of a sudden I feel myself falling backward. Re-lentless hold or no, I lose my bearings when we hit the water. Now we're both soaked head to toe and laugh-ing hysterically.

"Come, let me help you," Lyam says as he takes my hand and we make our way to the bank. "See, a gen-tleman." There's a smirk on his face that also fits him well.

"Will I see you later?" I ask wistfully.

My shoulders are in his hands, along with my heart. "I'll be here. I said I'm not going anywhere and I meant it." He picks up the pot of dishes. I assume he means to carry it home for me because he's already headed that way. I'm staring. He stops. "You coming?"

I drip toward him more quickly. Water is pooled at the bottom of a bowl, and I snatch it out of the pot, empty it over his head and promise, "This isn't over, by the way."

Lyam's lips pull up in one corner. "I hope not."

When we reach my home, Lyam hands me the pot. "Good luck with your brother." His sentiment carries a subtle note of cynicism.

So does mine. "Thanks, I'll need it."

TEN

betrayed

Being that I'm sopping wet, I feel relieved to find that no one's home. I change into a new dress. So much for soothing hues to combat Aeron's foul disposition. I hang the wet clothes on the line out back.

The rest of the morning is spent tidying up the house. Making my bed, ensuring that Lyam's shirt remains properly hidden. Gathering soiled laundry. Watering the herbs: oregano, chamomile, mint, and rosemary. Wiping down tabletops.

I've just finished sweeping the kitchen when the front door opens with a long, painstakingly slow *creak*.

That hesitant entrance can only belong to one person. Unsurprisingly, a sullen expression is still spread atop Aeron's usually pleasant one. "Hi," he says glumly. His eyes dart to my dress, my damp hair, but he raises no comment about either.

"Mother made lunch for us." I sound happier about this than I am. Inside, I'm a ball of nerves. "She thinks we should go to our spot and talk."

Aeron rakes his fingers through his loose curls, voice thick with irritation when he says, "We don't have to, though. I won't tell her."

As much as it pains me to say this, I reply, "I think it would be good for us, too." The basket now hangs from my forearm. "Ready?" I ask, forcing my enthusiasm.

"Sure," he grumbles. He's out the back door in no time, but not for anticipation's sake.

I follow, pace slow for procrastination's sake.

Normally, we would have walked side by side. I don't implore him to wait for me because I know it's better this way. I need time to think.

We head into the northeastern woods, where lofty boughs eclipse the full power of the sun, nature's generous reminder of the dread that overshadows me. Bumps spread down my arms, though it's a warm breeze that plays through the leaves. The stream crawls past us on our right. To the left, beyond the pines and cedars, the oaks and the maples, is the clearing. Up ahead is *our* oak, which looks down on *our spot*. The interlocking A's Aeron etched into the mighty trunk makes it official.

We have always treasured our time here. But what I have to do now, what I have to tell him, endangers nearly every precious memory our hearts hold.

This could go terribly wrong.

Aeron doesn't wait for me before nestling up against the base of the tree. He seems comfortable on the outside, but I can tell deep down he's still reeling from the thought of my new *friend*.

"Beautiful afternoon," I say. It's a weak start, but it's a start.

"It's nice enough, I guess." His tone is indifferent, too unlike the brother I know who sketches beautiful days like this even while he dreams. Does he really have to make this so difficult?

"I wonder what Mother packed for us. Wasn't that nice of her?"

"Sure."

Ignoring his surly demeanor, I pull back the cloth stuffed into the sides of the basket. There's salami and cheese and tomatoes and crackers. And the meal wouldn't be complete in our Mother's eyes without a bunch of grapes.

I stack cheese and salami on the crackers, Aeron divides the grapes into two smaller bunches.

"So," I begin, "tell me more about this girl in Jesyel Grove. What was her name?" I haven't forgotten, but the plan is to get him talking about her so he can more easily identify with me and my feelings for Lyam. It may be a longshot, but it's worth a try.

"Oh, uh, Mahdii. What do you want to know?" he says, reluctantly.

"What's she like?"

Aeron pops a grape into his mouth, perhaps delaying while he decides how to answer. "She's, uh, she's really great to talk to. And we have a lot in common."

"Like what?"

"Well, sketching, for one. I showed her my journal and she really loved it. She also loves music, and recently she started writing poetry. Mahdii's the one who showed me around her village and introduced me to a lot of the people there. They're all very nice, and everyone just adores her. She even took me to see the barvju grove. I can't even describe it, it's so beautiful. I really want to take you there."

I smile, noting his attempt to shift the subject from Mahdii, but it's a nice thought regardless. I do want to see the barvju trees one day, but for now I have to re-claim this conversation. "She sounds great. Is she cute?"

Aeron blushes, combs his fingers through his curls. We've crossed into uncharted waters. "Yes."

"What does she look like?"

Letting out a breath reminiscent of a laugh, Aeron looks off into the distance, eyes glazed as if in a love-struck trance. "She's got really dark hair. Dark as coal, and straight as a flame to the sky. And it shines so beautifully in the sunlight. Her eyes are dark too, but they're kind, like Mother's. I'm taller, and older— she just turned sixteen a few weeks ago. Oh, and she has these impossibly long eyelashes." He blushes again at his candor. Then he sighs. "She's really great. I sort of *miss* her. Is that silly? I barely know her enough to be thinking about her all the time like this."

"I don't think it's silly. I can understand how you feel." I pause for his response.

He doesn't give one.

"So, do you think you'll go back to visit her?" I ask, to keep the conversation from dying.

His reply comes swiftly. "No. It's too far to go there just to see her. I mean, I'll probably be there next summer for trades, but that's no way to build a rela-tionship. Besides, you know I'd never leave you behind, and we know how it ends up if we both go. It's just not meant to be." His voice is saturated with mel-ancholy. He's cutting at my heart. And my plan.

"I'm sorry. Maybe it's worth a try, though."

He shrugs. "It's not. I've gone over it in my head more times than I'd like to admit. It won't work. I have to try to forget her."

And I have to regroup. I come up with another tac-tic, but it's one that requires a certain degree of prudence. I'll have to tread lightly to avoid upsetting him. "It may be hard to imagine, but what if you were able to feel that way about someone here?"

Knots form between his brows. He sneers, "Like who? What chance do I have of finding someone in Avalon Valley? You and I may as well not even exist, you know that."

"I didn't want to tell you until I knew for sure, but I started picking up on something interesting. It involves a certain someone," I say, hiding half my face behind my curtain of hair to tip him off.

It doesn't. But it does perk him up, even if just a little. "Really? Who?"

My smile only shows on the inside, pleased that my brother's emotional state is headed in a more desirable direction. "Well, she's got sparkling blue eyes."

Excitement grows on his face as he meditates on the possibilities. I wonder if he's hoping for a specific outcome. The light in his eyes certainly suggests as much. "All right, what else?"

"Her hair is bright as the sun."

Aeron is quiet for a moment, as if consulting his mental list. "*And?*" He draws out the word, brows raised, his tone swathed in anticipation.

"*And,*" I say, mimicking him, "she's the daughter of a certain doctor." I wait for his reaction, which comes as slowly as my elongated *and.*

Finally, after the initial shock wears off, he says, "Satrie? You can't be serious. Satrie? Are you sure?" His eyes are wide and he's beaming in delight.

I nod, then proceed to tell him of her numerous furtive glances, how I caught her watching him while he worked yesterday, the way she hid her smile when we passed by her. Instances that neither of us had noticed before, Aeron because he was too busy being a brother, and me because I was too busy pretending not to exist.

He's speechless for several heartbeats. "I would have never guessed. Satrie. She's . . . she's . . ."

"Breathtaking?" I suggest.

"Exactly," he breathes, resting his chin into the cupped hollow of his hand. "*Satrie.*"

I feel somewhat slighted. "You never told me."

"It's just that we've never had those kinds of talks. I mean, I've always thought she was beautiful, even when we were younger, but what would have been the point of saying so? I never imagined, never *dreamed*, she'd feel anything toward me." He sits silently with his revelation. "*Satrie,*" he mumbles into the wind.

I'm unsure if now is a good opportunity to bridge the gap from this subject to the more pressing one, our entire reason for being here. I'm hoping this euphoric frame of mind will help him relate with my feelings, but doubt wrestles within me. Can Aeron cast aside his overprotective brother routine and truly listen and offer his support? I'm not so sure his understanding will reach that far. Regardless of my qualms, I have to tell him the truth. Perhaps he'll surprise me. He tends to do that now and then.

Distracted by our intriguing conversation, lunch has gone by with uncharacteristic slowness. When we finish, Aeron stuffs his hands behind his head, wearing a grin wider than the pines are tall.

This doesn't ease my tension though. It doubles it. My pulse quickens. Fear knots in the pit of my stomach, making me nauseous. Having to face Aeron, revealing what happened to me in his absence, petrifies me. As if that isn't enough, I desperately want his blessing. To know that he will stand behind me in my decision to pursue a relationship with Lyam. It would mean the world to me.

"So . . ." I swallow a deep breath. "You know how you couldn't stop thinking about Mahdii since you've been apart?"

Brows scrunched, Aeron says, "What about it?"

"I was going to say that I know how it feels, to miss someone like that." I fumble with my hands in my lap, avoiding eye contact. I imagine he'll inquire what I mean by that, though it's not hard to guess.

The downfall comes swiftly. "You mean your new *friend*?" His voice is choked with malice when he spits out the word 'friend.' He *is* going to make this difficult. Very difficult.

"His name is Lyam. And I think you'd like him if you gave him a chance."

"Doubt it," he snaps. "Sounds like a guy trying to take advantage of a lonely girl and steal her away from her family. Is that the kind of chance you want me to give him?"

"It's not that way at all. He knows how important you are to me, and he's certainly not trying to *steal* anything away from anyone. Nor did he try to take advantage of anything. We met by chance. It's not like he waited for you to leave and then went in for the kill. It just happened."

"But—"

"But," I interrupt, "then he went back to Garrison to make amends with his parents. I didn't see him for three days, and I thought about him the entire time he was gone. So I know how you feel about Mahdii. Don't you see the similarities, how you and I have struggled with the same thing?" I'm pleading for even a drop of understanding.

I get none.

"No, Aeria! This is completely different. Guys and girls don't think the same. It's night and day. A girl wouldn't take advantage of a guy the way some guys would. How am I to believe that you spent time with him and nothing indecent happened? I don't trust him!"

Aeron's accusing tone is grating at my nerves. *"Indecent?* I cannot believe that just came out of your mouth. He's not that kind of guy, Aeron! Besides, the consequence for those acts is the same wherever you go. You need to get your facts straight before you start judging him. I would think *you* would know that!"

"Maybe I don't care what kind of guy he is." He goes silent. Thoughtful. Somber. "He'll never be good enough."

I bring my tone down a few notches, but it still doesn't match his. "So it's perfectly acceptable for you to find happiness, but not me?"

"What happiness, Aeria? I've found nothing! My life hasn't changed because some girl in another village noticed me. Nothing will come from me pining over Mahdii. And Satrie? What if you're wrong? Or, what if things don't work out and I end up with nothing but a broken heart? Then I'll back right where I was, with hands full of dead possibilities." His eyes are watery now. "You and I, we were in this together. Aeron and Aeria till the end."

I move and sit opposite him. "Don't you see? We still are in this together. The story's just changed a little. Satrie and Lyam are unforeseen character additions, and if we don't at least try, you and I are going to die with that regret. Yes, we risk heartbreak, but that's what life is about, Aeron, taking risks. I'd rather die having a taste of love than none at all. Wouldn't you?"

"I . . ." His voice trails off. "I don't want to see you hurt."

I half groan, half laugh. "You sound like Mother. Look, you have a good heart, Aeron, but you can't always protect me. This is a risk I have to take. Lyam offers me a chance at a future, and I am not going to watch it slip through my hands. You shouldn't, either."

Aeron bites his lip, pensive.

"We have a real chance here, and I think it's time we rewrite our stories. I'll support you, whatever you decide, and I need to know that you'll do the same for me . . . whatever the consequence." I'm gazing into his watery eyes. Mine are watering, too. "Aeron, this changes nothing between us. Nothing ever will. You'll always be my brother, and my best friend."

We stay like that for a long moment, with tears hanging in our eyes. Finally, Aeron says, "I'm sorry I acted the way I did, Aeria. I really wasn't prepared for this."

"I know. I wasn't expecting it, either."

As tempting as it is to end our conversation on this note, I know I can't maintain this pretense any longer. I hesitate, swallowing past the thickness in my throat. Bracing myself for what's to come, I assume a small voice. "But I do have to be honest with you about how we met." My hands are trembling. I sit on them.

Confusion jumbles his features. "You said you met while you were doing chores. Why would you lie to me about it?"

"Well, this is just between us, and *please* don't overreact, but I couldn't sleep the night you left . . . so I sneaked out."

"You what? To meet *him*?" he shouts. The tears are gone; an icy stare takes their place.

"No, Aeron!" I shout back, then I lower my voice, mindful of my need to tread lightly. "I hadn't met him yet. I couldn't sleep, and it was still so hot out."

I don't want to go on. I see now that I've gone about this all backward.

99

Deep furrows run down his forehead. "So?"

"So, I went to the falls for a swim, and all of a sudden this guy—"

"He *followed* you?" He jumps up, seething. Blood surges to his face so that it's blazing red. Teeth bared, he snarls, "I'll kill him!"

"No! Please, no!" I scramble to my feet, but he's already tearing headlong down the trail. "Wait, Aeron, please listen." He doesn't slow. "Aeron!" I cry out, hot tears streaked across my face. I can only imagine the horror that must be going through his mind right now, the visions that have been scorched across his imagination.

I picture a horror of my own, wondering what Aeron means to do to Lyam. Whatever his agenda, I have to stop him.

Demanding more than I ever have before, I surge forward at unprecedented speed. Energy pulses through my limbs. My feet pound hard to the earth, cutting into Aeron's lead. My legs and chest burn with need.

I'm right behind Aeron as he nears the boundary of the woods. Screaming for him to stop has proven futile, so I don't bother. There is no stopping him. Not verbally, anyway. My new focus is to get to Lyam before Aeron does. Before there's an altercation.

We race past the plaza. I'm right on his heels. As expected, Lyam is outside the Browns' workshop, laboring over a length of lumber. When he sees us coming, he gives me a perplexed look, which is quickly followed by one of understanding. Shocked, he lifts his hands in surrender, letting Saeth's saw drop to the ground.

Unprecedented speed or no, I am too late.

ELEVEN

blessing

Before I know it, Aeron's fist cuts through air, hitting Lyam squarely in the jaw with a resounding thunk. Despite his stature, Lyam stumbles to the ground.

I saw on his face that he knew it was coming, yet he made no move to protect himself. Even now he stays down, refusing to get tangled up in Aeron's fury, refusing to even the score. What I see before me is a true gentleman, not the coward Aeron so explosively proclaims him to be.

My eyes dart about, searching for witnesses, but Saeth's shop is quiet and no one else seems to be around, and all the while, Aeron's expletives continue driving like gale-force winds. "You followed her?" he roars, hands balled into fists at his sides.

I spring forward and shove hard against Aeron's chest. We stand nearly eye level, and I have him by the front of his shirt, forcing his attention. Despite my anger, my voice is loud enough for only him to hear. "Shut up before you get him kicked out of here. You're being an idiot. I can't believe you! He saved my life, but you couldn't listen for five minutes without doing something stupid." I pause to collect myself, and Aeron's eyes dart to Lyam, staring daggers as if everything I've said has gone unheard. "Aeron," I say softly, recapturing his attention, "he saved my life!"

Aeron balks. "He . . . he what? But he followed you. You said it yourself." He's still speaking through his teeth, which makes me all the more irritated. I don't know this person who glares back at me with such malice.

"I didn't get to say anything because you wouldn't even let me start. Go home. Now. I'll be there when you calm down. Maybe then you'll listen."

My assertiveness stuns him, but he doesn't object as I expect him to. Mumbling, he punches his still-clenched fist through the air, kicking at the dirt on his way home.

I help Lyam to his feet, smooth a hand delicately over his cheek. "I am so sorry," I whisper.

He takes hold of my face, wipes away tears I hadn't even known existed. "*Shh*, I'm all right. We'll fix this. I promise."

How is it that he's the one comforting me?

Lyam starts to pull me toward home, but I am immovable. "Not yet. Give him a few minutes to cool off."

I consider giving Aeron a few years to cool off when Lyam begins to pull me to himself. Wrapping his arms around me. He is all pine and sawdust and absolute perfection. He kisses the top of my head, and there's not one bone in my body that cares if anyone were here to witness our embrace.

When Lyam and I come around the bend and my home is in sight, he relinquishes my hand.

My mother is outside, pacing frantically, arms folded across her chest to keep all the worry from spilling out. She runs to meet us. "What is going on? Why is Aeron so upset?" She seldom uses this stern voice. "He won't even talk to me."

"He overreacted, that's all. I was trying to talk to him, like you said, and we had a misunderstanding. We're going now to explain everything to him." I gesture to Lyam. "Mother, this is Lyam. I had hoped to introduce you under more favorable circumstances."

"Good to meet you, Miss Morgan," Lyam says politely, shaking her hand.

"Call me Nira. I've heard good things about you, Lyam. I hope you two can patch things up with Aeron." Mother regards Lyam with an expression I can't place. I think it's his eyes she's fixated on, but then she touches his chin, tilting his head slightly. "He didn't do this to you, now did he?"

"It's nothing," Lyam replies. "Aeron will go to any length to protect his sister, and I can respect him for that. Besides," Lyam chuckles darkly, "I've had worse."

I turn to my mother. "I'm sure we'll be able to sort things through." I will my words to be true.

"I hope so. It's a shame to see you two so disconnected. And I certainly don't want to hear any more about fighting, justified or not." She sighs, and leaves us to work things out with Aeron.

But Lyam doesn't budge. "Are you sure I should go in with you? It may make things worse."

"I need you there. Please."

"All right, but if you change your mind, let me know. I'll understand completely."

We go inside and I call Aeron's name.

No reply.

Our bedroom door is closed, so I knock gently, assuming that's where he's gone. "Can we come in? We really need to talk."

103

Aeron still doesn't answer but I hear movement from within.

I glance at Lyam. Should I give Aeron more time, or will his brooding only cause more damage? Neither of us seems to know.

So it's up to me. To the door I say, "Listen, Aeron, I'm really sorry about all this. I see now that I went about it the wrong way. This was a terrible misunderstanding, and we'd really like to explain what happened." I'm curious what he'll think about the *we* part.

Aeron mumbles a very reluctant, "Come in."

I enter the room slowly and sit on my bed. Aeron is lying on his side facing the wall so that his expression is hidden, though I probably wouldn't want to see it anyway. Lyam leans awkwardly against the doorframe. But we're in this together so I motion for him to join me. He does, but this involves standing beside me, looking more uncomfortable than a fish tangled in a net.

"I'm going to start over," I tell Aeron. "I sneaked out to swim, like I told you, but Lyam didn't follow me. He saw someone else who was." I pause to let my words sink in.

A very puzzled Aeron rolls to face me. "Someone else was following you?"

I feel my heart speed up. I hate to even think of the attack on me, let alone *talk* about it. "That's what I've been trying to tell you. Lyam knew you had left for the trades and that I was alone. So when he saw that I was being followed, he wanted to make sure I was safe."

Perched stiffly at the edge of his bed now, Aeron throws a quick glance Lyam's way, but his words are directed at me. "You said he saved your life?"

"I swam for a while, then I got hungry. When I got out of the water, someone was standing there. Waiting for me. He was huge, dressed in all black. He knocked me to the ground and I couldn't get away, but then Lyam came. They wrestled, and Lyam punched him. The guy ran off, and Lyam walked me home." I intentionally withhold the element of nudity from my summary of events, knowing what a disaster that would cause.

Outrage boils through Aeron again. "He knocked you to the ground?" He sounds hysterical. "Why would someone do that? Who was it? What did he want?"

The kind of physical assault I had suffered is so uncommon, so unheard of. I have an idea what my attacker wanted, but I refuse to throw wide that floodgate.

Now Aeron's on his feet, fists clenched and ready to fight, ready to defend my honor. "Who did this to you? Tell me!" I know he's already running through the villagers of Avalon Valley, working to sort out who could be capable of such a crime. A task easier said than done.

Suddenly we're all standing, amidst Aeron's tar-thick tension and hostility. Lyam and I hurriedly form a wall, shoulder-to-shoulder, to prevent him from leaving the room, and I'm praying this doesn't end with another fist to the face. This new version of Aeron isn't easily reasoned with.

"We don't know," I say. "It's not as if he told me his name, and all I could see were his eyes." My skin creeps, remembering those eyes. "He definitely isn't from Avalon Valley, though."

Aeron backs off slightly. "How do you know that?"

Finally Lyam speaks, voice subdued but very matter-of-fact. "I'm quite certain I broke his nose."

105

Recalling that distinct crunch I heard, I'm certain he did, too.

"Well, I haven't seen anyone with a broken nose," Aeron says. "He'd still have black eyes and a swollen nose. It would be impossible to hide."

"Neither have I," I agree. "I checked everyone. The whole village. They're all clean."

Aeron looks deeply unsatisfied. "What else can you tell me about him?"

"He was at least my height," Lyam supplies. "Maybe taller. Heavier build. Honestly, it all happened so fast, it's kind of a blur."

"Dark eyes," I add, and my tone sends the room into silence for several long seconds.

The tension is palpable, and it feels dreadfully inescapable. That's when Lyam laughs out loud. "Oh, and he has an affinity for women's clothing."

My jaw drops to the floor. I shove my elbow into Lyam's steely gut and he grunts, stunned rather than pained. A second later he realizes what he's revealed.

Teeth clamped, blowing hard through his nostrils, Aeron demands, "What the hell does that mean?"

I come up with a lie posthaste. "I— I brought along an extra nightdress, in case I wanted to change after my swim, that's all. He snatched it when he ran off." I'm getting better at this lying thing, but is that a positive development? Right now, being that Aeron seems to have bought it, I decide that it is.

I give Lyam a fierce look from the corner of my eye. He sees it, but Aeron doesn't. Aeron says, "You reported this, right?"

My eyes cut back to Lyam.

"Here's the thing," I say slowly. "If we report that Lyam was involved in an act of violence—"

It's Aeron who finishes. "He'll be forced to leave Avalon Valley."

Another moment of silence. It is the one and only thing that tethers my future to my palm. Silence. Lyam touches his fingers to mine.

"No one can know," I say. "We're lucky enough as it is that no one was around to see you throw that punch."

Aeron's eyes go wide with understanding, then tight with remorse. He sinks to his bed, as if the weight of his actions and the weight of telling our secret and the weight of Lyam leaving Avalon Valley are all too much to bear.

I cross the room and sit beside Aeron. "I am *begging* you. Promise me you won't tell."

Aeron's chewing his lip. He has to know that my fate is in his hands right now, and that is a very weighty thing. "Fine, I'll keep my mouth shut. But I'm not putting this to rest, that's for damn sure. I don't care if I have to bang down doors to get answers, I'm going to make sure no one here did this to you. And if it was someone here, I will find out!"

"I'll help you," Lyam tells him. "Anytime. It won't hurt to double check."

"I suppose I owe you an apology," Aeron says. He comes to his feet and stands before Lyam. "I'm really grateful for what you did for my sister while I was away. And I'm sorry I hit you. I should have listened to the whole story first."

Lyam's smile is anything but insincere. "No hard feelings. You did what you thought was right in order to protect your sister. You're a good brother."

"And you sound like a good enough guy," Aeron admits, though it comes out almost guardedly. "Tough as nails, too," he adds, getting a better look at Lyam's face, where a knuckle-sized splotch of red on the lower part of his cheek is the only evidence of Aeron's rage. "Thought I hit you harder than that."

"Tough as nails," Lyam agrees with a laugh. Stretching out his hand, he says, "Friends?"

With a hint of uncertainty, Aeron shakes his hand. "Friends."

"Lyam is a *great* guy," I amend emphatically. "And I'm not asking for your consent, but I do need to know that I—that *we*—have your blessing."

Aeron is thoughtful for a long second. Giving Lyam a pointed look, he thrusts his finger into his chest, cautioning, "You'd better be good to her!"

How funny it would be, I think, if Lyam were to puff up his chest against my brother's fingertip, but that isn't Lyam's way. Calmly he vows, "You have my word."

My heart stops as Aeron scrutinizes Lyam's face. Then Aeron turns to me, taking my hand. With a gentle squeeze, he says, "I love you, and I do want you to be happy. And if he makes you happy, then I'm happy. I shouldn't have acted so foolishly. Can you ever forgive me?"

"Of course I forgive you," I say. "You're my brother. I shouldn't have kept this from you as long as I did. And yes," I add with a grand smile, "Lyam does make me happy."

In my periphery I see Lyam's expression change, his face radiant. I'm amazed he hadn't fully realized my feelings for him until this moment. How does he not know that the mere thought of him makes my heart surge? I can't imagine my life without him, and now that I have Aeron's blessing, by whatever measure it was rendered, I don't have to. I am free to embrace the endless possibilities that have never been called mine before.

I am happy. Very, very happy.

TWELVE

beginnings

W're finally able to relax a bit as acceptance replaces the tension. Whether it is absolute acceptance I'm not certain, but it's acceptance nonetheless. My hand is clasped with Lyam's, as I no longer fear Aeron's disapproval.

Across the bedroom, Aeron leans against the wall, looking at ease, for the most part, while Lyam sits comfortably beside me on my bed. But me? I am rigid, unable to shake the tantalizing thoughts rushing through my mind with striking clarity. Images of Lyam, shirtless in all his muscular splendor, my fingers tangled in his artfully unkempt hair, his in mine, him drawing near to kiss my inviting lips. . . .

If not for our vigilant audience of one.

My hand feels scalding hot in his. My face flushes as if the room is on fire and I am in the midst of raging flames. I try to jerk my hand to my lap, but Lyam's fingers refuse to be denied the presence of mine.

Lyam gazes over at me, eyes pulled into tight slits. "Are you feeling all right? You look feverish." He lifts the back of his hand to my forehead.

Aeron sits taller, peering on in concern, but he graciously allows Lyam to assess the situation, a stark contrast to his usual behavior. But then, a lot of things are a contrast as of late.

I evade Lyam's gaze. "Really, I'm fine."

Cupping my chin, he drags my face to his. "Are you sure? I can take you to see the doctor."

I laugh. Not even Doctor Solmon's magical medicinal roots can cure this fever. "That's not necessary. It's just hot in here, that's all."

Lyam's mouth goes "Oh," and I am surprised he was able to interpret my meaning. He steals a glance at Aeron to see if he's privy to our unspoken exchange.

Mercifully, he's not.

"So," Lyam blurts, changing the subject and quenching the fire between us, "since I have the two of you together, I thought maybe I could ask you some questions."

Aeron's features harden, along with his posture. "Questions?"

"If you don't mind. I was just wondering . . . about your family." Lyam seems equal parts curious and unsure.

"What did you want to know?" I chime in, to prevent Aeron's temper from flaring up again. Lyam means no harm by his inquiry, I know that, but this is such a sensitive subject for Aeron and me. Keeping the tone as light as possible will be key.

"Well, when I tried to ask about you two, people were not forthcoming with information." He stops, assessing my brother's demeanor, then goes on. "I've heard the stories from ages ago about parents having more than one child, but never were they carried at

the same time. *Dviinu*. Is that right?" His pronuncia-
tion is spot on, a lot like *divine* with the long *oo*
hooked on at the end. Aeron and I had discovered regretfully early in life that to be *Dviinu* is anything but
divine.

"Yes." I laugh softly. "That's the word our mother
came up with the day we were born, since no one had
ever heard of a double birth before."

Lyam's confusion and curiosity makes a jumbled
mess of his perfectly sculpted face. "How did it happen?"

"Another long story," I reply, evaluating Aeron's
uneasy expression. It says, *Are you sure you want to
do this?*

Lyam meets Aeron's eyes. "I'm game, if you are."
He says this like he's seeking Aeron's permission
more than offering to lend an understanding ear.

Their gazes lock for a brutally long minute.

Aeron returns to his back-to-the-wall position,
arms outstretched over bent knees. "What the hell,
why not?" Under his breath, he tacks on, "It's your
funeral."

He thinks our past will drive Lyam away, that he'll
refuse to get involved with some with a family history
such as mine.

Before, when Lyam was just another one of Aeron's
tales, the newcomer from afar trying to start anew, I
had accused him of being this very person. But actually knowing Lyam, knowing his character, his heart, I
am confident he is beyond such childish prejudices.

Determined to prove Aeron wrong, I figure there's
no better place to start than the beginning. "Has anyone told you the history of Avalon Valley? How it was
founded?"

Lyam crosses his legs, shuffles closer to me. "I
know nothing about it."

Suddenly I am my mother, with my mother's warm, enchanting voice, painting a picture of how Avalon Valley came to be.

"Hundreds of years ago, back before the Darkness, Zeccion Morgan, who was only sixteen at the time, set out from the west with his young wife, Jautrith. They sought a new life, one with more beauty than their desert-dwelling past had offered. Leaving the land of Mitrs behind, they traveled a great distance over many weeks, the sun guiding them by day, the silvery moon by night. But they never really found what they were looking for. That is, until they spotted a breath-taking wilderness filled with endless possibilities." I lose myself for a moment, drinking in the rapture in Lyam's eyes. "Do you know what *Avalon* means?"

"No," he replies, interested.

"It means *paradise*." I pause again, this time for effect. "Zeccion and Jautrith found their own piece of paradise right here, naming it Avalon Valley. They were delighted by the potential all around them. Trees as far as the eye could see offered shade and lumber. The soil was soft and fertile, perfect for plant-ing. The majestic waterfall furnished an endless supply of fresh water, and wildlife was just as abun-dant."

I continue, revealing that the wide-open space we now call "the clearing" once teemed with hundreds and hundreds of trees, and that they built this very cottage of the choicest cedars cleared from the heart of the woods. The vineyard, the main crop field, and a small orchard were planted. They even worked to do-mesticate some of the animals that once roamed free, the horses, goats, and sheep.

It took several long years of hard work, but Zeccion and Jautrith's devotion was tireless.

In the end, they not only established a place that would sustain them for the rest of their lives, but they started a family. They made Avalon Valley *home*. It truly was paradise.

After seven solitary years had passed, a small, weary family wandered onto their land. Zeccion, having compassion on them, agreed to let them stay. At that time, three of their four children had already been born, and the extra help eased Zeccion's heavy load.

Soon after, another family joined, then another, and within a few more years they had a thriving community on their hands. The entire village held the Morgan family in the highest respect, and that is how it had always been. Until recently.

I break in my story, directing my attention to Aeron. His head is to the wall, tilted toward the ceiling, his eyes closed. He's stretched out his legs, ankles crossed, feet dangling over the edge. I can't tell if he's utterly tired or utterly bored. I decide I don't care.

My focus shifts back to Lyam, who waits patiently.

"Over time," I say, "Avalon Valley grew overcrowded. Many wanted to level more trees to expand the village to the north and west. Being chief, however, Zeccion ultimately had the final say. He was unwilling to lose more of the beautiful woodlands he and his family so loved.

"When he denied their requests, hostility mounted in the newcomers' hearts. They became defiant and disorderly, and began stirring up dissention among the others. But because Zeccion was so highly regarded, they failed, and the rioters were exiled from the land. Most went south and founded Garrison and Crowellhaven. Only a few went northwest, to start Jesyel Grove. Over time, those villages also grew and became well-established communities of their own."

"Established by rioters," Lyam scoffs. "Good leadership qualities they must've had."

"It is what it is," I say. "They're all very nice villages, I'm sure. And there's no animosity between them now. Our men go to Jesyel Grove for supplies, sometimes twice a year. We don't go as far as Garrison, though. I'm surprised you don't know about Garrison's history."

"Maybe I never paid enough attention. *Or* maybe it's because we don't have a proud history to tout, such as yours," he teases.

Aeron chuckles, proving that he hadn't actually been asleep.

"It *was* a proud history," I amend. "Not anymore. People here don't care so much about our beginnings. Their minds are clouded by more recent events."

"Such as?"

Here's where things get tricky. "Well, after the Darkness, the Morgan line eventually died off, except for one. Levvi Morgan was the last remaining son. After he was grown and married, he and his wife had a son, who had a son, who had a son, and so on."

Lyam's dark brows draw low over his ochre-colored eyes. "Only sons? No daughters? Ever?"

"That's right, but that all changed. 'Here's the end of the renowned Morgan family name,' everyone said the day our mother was born. She grew up feeling . . . *inadequate*, to say the least. She worked hard, learning the family trade so that when she married she would be able to care for the vineyard herself."

It has never been a stretch for Aeron or me to identify with our mother's feelings of inadequacy. Her parents, Caastan and Scarlet, loved her very much and always told her how special she was. Like our mother when we were born, they didn't regret having a daughter rather than a son. Still, Mother felt she wasn't good enough. She hated to be the one to bring an end to her family's proud lineage.

My stomach feels deathly hollow and repulsively full all at once. But I press on, reciting the horrific accident that still affects our family to this day. My voice is my own now, not my mother's. "Then a series of unforeseeable events were set into motion one summer day. Our mother was only seventeen and, like me, she loved to swim. She decided to go to the falls after her chores one morning, but as she started home the sky turned dark and sinister."

The images are so clear in my mind, as if I am the one standing under that haunting sky, watching as the sun is consumed by choking, black clouds. I feel the rain wetting my face. Hear the thunder crashing in my ears. I see my mother's father as if through her eyes, racing toward me to bring me home. His mouth forms my name, but the sound is stolen. I'm running, running, running, fast as my legs will go, drenched to the bone. I'm almost there, in the safety of his arms.

Then I'm blinded by a sudden burst of light. Chills slide through me as I run harder. Faster. Another crash of thunder. Another bolt of lightning.

And I am left lifeless on the ground.

THIRTEEN

the dviinu

Lyam wipes away the tears that roll down my cheeks. "You don't have to go on. I'm sorry. I had no idea . . ."

Sharply, Aeron insists, "That's enough for today."

Equally insistent, I say, "No, I want to go on."

Brushing away the remaining tears, I continue, still not quite myself. My heart laments Caastan Morgan's plight as he looks upon the limp, unresponsive body of his only child, knowing there is nothing to be done to bring her back. I see him as he lifts his face to the heavens and weeps into the pounding rain.

Then the menacing clouds vanish in an instant, taking their tears with them. The sun takes back its rightful place in the sky, brilliant and calming. A vivid double rainbow, one atop the other, stretches as far as I can see in either direction, so lovely that it makes the tears all the more fierce. But even the beauty overhead is no remedy for a father's broken heart.

He means to gather his daughter into his arms, needing her closer, unable to let her go. But when he

117

looks upon her, he finds that she is no longer lifeless. Breath passes through her lips. Her eyes stare back at his, glittering in the sunlight. She wears a glowing smile that transcends all the pain he just endured.

"He carried our mother home," I conclude, "drenching her with new tears. Tears of joy."

"That is amazing." Lyam's voice is full of wonderment.

But the story doesn't end there. "Yes, it was a miracle," I say. "But the weeks following her accident were very distressing. When it seemed her health was improving, she would suddenly take a turn for the worse, becoming more weak and ill than she had been before. She was unable to hold anything down, so it wasn't long until her body became emaciated. Her parents felt completely helpless, exhausting every means they could think of to bring her comfort and make her well again. Nothing worked, and they thought she wouldn't survive.

"A few weeks later, our mother started to feel normal again. Her body no longer violently rejected food, and she had an insatiable hunger. She was finally able to regain her weight. Only she put on more than she'd lost. No one could understand what was happening, not even her."

I feel somewhat out of place, trying to paint this picture my mother portrays with such delicacy and poise. This is her story, one I have never been able to relate to. She used to tell it to us when we were young, again and again, because this was our favorite part. I remember how I would hold a hand to my belly, pretending I could feel the tiny nudges she felt that day. But then I grew up, and I had to accept the fact that I never would. I would never truly understand what it would be like to have my belly swell with child.

I don't know how she knew, because her being pregnant was impossible. Perhaps it was intuition, but somehow she knew. She hid her secret for as long as she was able, but instead of letting her parents grow suspicious of her ever-expanding midsection, she decided to tell them the truth, afraid they wouldn't believe she had never been with a man in that way. They did, though. After all, her father had watched her die months prior, and yet she was very much alive.

"Her parents hid her away after that, claiming she'd fallen ill again. Of course, they couldn't conceal her secret for long. Try as they might, they couldn't explain how she came to be with child, for no one believed she was still," my eyes sink to my lap, and the room is on fire again, "a virgin.

"Our mother was treated very badly after that. People whispered things behind her back, called her names. She was an outcast. Nearly the entire village turned against her. The greatest miracle was that she wasn't stoned or hanged for her *crime*, though those things were frequently topics of discussion.

"The respect that had been held for our family for hundreds of years was lost," I say, "but perhaps a little remained, which absolved her of that fate so many thought she deserved. Still, Mother felt her only allies were her parents and her best friend, Tavine."

Lyam is aghast. "That's terrible! To have nearly everyone you've known your whole life forsake you like that. And at such a young age, too, to have to bear such an unorthodox burden. Your mother is living proof that nothing is impossible."

"That isn't the half of it," I say, whisking Lyam away to the day of our birth.

My mother's face replays in my mind as she tells us of the spiteful comments from ignorant, judgmental

119

hearts, which drove her to seek escape on that unsea-
sonably warm February day. Eight months pregnant,
she stole away for the clearing, heedless of the extra
life she carried inside her. Tears came down in tor-
rents, as did the water that rushed to her feet. She
was in labor. And she was alone. She screamed out in
pain, though no one would come to her aid, making
the fear all the more crippling.

Then my mother's expression changes in my imagination, from troubled and faraway to shining and
peaceful, describing the calm spirit that swept over
her, as if the gods were with her that day, comforting
her. A new sense of joy shattered the fear, and she no
longer felt alone. Within minutes she was looking into
the bold, green eyes of her baby girl, sensing that she
was different, special somehow.

Not long after that, another bout of paralyzing pain
stabbed at her from inside her womb. She bore down
while another birth pang overtook her, and she delivered a second child. Again, she gazed into the eyes of
her baby, this time a son. She held her two infants—
Dviinu, as she called us—in her arms, knowing that
our lives were set apart from others.

Naturally, news of our arrival was not well received amongst the villagers. It was bad enough that
the unwed 'virgin' girl, the same one who had died
from a lightning strike and miraculously lived again,
had now given birth.

The fact that she'd birthed two babies was more
than they could handle. We were called nothing short
of an abomination. Somehow we were spared from
death. I always suspected that Caastan Morgan re-
nouncing his title as chief played a role in that
decision, but our mother has yet to affirm that. Perhaps that was the negotiation, our lives for his
authority.

I go on without missing a beat. "Our mother knew without a doubt that those two tiny lives she'd carried would forever change hers. That we were born for a purpose, and she was specifically chosen to be our mother, given the supreme responsibility of raising the first set of Dviinu in existence. And now, with a son born to her, the Morgan family name would live on.

"That was the second day of February, a little over sixteen years ago," I conclude. My lips curl into a tight, crooked smile, hoping Lyam is the man I think him to be.

Aeron's eyes open, also anxious for Lyam's reaction. I can read the question in them. Will Lyam walk out, wanting nothing more to do with me?

The sudden nerves of it cause my stomach to quiver. In theory I'd found it hard to believe Lyam would be anything but understanding. I only wish I still had that steadfast assurance.

I find Lyam's expression unreadable. "That's quite a history. Unbelievable, really. It's no surprise you two are so close. I think I would have been crippled under all that condemnation. But it's been sixteen years now. It's not that way still, is it?"

I release a breath I've been holding in. "No, the hostility has subsided. The most belligerent have passed now and just their children remain. Like our mother, many were teenagers at the time. They saw the torment their parents put her through, and as they grew and had families of their own, they assumed a different approach. Though the original respect for our family has long since faded, a new respect has risen. We were recognized as Zeccion Morgan's heirs, therefore rightful owners of this land. Because of that, they've learned to be civil. Not kind, just civil."

"It's as if we don't exist," cuts in Aeron bitterly.

Satrie knows you exist, I almost tease, but I think better of it lest I risk embarrassing him.

For both his sake and Lyam's, I clarify. "Not everyone is that way. Aeron has a good relationship with Doctor Solmon. He's not like the others at all. He was a teenager when we were born, too, and he and his father were there for our mother from the start. And Mother is still friends with Tavine Mercer. She's never cast judgment on any of us, but I keep to myself when I'm not with Aeron or Mother."

In truth, I've never had a friend, which is easy to know but hard to say, because the saying stings more than the knowing.

"We've mostly gotten used to being outcasts, being invisible. Some days are harder than others, but since we have each other, it's easier to bear. Sometimes we feel like we have some kind of plague or something." I laugh, just a small one. "Like being Dviinu is contagious."

"That's absurd," Liam says with a laugh of disbelief. "What happened to your mother was not by choice, yet your family is treated as if it were." He gathers up my hands and pulls them to his chest. "I want you to know that I will never judge you like that, ever. I am so sorry you've had to live like this so long. Something has to change. This cannot continue. I won't let it."

"Lyam, that's very noble of you," I say, "but this is nothing new to us. I don't expect anything from you, I just ask that you accept me as I am." There's an apprehensive note in my voice that I can't shake, no matter what I tell myself.

"Aeria, you are perfect. Do not let anyone ever convince you otherwise."

My hands are still pressed to Lyam's chest, and I feel the rapid beating of his heart. Mine goes *ba-ba-boom* and I can't tear my gaze from his and I'm in a thousand places at once, some born of hope and some precious remembrances. I don't know what the future holds for us, which both thrills and terrifies me, but I also know there's nowhere else I want to be so long as we're together.

Noisily, Aeron clears his throat, reminding us of his presence and his overprotective nature. A warning in his brows says we're being too intimate.

I linger a moment longer at Lyam's chest, then scowl at Aeron with a warning of my own. If he's to accept our relationship, this is something he will have to get used to, and there's no better time to start than now. I slide closer to Lyam, wrap his arm around me so that his hand rests at my side. Aeron delivers another stern look. Which I ignore.

But Lyam does not. "Are you sure about this?" he whispers in my ear, causing my skin to prickle at the touch of his breath.

Dizzily, I manage a nod.

Let Aeron cast all the withering looks he wants, but he will be powerless to compel me to leave this embrace. I hadn't realized how much it had been weighing on me, the secrets of my past, and how freeing it would be to have Lyam know the truth. Now his embrace represents so much more than it has before. This limitless acceptance I find in his arms is so foreign, and with that heaviness lifted, I have nothing to fear. I can just be me.

And to Lyam, that is perfect.

I am perfect.

FOURTEEN

company

Aeria? Aeron?" Mother calls from down the hall.

"In our room," Aeron says, cutting a warning glance at me. We both know Mother won't feel too kindly about the way Lyam and I are snuggling.

That is not a battle I am prepared to enter into. Neither is Lyam. He shoves away from my bed, crosses the room in three quick strides, and stands stiffly at the foot of Aeron's bed.

Soft footfalls draw nearer, followed by three taps. "Is everything all right? May I come in?"

"It's safe," I assure her.

Mother pushes the door open enough to peer in; I see her eye and a sliver of her cheekbone pressed against it.

"Really," I say, "Aeron and I worked everything out."

She pushes the door slowly still, as if her appearance will somehow disrupt the delicate balance of Aeron's mood, and everything I've worked toward will be for naught. I urge her on, and when the door

125

swings wide she is immediately taken aback, eyes trained on Lyam. It's apparent his proximity to me makes her apprehensive. And him being in my room behind closed doors has likely doubled her trepidation. She trusts me, I believe, but she doesn't know a thing about the boy who's suddenly entered my life.

"Oh, Lyam. I wasn't aware you were still—"

My voice cracks as I break in, "Mother. I told you we'd talk to Aeron, remember?"

Her wide-eyed expression begins to relax. She smiles sweetly. "It's getting late."

"Of course, Miss Morgan. I was just about to go. Thank you for allowing me to come and make peace with Aeron. I believe we can be good friends now." Lyam hurries past her to the door.

I ask, "Wait. Mother, couldn't he stay for supper?" After all, she's the one who suggested he come for a visit, so why is she now so anxious for him to leave? I can't believe my family, what fickle creatures they have become.

I hear her "No" before she says it. "Aeria, I—"

"No, she's right," cuts in Lyam delicately. "It's late and I've got to get back to the Browns'. I have some work to catch up on before daylight's gone. Another time, perhaps." Though there's more hope than confidence in his words.

Mother is tongue-tied by Lyam's level of maturity and humility. It shames me. I sound like an argumentative little girl, with more demands than experiences and nothing to show for either.

Still, my request hangs in the air, and I can see the consideration in my mother's brown eyes. I think back to our conversation the night before, of her secret admiration for Lotz Drake and the heartbreak of those unrequited feelings, wondering if her pain then will influence her now. But I also think of this supposed purpose she speaks of, wondering if that will win out over love.

Finally she says, "How about dessert?"

"Dessert's great, if it's not too much trouble. Please, Miss Morgan, don't feel pressured. If another night would be—"

"Call me Nira," she reminds him softly. "While I know my daughter can be quite convincing at times, I have been known to make my own decisions. Tonight would be lovely. I'm looking forward to hearing more about you."

"Thank you, Miss Mor— uh, Nira. I'll be here." To me he mouths a jovial "Bye."

Then he's gone, and my heart is left with hollow yearning. I've spent so much of my day with him that I hate for him to go.

"Well," Mother says, "I'm glad you were able to talk things over and make up. I don't relish all this disunity. Or *fighting*," she chides gently.

Aeron bows his head. "I was out of line. It won't happen again."

Mother looks on him with compassion. "It's behind us now. We can all move forward in forgiveness."

She's right. It's all behind us. My sadness over Lyam's absence, Aeron's misunderstanding and animosity, the revelation of our family's history. It's all behind us. All except for the attack on me. I have an eerie suspicion *that* is not behind us. But for now I can accept that.

The minutes pass dreadfully slowly after that.

It's my turn to help with supper, so Mother and I prepare a simple leek-and-potato soup, then I ready the crusts for apple pie. I realize, a bit belatedly, that Mother's basket sits abandoned beneath our favorite tree. Mother sends Aeron to retrieve it while I finish up the pie. I spread spiced apples over the crust and top it with the second crust, pinching the edges together to resemble cresting waves, and slide the dish in the oven above the stone hearth to bake.

Over supper Mother asks about our lunch, curious as to what had led to such violence, while also reminding us of the implications of anyone discovering Lyam had been in an altercation. Voice laden with shame, Aeron explains how he took off without hearing the entire story. How he thought I'd found Lyam's presence unavoidable while I went about my chores. Mercifully, he honors my request to keep the night I sneaked out a secret.

Aeron finishes off the last of the soup and takes the dishes and the soup pot to the stream for washing. I wipe down the table and dress it with Mother's fine linens, which seldom see the light of day, and set out four small dessert plates and four forks. It's been ages since we've had company for dessert, or any meal for that matter—putting aside Tavine's visit when Aeron was gone, so it was still a party of three.

Really, it's a wonder we even own an extra chair. We're so used to it just being the three of us, and though four is an even number in the traditional sense of the word, it's odd for us.

With nothing left to do, I take to pacing between the kitchen and the front room, which would actually be one big, open space were it not for the partial wall that divides them. We don't have much in the way of decorations on the walls, save for rows of horseshoes that hang above the divan. They are aged and worn, some rusted, others still caked with dirt from better days. They date all the way back to Zeccion Morgan's horse, Chief, to my mother's father's horse, Maelco. The last horse that ever carried a Morgan chieftain.

Pacing back and forth, the heat from the hearth makes it like stepping from summer to fall, summer to fall. Especially when the house is so piercingly and delightfully infused with the warm scent of apples and spices.

This goes on for some time before Mother's had enough. "Breathe," she tells me, cupping my shoulders, and I do, inhaling through my nose and blowing the air out through my mouth. It helps a little, but my stomach is still tied up in unruly knots.

Concluding that pacing is of no benefit, I commit to being still. I stand in the kitchen, gazing out the tiny, square window. Though light remains, the moon gradually mounts its lofty throne, our peaceful keeper of the night.

Though I still my body, I cannot still my mind. What is taking Lyam so long? Has he decided not to come? Maybe what he learned about me has shifted from a story told to a reality lived, an inescapable lifestyle, and he can't bear the thought of getting mixed up with that.

That's when I hear the front door open.

But it's only Aeron returning from the stream. I try to keep the disappointment from showing, but it is regretfully evident.

I hate to think the worst, but as of late it's all I can come up with. I imagine Aeron going back on his word, and never seeing Lyam again. The thought pricks at my insides, rattles my core, sends my feet back to pacing. Over in "fall," Mother and Aeron look on helplessly.

I've crossed back over to "summer," spying on the pie while I'm there, when a series of light knocks rap at the door. "Lyam," I breathe, as a fluttering being takes flight in my chest.

Mother is first to the door. She smooths her hair from her face, lets out a calming breath. She's just as nervous as me, yet she's shown no signs of it until now. When she swings the door open, she reveals a devastatingly handsome Lyam. He's changed into a dressier shirt, designed for wearing rather than working, similar to the one tucked beneath my pillow for safekeeping. In his hands are two long-stemmed purple orchids.

"Good evening, Nira," he says, presenting the first flower to her. Four brilliantly-colored orchid blooms grace the gradually arching stem.

She smiles, slightly embarrassed. "Good evening, Lyam. Thank you, these are lovely," she says, absently lifting the topmost flower to her nose. I wouldn't be surprised if Lyam's the first boy to ever give my mother a flower.

I can only imagine the simple things she never got to experience throughout her life. Has she ever been kissed? It breaks my heart, because I don't think she has.

Lyam steps inside. "Thank you for having me over on such short notice." Then he's standing before me. "Hello again, Aeria." He holds the remaining orchid in his hands. Unlike my mother's, the stem boasts a solitary, deep-purple flower. With one quick motion, he snaps the stem in two, making a crunching sound as if he's broken a twig in half. My mouth gapes. I think I hear Aeron chuckle.

Lips turned up in a crooked half-smile, Lyam offers me the docked flower. I reach out to accept it when suddenly he pulls it to his chest. My face scrunches up in confusion. Lyam gives a soft laugh, and he offers the flower once more.

Only I don't reach for it this time.

He tucks my hair behind my ear and threads the orchid through so that it rests alongside my temple. As he lowers his hand, he softly caresses my cheek.

We both start when, out of nowhere, the door crashes shut. Aeron claps his hands together, glances around the room. He says, "How about that pie?" even though he knows it's not done yet.

Mother shakes her head at him. I make a dark face, and only then does his expression turn rueful.

I tell Lyam in a low voice, "I'm so glad you came."

His fingertips graze mine. He whispers, "Why wouldn't I come?"

I don't think Mother's too keen about our whispering, so she says, "Would you like to have a seat, Lyam? My daughter has prepared a fabulous pie, but it's not quite ready." She's gesturing to the worn, leather chair adjacent to the divan. It's oversized by normal chair standards, but as normal chair standards go, it still seats only one.

Lyam is quick to appease my mother, though I am confident we're both thinking we'd rather take up two-thirds of the divan than split us down the middle. Frankly, I'm growing tired of people wanting to split us down the middle. As it is, Lyam's got the chair, so I sit at Mother's right, closest to the chair so that if we lengthen our arms a bit we can hold hands. Aeron drags a chair out from the table, twisting it around so that it faces the rest of us.

"Aeron, would you join us, please?" Mother pats the empty spot beside her. It's not a request.

"I'm fine here, if it's all the same to you."

I recognize the tone instantly. It is the one he uses when he's in overprotective mode. Standing guard. Taking first watch. Keeping an eye trained on the threat. It's a message: I am here, and I am watching.

FIFTEEN

loss

Mother dismisses Aeron with a wave of her hand and turns back to our guest. "So, Lyam, tell me about yourself. I hear you're from Garrison. I've never been there. What is it like?"

"I certainly can't tout its great history, as people here can." He says this earnestly, and he's rewarded with one of my mother's vibrant smiles. Lyam goes on. "I never knew any different, but in all honesty Garrison pales to Avalon Valley. It's much smaller, and the homes are crowded so close you can hear the wind whistle between them at night. They seemed to have been constructed hastily, and the weather has really taken a toll over the last few decades. We get a lot of wind, you see, so we've had to do some rebuilding over the years, my family's home included."

"Aeria mentioned you're a carpenter," Mother says. "Were you involved in the rebuilding?"

"Yes. My father and I led the project for many years, and it was his father who led it before us, and his father before him."

"Tell me about your parents. What are they like?"

"My father, Vitar, was born and raised in Garrison. People say he was born with sawdust in his veins and tools in his fists," Lyam says with a smile, "not because it was the family trade but because he always had this natural aura about him. He could mend *any-thing*, and the whole village knew it. It was my father, at the age of twelve, who developed a method of notching beams to strengthen the joints, providing greater integrity and longevity.

"He's a serious kind of man, but very loving. The story goes that he met my mother, Myriam, the day she moved to Garrison. She grew up across the river, but there was a fire that forced many to seek refuge. When my father saw her, it was love at first sight. But my mother was stubborn in her youth. My father says wooing her was like talking a horse into branding itself. But eventually she fell victim to his charm. They married, and I was born the next year."

"So what brought you here?" Mother asks.

Lyam hesitates, a wry smile tugging at his lips. "They are wonderful parents, but their persistence over . . . certain matters . . . was taking a toll on me."

"*Matters*?" Mother and Aeron say in unison.

Lyam laughs nervously. "Uh, yes. They were concerned for my future, which is understandable, but they became quite proactive about finding me a wife. That's why I left. I wanted the freedom to make my own choices."

I feel my mother become smaller and smaller beside me, shrinking back into the divan cushion as if she's being swallowed whole. She stares ahead with faraway eyes. Noticeably flustered, she says, "So, you came here to— to find a *wife*?"

"Not at all," Lyam chuckles. "I came here to escape my parents' pressure, to choose my own path. Now, if that means getting married one day, I'll be open to that. But I came here with no agenda, no expectations. I always imagined that if I was meant to find love, it would find me." He squeezes my hand, glances at me from the corner of his eye.

Suddenly I'm there in the clearing, lost under that bold, night sky, wearing nothing but Lyam's shirt, his eyes on me so intently. A finger pressed to my lips, his voice is sweet in my ears. *What if I've already found it?*

The thought that someone could love me had been such a foreign concept all my life that my heart couldn't properly grasp it, couldn't hold onto that much hope. Even now, it's hard to believe that Lyam is here in my home, squeezing my hand in a single, tiny gesture that could fill an entire ocean to overflowing with hope.

Mother's voice cuts through the warm night air and I'm no longer sitting with the grass licking at my ankles. The scent of spiced apples replaces the solid pine of Lyam's shirt. "So, *Lyam*, what does that mean?" She crosses one leg over the other, resting her hands on her knees, at ease now that the subject's shifted.

Lyam's mouth works to keep a smile at bay. "It means," he gives pause long enough to pique my curiosity, "*protector*."

I choke. Aeron's eyes flash wide.

I'm already on my feet, stumbling toward the kitchen when Mother asks, "Dear, are you all right?"

I clear my throat as quietly as possible and answer, "Checking on the pie."

"My Aeria makes a wonderful apple pie," she tells him.

"It smells heavenly," Lyam says loudly, to be sure the compliment reaches my ears.

I smile at the pie, though he can't see it. The once-pale waves are now golden brown. A bit of the liquid center has escaped around the edges, coloring them with promises of sweetness and cinnamon. I remove the dish, carefully, and bask in the aroma and the steam that rises against my face.

"Your name has very strong meaning, Lyam. Was it your mother who named you, or your father?" Apparently my mother still thinks this to be a safer topic than the one that involves Lyam finding a wife.

"It was my mother. One of my earliest memories is of sitting on her lap and, very seriously, she says to me, 'Lyam, you'll save someone's life someday. It is a great responsibility you bear, my son.' I couldn't have been more than four or five, but those words have always stuck with me."

"Well, I'd say you were born with a special purpose, like my Aeria and Aeron."

I can hear the smile in Lyam's voice. "I believe so. More strongly now than ever."

My mother *hmm*s thoughtfully. At the same time, she and Lyam call my name. I jerk my gaze away from the pie, set it down to cool, and return to the front room, my face warm with both steam and the truth my mother can never know.

"There's something I'd like to ask. Please, sit." Lyam's standing, but he's far from stationary. His feet move, yet he goes nowhere, and he's stuffing his hands in his pockets and pulling them out, only to put them back in again.

I sit, curious as to what's got him this undone. He's a horse champing at the bit.

"Nira, I was wondering if you would give me your permission to—"

BOOM!

My skin pricks as another *BOOM* thunders throughout all of Avalon Valley.

Lyam falls silent. We sit unmoving.

BOOM!

BOOM!

BOOM!

I count them. My heart grieves more and more, as each one bespeaks a deeper sense of finality than the one it preceded. The realness of it is as harsh as it is inescapable.

"What's going on?" demands Lyam after another *BOOM!* There's a healthy dose of terror in his eyes.

Mother's face is grave. Voice weighted with sadness, she replies, "The drums. Someone's passed."

At this, Lyam bows his head.

I continue counting. Another. And another. And yet another still.

The drums finally cease, but our silence lives on, nearly as loud.

The sadness of it draws a sigh from my mother's lips. "The announcement will begin any minute. We should leave before we're late." She motions to the door.

"Leave?" Lyam asks.

"We all meet at the plaza," I explain. At his side now, I slip my hand into his.

"Why'd the drums carry on so long?"

"We call them *marks*." This is Aeron, deadpan. "Every drumbeat marks a year of the person's life. It's one of the ways we honor them."

"Any idea who passed?"

"Not sure," I reply, more hushed now that we're outdoors. At first, I feared it might have been our leader, Chief Cole, but the number of marks doesn't support that. At forty-five, he's the oldest member of the village, and truth be told, he doesn't have much longer since the Darkness has driven a knife through life expectancy. I have a sneaking suspicion who it might be, but I don't say anything except, "We'll find out when we get there."

There is no urgency in anyone's gait tonight. The sun has settled, and the moon and stars shine in full glory. The torches that flank the footpath are alight. They are as tall as my shoulders, and their dancing flames cast ever-shifting shadows at our feet. My fingers are twined with Lyam's, seeking the safety of his touch, the darkness too much of a reminder of things that hide in wait.

The village is silent. Every living thing is soundless to honor the life lost.

Except Lyam, but I can't begrudge a newcomer his curiosity. At least he's keeping it at a whisper. "How many marks?" Of course, he doesn't know to count them as everyone else does.

My answer makes my stomach turn. "Eighteen."

I think it has the same effect on Lyam. I see his eyes narrow, his mouth work, his brows join together.

We approach the brightly lit plaza where the others have already gathered, faces awash with shades of loss. They huddle together, family and friends, in solidarity, shoulders hunched against the pain. Some cry openly. Some weep inwardly. And still some wear a look of shock that will soon turn into one of the two former things. For no one can't not cry.

Us included.

We go to the back, as usual, and Lyam stands with us. We are the last to arrive. As Aeron's gaze sweeps over the crowd, eyes jumping from man to man in search of evidence I know he won't find, I search for the girl I don't expect to find.

She isn't here.

From the heart of the crowd I see the top of Chief Cole's head glinting under the moonlight, see splashes of his ceremonial robe as he makes his way to the dais at the front of the plaza.

I watch as he mounts the steps, one, then another, and another after that, and finally the last, as if his reluctance could undo the reason for us being here tonight.

Chief Cole's face is pale in contrast to his blood-red velvet robe. It is unadorned, save for the braided gold cord around his waist and, embroidered on his right breast, the Cole family brand, a C that very much resembles a horseshoe.

For sixteen years he's worn the chieftain's robe, but one day soon his twenty-seven-year-old son Zede will succeed him, and he will don the same unadorned robe with the golden braid for addresses such as the one his father will make tonight.

Chief Cole raises a hand to silence the murmurs. He looks tidy and official, but I can never get over the way his stomach protrudes as if he's stowed a sack of grain beneath his robe. As always, his thin, black hair is slicked back and gathered at the nape of his neck. From this distance he seems to have almost no eyes, with those big, bushy brows of his. Especially when the sadness of his address weighs them down so.

"There is much grief in the air tonight," he says, remembering to project his voice halfway through. This stirs a few sleepy children who repose limply against parents' shoulders. "As you have heard the marks of the drums, you know why we gather. It is with great sorrow that I inform you that our dear Debayah has fallen victim to the Darkness."

A collective moan hums through the crowd. Heads bow.

I feel like something inside me has snapped. Only two years my elder, Debayah's death hits so, so close to home. I look to Lyam through watery eyes.

Chief grants a moment of silence, then continues. "We were blessed with Debayah's radiant smile for eighteen glorious years. As a village, we grieved alongside her when her beloved Javiss passed last August. Then again, two months later, when her mother and father passed in the same night. Tonight, we gather together to remember her life."

He motions to someone in the crowd, and we all search to see who is moving.

Finally, I see her. Ruuah Harris is four years older than Debayah, but they were always close friends. Ruuah is a slight thing, made smaller by her grief. Before she turns to face the crowd, she scrubs away tears. "Debayah suffered more pain in her short life than any one person ought to," she says, and each word sounds like a stifled sob.

I was fourteen when Debayah and Javiss were married. It was only three weeks later that he fell deathly ill. And when he passed the following summer, I remember questioning how it was that Debayah could wear such a brave face in light of what had happened, in light of what would happen since her chance of becoming a mother died along with her beloved. Mother told me it was because she did not want to be pitied. I imagined she must have cried and cried and cried, but that was something she kept hidden away for only the gods to hear.

What I remember most is how the news of Javiss' death broke me that day.

Now again I am that young girl, feeling small and powerless, and pitying Debayah Baynes and the future version of myself. I identified with her in a way others never would. I understood that her fate would become my own. I accepted it long ago, though I can't quite put a finger on the day. It became a given, like the sun rising in the morning and the moon at night. I knew I was too different and my past was too dark for anyone to ever look through them and see me for me.

It hadn't felt right then, losing Javiss, and this doesn't feel right now, losing Debayah for the sole reason that she couldn't have a child. Life shouldn't be this way. It was meant to be enjoyed, not spent mourning over loved ones who were never given the opportunity to live to a ripe old age, the way it used to be before the Darkness. It grates at me how lives are always cut short. Stolen. The brevity of it all is a grave injustice.

Standing in the midst of all this heaviness, I am forced to wonder when loss will strike my own life. My mother's parents passed when I was young, too young to recall. I know nothing of this intimate loss, the kind that causes even your spirit to weep, the way she and nearly every other person here does. I wish to keep it that way.

Of course, the fate of my loved ones is not in my hands. I can only have an immense appreciation for the fact that it was not me who had to present a tearful eulogy tonight.

A tear hangs in my eye as I look from my mother to Aeron to Lyam. Three people I love too dearly. Pain throbs in my chest, but I push it down. Words play in my ears, shapeless sounds. Tears rain down, but they feel strangely out of place, for all I can do is think how blessed I am to have these three in my life.

SIXTEEN

White roses

C hief Cole returns to his position at the head of the plaza and thanks Ruuah for her beautiful words. A low, respectful applause surfaces for a moment as Ruuah returns to her husband and their three-year-old son, fast asleep on his father's shoulder.

"We will mourn Debayah's passing," Chief Cole says, "with the preparation of the ceremonial funeral table, then we will lift her spirit to the gods. After that, we shall join for the Celebration of Life. Let us sleep well tonight, for there is much to be accomplished. Duties are to be assigned in the morning." Chief Cole steps down from the dais, joins his wife, Iris, and pulls her into a tight embrace.

With that, we are dismissed. What was once relative silence now climbs to a soft, collective whisper. Condolences are offered to the Harris family, as they had opened up their home to Debayah after her parents passed, so her loss is especially hard on them.

I watch the crowd slowly dwindle to just a few people scattered here and there. My gaze finds my mother, her eyes red and glazed. She doesn't blink for a long minute. And when she speaks, there is no life in her voice. "You should get home, Lyam. We will see you in the morning."

I'm curious if Debayah's death causes her to reconsider whatever reservations still linger regarding Lyam and me. This is irrefutable evidence that, without him, without him giving me a child, it will be me she mourns in two or three years. Four, if we're lucky.

Lyam nods respectfully, first to Mother, then to Aeron. "Thank you for your hospitality tonight. I look forward to another opportunity to try Aeria's pie." He smiles warmly, giving my arm a gentle squeeze. "Sweet dreams, Aeria Morgan." He says my name as if he cherishes the sound of it, the feel of it on his lips. It makes my pulse trip and my insides flitter.

"That's too bad about Debayah," Aeron remarks dolefully when we're back home. "If only she'd had a child, how different her life would have been."

"Debayah lived through many sorrows over the last year. I can't imagine the pain of never becoming a mother. Losing Javiss must have been unbearable. The Harris family must be devastated." Mother's thoughts are clearly jumbled. "She will be greatly missed," she adds.

Part of me wonders if she sees herself in Ruuah's place tonight, scrubbing away tears and holding back sobs as she speaks of my own life cut short. Perhaps now she will appreciate what Lyam truly means to me. More than a friend. More than a chance at love. But hope.

Hope that my future may be rewritten. Hope that my days will not be as a vapor, here for just a short while and then gone, but as numerous as the stars.

Mother bids us goodnight and retreats to the sanctuary of her bedroom.

"I'll be a few minutes," I tell Aeron, but he won't budge until he sees that I'm only tidying up. I clear the dessert plates from the table, fold Mother's linens, cover the pie, and heave a lengthy sigh that no one hears. I had pictured this night ending so differently.

I pick my way through the darkness to my bed and bury myself beneath my blanket, though it is ineffectual at concealing me from the sadness of tonight. My hand slips under my head, under my pillow, such an unconscious action now that I must have been rubbing Lyam's shirt between my fingers for several minutes before it ever dawns on me that I'm doing it.

I force my fingers to another victim of my mindless manipulation, a button, lest I wear a hole in the fabric. I trace the circular shape of it, play over its smooth surface, but it is a vastly poor substitute for the smoothness of Lyam's rich, sun-tanned skin.

Try as I may, my lids just won't close. If Aeron's still awake, and I'd bet the goat I don't have that he is, he doesn't let me know it. Sleep is a cunning thing to chase tonight.

When I wake the next morning, it's as if the new day is a deep well which has collected all the grief my slumber took and has hastily poured it right back in. I feel groggy and sad. And still broken.

I'm surprised to find Aeron across the room sleeping soundly. How early have I awakened that I've outslept him?

"Morning," Aeron croaks not two seconds later, but it couldn't have been me that roused him. Dark circles ring his eyes, giving him a haggard expression without having to work at it. He's slept about as well as I have.

145

My "Morning" sounds equally jaded, heavy with consonants and not enough vowels. I clear my throat a bit as Aeron comes to a sitting position.

He buries his face in his hands, leaving enough room for his words to pass. I can only see his lips. They part, and he lets out a frog-like groan. "I had the strangest dream. I was trapped, but I don't know where." Now he's looking at me, eyes round and intense, as if this dream world and our reality coexist and he can't decide which world I belong to. "And I don't know how, but I could see *everything*. There were so many colors, bright colors like I've never seen before. Someone was in my head, and we were talking back and forth. I can't remember what I was doing, but I know it was important, as if someone needed my help. It was all very strange." He rests his head against his pillow. "I wonder if it means anything."

"Of course it means something. It means I've been right all these years. You do hear crazy voices in your head."

He rolls his eyes, and then all I see is his pillow cutting through the air. I dodge it, but only barely. I chuck it back at him, but he's already traded his playful side for one that says, *It's time to get to business.*

Bed made, he tells me, "We should get a move on." He tucks a change of clothes under his arm and mumbles to himself as he makes his way out the door. "It's going to be a busy day."

For my family, someone's death means more than just the normal ramifications of mourning. It means that the three of us will spend the day intermingled uncomfortably amongst the villagers. My heart knocks anxiously at the thought, and I take several purposeful breaths to calm myself.

Following tradition, I dress in a long, black mourning gown, representing the Darkness that covered the entire earth so long ago. Had it not been for those three dark, fateful days, Debayah Baynes and everyone else who passed far before their time would still be here with us.

We settle down to eat, but no one speaks. What is there to say when such sadness looms? Mother looks as worn as Aeron and me, which is so far from her usual appearance that the image doesn't sit well. Black does not suit her.

As a single unit, we wend through the village to Central Plaza to receive instructions for the day. There are many preparations to be made, and I'm mentally preparing myself for a repeat of last fall, when I worked invisibly alongside Shara Lofton and Aarzay Mason. We're not the last to arrive, so Chief Cole hasn't yet taken his place. The somber mood has survived the night, touching every member of the gathering with the same unforgiving potency as in the moment it was delivered.

I spot Lyam toward the front. He's standing at Saeth Brown's shoulder. From this view, neither of them can see me but I can see that they're talking. I watch the way Lyam's lips move, the way his mouth forms the words I cannot hear, the way his eyes tell a story I wish I could understand. Was this how he felt that day before we met, when he'd seen me all over the village without me noticing? It feels wicked and wonderful all at once.

Lyam, knowing where to find me when I arrive, turns and catches my gaze. He fights back a smile, but it breaks through the hard set of his eyes, softening them if only for a moment.

After what seems an eternity, though it was probably no more than an hour, the list of roles has been read. It's no surprise that Lyam will help Saeth and his father, Thellan, with the funeral table, but a foolish part of me longs to hear his name called out along-side mine.

I have no room to complain, however, for Mother and I have been entrusted with the distinguished role of gathering the roses, which will line the table like a pure white, satin blanket. What's more, the list is mercifully short. It's just us and Mother's friend, Tavine, which means I won't have to play invisible all day.

Aeron's more than pleased to hear his name called a few beats after Satrie Solmon's. They'll be part of a team of seven responsible for gathering the food for tonight's Celebration of Life feast.

As the crowd begins to split into groups, Saeth starts toward his workshop, tugging at Lyam's shirt-sleeve. Lyam throws another glance my way, and I think he means it as an apology, but his lips don't move. Then Saeth says something that reclaims his attention. Lyam doesn't look back.

I give a start when Tavine flutters to a stop in front of us. "Good morning, Morgans." Her singsong voice is good medicine against the melancholy, and if that isn't enough, her fiery, red hair is sure to do the trick. "Looks like we're on finger-pricking duty."

"You always have the best outlook on life, Tav," Mother pokes back, wrapping an arm around Tavine's slender frame.

"I'll see you later." Aeron's tone is the same shade of enthusiastic. "I'm going to join my group."

I can't help but wonder if Aeron will actually sum-mon up the courage to talk to Satrie now that her infatuation with him has been brought to light. I en-courage him with a whimsical smile, wishing him luck in a way only he will understand. He smiles back and strikes off with more confidence in his step than I've seen in a long time.

Aeron's the last to arrive. Satrie, who had slyly watched his approach, is now engaged in a conversation she didn't start, going out of her way to pay him no mind. Doctor Solmon, on the other hand, takes him by the arm. They've always had a friendly relationship, but I puzzle over what the good doctor would think of Aeron's interest in his daughter.

It's a ten-minute walk to the gardens from Central Plaza. We stop first at the barn. Mother and Tavine go inside for supplies while I go around the back to retrieve a large wheelbarrow.

We continue to our appointed location, chatting in hushed voices. Mother and Tavine dominate the conversation, which is fine by me. They're entertaining enough to listen to. I'm glad to have been grouped with them; it'll be nice not having to receive the cold shoulder all day.

The gardens are enclosed by a fence identical to the one that surrounds the orchard. Mother pushes the gate open, allowing me to get the wheelbarrow through. I trail behind Tavine, whose familiarity with the gardens is the result of years of tender loving care for the plants here. The warm air is sweet with the fragrance of blooms that color the picturesque stretch of land.

"Here we are," Tavine says, gesturing with a flourish to the white rose bushes.

Mother passes out the gloves she got from the barn, keeping a pair for herself, and we get to work, cutting roses from the plentiful bushes, selecting only the purest, whitest blooms. The stems are left long, and soon Mother takes to the task of removing the thorns, adding immaculate rose after immaculate rose to the barrow. Now and then, the sharp points sneak through the fingertips of my gloves, quick and temporarily bothersome.

149

"So, Aeria," Tavine says, "your mother tells me that you've gotten friendly with that new boy. How's that coming along?" Her brows dance in curiosity. Freckles swirl beneath her striking, blue eyes from one cheek-bone to the other, splattered even more prominently across the bridge of her nose. She hovers a sliver above five feet, which never ceases to amuse me when she's standing opposite her mountainous husband. Tavine's hair falls below her shoulder blades, and it appears even more aflame when backlit by the sun.

I can't decide if I'm shocked that my mother's told her about my relationship with Lyam. "It's going fine."

"He's a handsome young man."

"He's great," is all I say, knowing that Tavine's fishing for spicier details. Which I am not willing to divulge.

Mother stands to stretch her legs and adds, "He is very well-mannered."

I say nothing more after that, and the subject quickly turns from Lyam to Debayah, which is more fitting. I hadn't ever talked to her personally, but I don't think either of us can be faulted for that. It stems from the sad union of her circumstances and mine. From what they say of her, I have to admit she did sound wonderful. Like we might have been friends, had we lived in some other world.

SEVENTEEN

last goodbye

I've been cutting roses so long that my legs and feet are tingling from the lack of circulation, and my muscles are as stiff as Sebaan gets at bath time. But when I come to my feet a sudden onset of dizziness strikes me. I brace myself until my vision clears and everything is right back where it's supposed to be.

Tavine whispers something to my mother that I can't make out. Mother turns around, so I twist in the same direction to see what caused her mouth to drop. Mine gapes, too, and I shut it promptly, biting the side of my tongue in the process. The metallic taste of blood floods my mouth and I swallow it down, unwilling to spit it out in front of Lyam.

"That's a whole lot of skin," Mother says, not bothering to mask her flustered tone. I can sense a bit of irritation there as well.

"That's a whole lot of *muscle*," Tavine corrects, not bothering to mask her fascinated one.

It's not all that uncommon for men to work around the village shirtless, especially in such kind weather, but to be honest, I can understand my mother's reaction. Never before has her daughter found one of those men so attractive.

Lyam makes his way toward us, his bare chest glistening as the sun trains a generous beam on his form, and everything else has been eclipsed by his glory. My world sways and swirls about, but everything is precisely where it ought to be. I am, once again, frozen by the mere sight of him.

He greets us each by name. He's got a basket in one hand and a blanket in the other. He raises the basket. "I brought some food, if you'd all like to take a break."

"That would be lov—" Mother starts, and I already know what's coming, but Tavine is quick to interject.

"That would be lovely, Lyam, but Nira and I were just talking about having lunch at my place today. You and Aeria are welcome to join us, but you two may as well stay here and have your lunch, since you've already got it. And you even have a blanket." She can't hide the fact that she's charmed by Lyam's gesture.

Mother snaps her head in Tavine's direction, but Tavine takes her by the arm and begins to tow her off. "Come, Nira. I'm hungry. And I'll bet anything Daveed is wasting away to nothing, waiting for me to feed him."

As she's whisked down the path, Mother looks over her shoulder and says, "See you in a bit." Her reluctance makes me equal parts disappointed and humored.

"What must his father look like?" I overhear Tavine say when she thinks she's out of earshot.

Lyam wastes no time. He folds the blanket length-wise and spreads it over the dirt path. "Alone at last," he says with a crafty smile.

"Thanks to Tavine."

"Good thing, too, because I only have enough for the two of us."

I shake my head in wonder, but I'm grinning like a fox that's gotten away with a chicken. We sit on the blanket, which I assume belongs to Saeth and Emay, and I can't place why, but I unexpectedly feel self-conscious. "It's a beautiful day today," I say, simply because I can't think of anything else.

"It is now," Lyam says. His eyes are as hypnotic as on the night we met.

I blush and my head is rushing and my heart is pushing against the walls of my chest. Will this feeling ever pass, or will he always have the power to steal my breath away?

Proving the latter is more likely true, Lyam takes my hand, slips off my glove, and presses a kiss to the tips of my fingers, measuring my reaction from under dark lashes. My skin prickles and my cheeks go hot, and I'm pretty sure he can feel my pulse racing where his thumb is pressed against the inside of my wrist.

"I'm sorry," he says. "Did I make you uncomfortable?"

I don't mean to, but my "No" sounds desperate, hungry for more. "It's just that this is all new to me. I've never felt this way before."

He swallows hard and whispers, "Neither have I." He removes my other glove and kisses my fingertips once more, and I find myself wetting my lips, wondering how his would taste on mine, and whether or not he's thinking the same thing.

But then he trades my hand for the basket, and he's serving me while asking about the rose gathering.

I tell him, though there really isn't much to tell, and then he talks about how the funeral table is coming along.

"Saeth's having me do the sanding and polishing when it's finished."

"Is it much different here than the way it's done in Garrison?" I ask.

"Not a lot, but there certainly are differences. Definitely no drums. Our mourning period works the same, though, one hour to represent every year."

"I can see why, being that your founders knew so many of our customs."

"But," Lyam says proudly, "we have adopted a few customs of our own. I'll have to tell you about them sometime."

"Can you tell me one now?"

"All right. We construct a raft rather than a funeral table. We line it with straw and send it down the river ablaze."

"I didn't know that. Do you celebrate afterward as we do?"

Lyam nods. "Lots of food, music, drinking . . . and *dancing*. You like to dance?"

My gaze falls. My voice is small. "I've never been asked before." I can call up too many times when I've only watched the dancing, watched the merriment, watched everyone else forget their cares and enjoy themselves.

"Well, that is going to change tonight. You're dancing with me, Aeria Morgan, and I won't let you talk or *charm* your way out of it." A wry smile turns up his lips, and a sensual look sparkles in his eyes. It's so intoxicating to feel his lure.

My heart is aflutter. "Talk about charming."

But I haven't said yes, which is clearly what he wanted to hear. "*Aeria.*" He draws out my name, pushing for surrender.

"All right. All right. You twisted my arm. How can I say no?" I make a show of it, though truly I'd never dream of passing up the opportunity. Something about this conversation reminds me. "I have a question."

"Sounds more like a statement to me." I quirk a brow at him, which makes him laugh. "What's your question?"

"What were you going to ask my mother before the marks started?"

"Oh, that? That was nothing."

"Nothing? Lyam, you were so restless I thought you might self-combust and burn down my house. You were going to ask my mother's permission for something, so what was it?"

Silence. Then, "I've changed my mind. Now you'll just have to wait and see."

But waiting isn't my forte. "Or you could tell me now and I'll act surprised later." I flash my big, green eyes at him, hoping to soften his resolve. Regrettably, my flattery gets me nowhere.

"Ha!" he says. "That eye-batting thing won't work on me. Not this time. I'm keeping my lips sealed on this one."

"Fine," I huff in mock irritation.

Soon Lyam's smile fades, and fades fast. I immediately know why. Mother must have rushed through lunch to ensure our time alone was limited. I should have expected it.

We've already finished our food, which is a good thing, because Lyam hastily pulls me to my feet and gathers his things. "See you tonight." Then he shoots down the path like an arrow, my mother his target. Her pace is just as brisk and purposeful.

"Bye," I mumble, but he's already gone. As always, I'm left unsatisfied by the abrupt end to our brief time alone.

They meet halfway between our picnic spot and the garden's entrance, out of hearing range, and I stand there wishing I had the ability to read lips. Lyam's back faces me, a nice view for sure, but Mother's expression is anything but. She looks angry or worried or something of that color. And it appears they are having a disagreement. She lets Lyam speak his piece, her lips pressed into a straight line as she weighs the merits of his argument. Slowly they curve upward. She nods. Then it's over. But does that mean Lyam's gotten his way?

When she reaches me, she asks, "Did you have a nice time?" as if the last handful of minutes hadn't happened.

In no mood for pleasantries, I snap, "That's up for debate. Did you swallow your food whole, or shove it under the table?"

This shocks the both of us.

"Aeria, I'm sorry," she says. She looks a great many things, but *sorry* isn't one of them. "I'm not comfortable with you two being alone. But I am trying. Please know that." She tries to stroke the side of my head, but I dodge her advance. "I just want to protect you."

"What, am I like one of these roses here? Fragile and impossibly vulnerable, easily withered by the sun? You know how I've been shunned all my life. And yet, here I am." I toss my arms out at my sides, my volume elevated. "I've survived. So why is it that when someone wants to be with me I need extra protection?"

Mother bites back her response and goes to work, and I quickly follow suit.

Tavine returns shortly after, and the reason for the deafening silence between Mother and me is not lost on her. She likely expected it, actually. I bite back the myriad things I'd like to say and keep to my work, cutting the roses less gingerly now. My hands turn forceful as I cut the blooms free from the bush that once provided for, nourished, and protected it. How I long to be cut free, to live my own life as I so choose.

The wheelbarrow is brimming with hundreds of flawless white roses, but they are not the cause of my slow clip as we head back to Central Plaza. I remain behind Mother and Tavine, who walk arm-to-arm, but no one has uttered a word since the argument.

We are meant to line the funeral table next, but Mother deems herself more useful in the area of food preparation. While she does wield a certain kind of magic in the kitchen, it's not for the sake of our stomachs that she leaves us. So in silence Tavine and I begin to fashion a bed of roses atop the lovely masterwork of our carpenters' hands. Even the poles that run along the underside of the table for carrying it have been sanded to a perfect smoothness. The sides of the funeral table gleam and wink in the late day sun. It's been nearly eighteen hours since Debayah's death. Soon the mourning period will be over, and her spirit will be lifted to the gods. Then the Celebration of Life will begin.

A drumbeat marks that it's time.

We circle the table, everyone, young and old. It is our last chance for goodbyes. Debayah, lying upon her roses, has been wrapped in pure white so that only her face is visible. She looks peaceful, but the pallor of death has replaced her once sun-kissed skin, an astringent reminder of how quickly one can fall victim to the Darkness.

Chief Cole motions to the pallbearers. They take their positions, four of them, one at each corner, and hoist the table to waist height. The crowd parts to let them by. Flanked by torchbearers, they march in time to the drums, leading the procession away from the village toward Spirit Hill. With torches aloft, we move as one body. The sound of drums rolls throughout the vast night.

We stop. The drums die. Silence touches us. A breeze moans through the tight spaces between bodies as the sun disappears behind a dark cloud and Spirit Hill mourns yet another loss.

Back to front, an aisle is formed down the center of the crowd, granting passage for two archers, along with their respective torchbearer. From leather quivers the archers each draw an arrow fletched with pristine, white egret feathers. They string their bows. The tips are set aflame. Training on the funeral table a good distance away, they take aim and release a rainbow of fire. It consumes the pyre slowly, intentionally, glowing red-orange against the suddenly-twilight sky. The smoke rises, both a guide and ferry as it lifts Debayah's spirit to its eternal place among the stars, where she will be with her beloved once again.

EIGHTEEN

celebration

The resounding grief of Debayah's passing," Chief Cole says back at Central Plaza now, "can be felt in the hearts of all who stand here tonight. May her memory never fade, just as her spirit will now shine upon us from the lofty heights amongst the stars of ancestors past. We join together, shoulder to shoulder, not to grieve, but to partake in celebration."

A medley of applause and joyful shouting stirs up from the crowd.

"The Celebration of Life," he goes on, a bit louder, "serves as a reminder that we must take nothing for granted. Not one day. Not one breath. Not one of these lives that surround us here now, for we know not when tragedy will befall us. We cannot know when our time will come. This moment may be your last," he points to a face, "or yours," then another, then turns his finger on himself, "or mine."

I can feel Chief Cole's words work their way through me. Somehow, they have the power to penetrate the outermost layer of my hardened heart, burrowing deep inside so that my anger toward my mother turns to shame. I regret how I'd wished to be like the roses, to be cut free from my family branch. That isn't what I want at all, for my family means everything to me.

Leaning over my left shoulder, I say quietly in her ear, "I'm sorry." I take her tiny hand in mine.

"May we be mindful of our gratitude," Chief continues, "not only as we celebrate tonight, but tomorrow, and the next day. May our devotion to one another withstand the test of time. Let us all remember to serve one other with blind abandon. Let us offer greater understanding, and extend the hand of forgiveness. And let us appreciate every moment spent in the arms of the ones we love."

Though beautiful in theory, I can't help finding this declaration more hypocritical than inspiring. Had I not known better, I would have thought this to be a pivotal moment. Eye-opening. Life-altering. Heart-changing. And above all, redeeming.

But I do know better.

There will be no change in people's hearts tonight.

Despite Chief Cole's admonition, this love and grace and devotion he speaks of has never stretched as far as to supersede the bias covering my family. We have yet to feel any acceptance, ever, and I don't expect tonight to be the start of anything to the contrary. We'll still be outcasts, negating the entire intention of this speech. And the celebration.

Perhaps, perhaps this time will be different. At least by some measure. It's a good bet that the villagers won't change, but that doesn't mean my outlook on the situation can't. It's not easy to tell the past not to creep into your present and show you what it thinks your future holds, but with Lyam by my side, maybe those constant feelings of rejection won't be so loud. Maybe his presence, his compassionate embrace, the acceptance I find in his eyes, will quiet the pain of the past and I can allow myself to actually enjoy tonight's celebration.

This time *will* be different, I determine.

We remain silent, pensive, as the message continues. "Again, I thank you all for the preparations made for Debayah's farewell, as well as for our celebration. May the gods find pleasure in your sacrifices, and may the works of your hands be rewarded. I count my blessings for each one of you here tonight. I look forward to celebrating at your sides. Let the Celebration of Life commence!" Chief exclaims, arms raised high.

At this, the crowd roars to life. My applause is more animated than ever before, focusing on Lyam's words as an anchor. *You're dancing with me, Aeria Morgan.* My heart already dances in anticipation.

It's likely Mother and Aeron will be sore about it, about our being so close, but it will be futile for them to oppose me. Everyone dances during the celebration, so how dare I be denied that same right?

Tavine is quick to drag Mother off without offering any specified reason, and I assume she's thinking Mother and I are still at odds. Mother winks at me.

All the while, even throughout Chief's speech, Aeron has been seemingly at odds with no specified person for no specified reason. He's fidgety and impatient for something without a name. He's seeking, though he moves not more than a few inches. I rarely see him this way, and I'm puzzling over what has caused this restlessness.

This goes on until Doctor Solmon comes out of nowhere and rejoins his wife and daughter. I see Aeron swallow, lift his brows, make his move. He strides toward them, heedless of the sea of people, and I think his plan of action is to use Doctor Solmon to get closer to Satrie. I smile at his back, at his gall, at how fortune has decided to shine upon the Morgans for a change.

Alone now, I watch with wonder as, in a matter of minutes, the plaza is transformed from a place that remembers the loss to a place that celebrates the life. People laugh and talk and embrace one another. Bodies move jovially to the harmony of drums, flutes, and stringed instruments. The torches outlining the perimeter of the plaza have long since been returned to their bases. Their odd-shaped shadows skip around under lithe footsteps.

At the plaza's center sits a stone pit, fire raging. It crackles and bends and throws twirling sparks into the air. Above the blaze, a boar is strung upon a spit, skin sweating with the heat of the wild flames that reach up and up and up.

I'm standing near the back as usual, where long tables boast bountiful platters of meats, cheeses, nuts, roasted apples, breads; salads tossed with pine nuts and hazel nuts and boldly-colored vegetables; and a sinful-looking assortment of cakes and pies, cobblers and turnovers. My stomach sings in delight. Also in attendance is a flagrant quantity of uncorked wine bottles, all to make for a lively celebration.

And for the first time, I'm actually looking forward to it.

My eyes sweep the plaza in search of Lyam. I spot him near the right side of the dais, apart from the others, talking with Saeth and Emay Brown, though they noticeably monopolize the conversation. Lyam's lips are pursed, his forehead furrowed in response, and at one point he folds his arms and shakes his head, unmistakably displeased.

I feel worry squeeze the air out of my lungs, fill my head with piercing images of Lyam with his back to Avalon Valley.

Lyam offers his retort, but the Browns look just as displeased. There is a moment when only their eyes speak, then it's over and the Browns take their leave. I don't know who's won the battle, or what the battle was about, or why it happened. I do know that when Lyam's eyes meet mine, his features brighten as if it were nothing.

But I don't think it was nothing.

He gives me that crooked half smile, curling his finger at me three times, beckoning me to join him. The lure.

Before I realize it, I'm wearing a smile I didn't authorize. The traitorous thing is gone in a blink. Dropping my eyes to the ground, I move toward him with uncertain feet.

"What is it?" he asks, inclining my chin with a bent finger.

I say nothing, my eyes avoiding his in spite of the way he still demands my attention.

"You can tell me anything, you know." His tone is calm. Too calm, considering what I've just witnessed.

To the night and to the stars and to the distant smoke that once was a beautiful young woman, I say, "What were they talking to you about?" My words are small and weak and unbelievably shaky.

There's a smile in Lyam's voice. "Aeria, look at me."

I don't.

"Aeria," he breathes. "Please. Look at me."

I succumb after a second, only because it pains me so to hear the desperation in his voice. "What were they saying?" I ask.

Thoughtful lines wrinkle between Lyam's brows, a decision to be made. To tell me, or not tell me. I want to reach up and smooth away the lines, as if to some-how wash away all that threatens to do us harm. "It doesn't matter," he says.

More insistent this time, I press, "What did they say?"

He exhales gustily. "They said that I—" He pauses, as if having the words replay in his ears causes physical suffering. Or worse, that his own lips have to give them shape, and each and every syllable is pure poison. "—that I should stop . . . seeing you." This cuts me, and I understand now why Lyam was less than forthcoming. Not that it makes me feel any better. "But it's nothing you need to worry about."

Still, I do. It's hard to stand on solid ground when the earth tilts and steals your footing. To have clear vision when the subtly shifting line between reacting and overreacting is so easily blurred.

"I see." Assuming a less frantic demeanor, I try humor to hide my fears, something I've picked up from Aeron. "So they're your stand-in parents now? Then where does that leave us?"

The way he stares at me, with such unadulterated fervor, his eyes aflame in the ambient light, takes my breath away. "Nothing they say could ever change my mind. Even if they told me that being with you is to forfeit my own life, I would still choose you. A million times over, and a million times after that." His voice, softer than a whisper, is louder than my fears. "Aeria, I'd choose you every time."

I feel tears coming on, and though it wouldn't be the first time he's seen me cry, for some reason I can't let these fall.

"Now," Lyam says, capturing my hand in his, "how about that dance?"

I hope my smile isn't too eager.

Then it's just his eyes on mine, his hand at the small of my back, our bodies nearly touching, swaying slowly despite the way the upbeat tone charges for more lively footsteps. And when he pulls me closer, and mere inches separate my breaths from his, the memory of our encounter at the shed is alive in my mind and it's all I can do to keep the tremble from rattling through my body to his.

"Is this all right?" he asks, and his smile tells me he knows full well the effect he's having on me.

Because I'm afraid he'll withdraw if I appear too uncomfortable, I nod and work to still my nerves by focusing on my footing, though given our pace it's not much in the way of distraction.

"So," I say, "tomorrow is Rest Day."

"Yes it is."

"Do you have plans?"

"Yes."

I wait, but get nothing more. "Are you going to tell me what they are?"

Lyam doesn't indulge my curious nature. Instead, his "No" intensifies it.

I wonder what it is he's doing, but more so, I wonder why it is that he holds back. I also wonder something else, something that perplexes me. "Will you tell me something?"

"Clearly," he says, "that depends on the question."

I bite my lip, more nervous than a bride on her wedding night. "Why me?"

Lyam's countenance is skewed, as if my words were unintelligible. "*Why you?*"

"Yes. I mean, how could it be that your parents introduced you to a host of young women, all beautiful, I presume, and yet, of all people, here you are . . . with *me?*"

Lyam sends a laugh into the blackening sky.

"What's so funny?"

His reply is accompanied by a stronger pull of my body to his, but what we're doing can no longer be defined as dancing. "And how could it be that you have no idea who you are?"

I'm baffled. "Who *I* am?"

"Aeria Morgan, never have I met anyone like you in all my life, and I can't seem to get enough of you. I'm drawn to you in a way I can't explain. I felt it the very moment I saw you. It wasn't merely the physical attraction, because believe me, I find you so beautiful that it hurts, but there was something more. Something internal drawing me to you. I desperately wanted to talk to you, to be near you.

"Then, when I thought you might be in danger that night, I had no choice but to follow. And when we were alone under the stars I was so captivated by you. You took my breath away. That's when I knew that you were the one. The one I've been saving my heart for."

He's taken my breath away. "I . . . I don't know what to say."

Lyam grins. "I can keep going if you'd like."

I can feel the knot form between my brows. "There's *more*?"

"You may want to pull up a chair, we could be here all night," he says before turning serious again. "I see strength in you, Aeria, even if you don't see it in yourself, but at the same time, you don't pretend to be immune to vulnerability. You're more humble than anyone I've ever known, and I don't think it has anything to do with how you've been treated. It's in you. It's who you are.

"And despite everything you've been through, you don't demand justice or recompense. Hell, half my village would be shouting from the mountaintops if they were slighted in even the tiniest thing. But you're not like anyone I've ever met. But the thing that really gets me about you is that, though you've been wronged in the worst ways, you aren't afraid to love or be loved. You make me laugh, Aeria, like side-splitting laughs that have me chuckling to myself like a fool even hours later, and there's something so *unbearably* adorable," his eyes flutter, drunk with the thought, "about the way you bite your lip when you're nervous."

His thumb to my lip draws a soft sigh of pleasure from me. My eyelids slip closed.

My name falls upon my ear as a feathery whisper. I meet Lyam's passion-filled gaze. "There really are no words to express how exquisite you are," he says. "I melt every time I look into those brilliant, green eyes of yours. We're connected, you and me. We were meant to be, even from the beginning of time." After a pause he adds, "And I am insanely jealous of your clothing."

"My *clothing*?"

His fingers slide down the length of my arm, his touch velvet. "The way they're free to hug and caress your body, every inch of you, without fear of repercussions."

My face is warm and my pulse is racing in response to the longing in Lyam's eyes as they touch me. I am vibrantly aware of how near his mouth is to mine and how my own longing pulls me nearer, closing the space between us.

NINETEEN

amends

I think Lyam is going to kiss me, but then my mother sidles up beside him and asks, "May I have a word with my daughter? It won't take long."

Flashing one of his brilliant smiles, he replies, "Of course, so long as I get her back." And just like that our dance ends. Lyam steps away.

I can't tell if the disruption was my mother's intent or a rare case of her obliviousness. Either way, I can't shake my disappointment.

My mother and I stand there face to face, so far removed from the crowd that I realize only now that Lyam and I had been unconsciously moving away from it.

"Mother, I—"

"Wait," she cuts in. "You need to hear what I have to say. I was wrong to treat you the way I did this afternoon. There was no excuse for my behavior. I should have trusted you. Respected you. I told you I would support you, and that's what I am going to do."

Mother shakes her head and sighs. "You have no idea how hard it is to be a mother. It's my job to protect you from harm. I know Lyam means you no harm, that's not what I'm saying, but I want you to know that from now on I will make a greater effort to allow you more freedom. Not too much freedom, mind you. I am still your mother, after all, and there will be expectations. You need to remember to maintain appropriate behavior with that boy. You aren't married, you know."

"I know, but it's nothing you need to worry about. Lyam wouldn't do anything to take advantage of me, or the law. Besides, he hasn't even kissed me." My stomach twists at my transparency. *Why am I telling her this?*

Mother is beside herself with shock. And possibly relief. "Really?"

"Yes, Mother." I regret that I look as crestfallen as I sound. "I told you, Lyam is a good guy. A gentleman to a fault, really."

"It seems," Mother replies, "that I am constantly being reminded of that."

"Look," I tell her, "I have something to say to you, too. I shouldn't have snapped at you earlier. I know you were only protecting me, and—"

"Oh, sweetheart, you have nothing to apologize for. All I've ever wanted is what's best for you, and I'm beginning to realize that it's coming in a different package from what I imagined." Mother's eyes flit to the space behind me, to whoever now occupies it. She says, "Someone else would like to speak with you."

I turn on my heels. Hands stuffed in his pockets, Aeron wears a boyish, guilty grin. To Mother he says, "Mind if I dance with my big sister?"

"She's all yours." Mother gives my arm a little squeeze, a parting gesture that draws a little hope from somewhere deep within me. Hope that this concept of more freedom is more than words spoken in private for the sake of making amends.

I hadn't considered it before this moment, as Aeron stands before me ready to take my hand, that he and I have never danced together. It seems silly now that we haven't. I mean, why not? Wasn't that something siblings used to do long ago?

I slip my hand into Aeron's and rest the other atop his shoulder. He does the same, and I'm surprised at how natural this is, dancing with my brother, as if we've become one being.

"Your boyfriend makes one hell of a funeral table," Aeron says. Surprisingly, there is no animosity in his voice when he labels Lyam as my *boyfriend.*

Is Lyam my boyfriend? The hair at the back of my neck prickles at the thought. I don't even know how it works. Is there some kind of standard protocol to be followed? Or rite or tradition that seals the deal? As far as I'm concerned, the position is his if he wants it.

Aeron says, "So how was your day?"

I look down the length of my dress to the shadows at my feet. "I was rotten to Mother."

Aeron wears a crooked grin. "I know. We talked." This does not surprise me. "We came to the conclusion that we both had some apologizing to do. To you and to Lyam."

Sometimes, when the darkness dulls the green of Aeron's eyes, they look exactly like Mother's. Right now, the way the light of the torches plays over his penitent face and flickers behind his back, there is so much of my mother in him that my heart swells with pride. He's been disturbingly rotten lately, more so to Lyam than me, but I can see already how he's grown, how it's matured him.

"I had no reason to be like that. I can't imagine how I've made you feel. But seriously, it was *killing* me, the way he was touching you, and . . ." He shudders. I laugh. His scowl shuts me up and he continues. "I felt like I was going to go insane! He was putting that flower in your hair and I thought he might just have the nerve to— to . . . Can you just promise not to kiss him around me? Because I really won't be able to stomach that." His teeth are clenched and his lips have twisted into a snarl, disgusted.

My chest heaves with laughter, only this time it's harder to check. "Does Satrie know how squeamish you become at the mention of kissing?" I tease, then I press my finger to his chest before he can react, serious now. "But you better get used to the idea of Lyam and me." Spotting Lyam across the plaza, I add, "Because I'm going to marry him someday."

Aeron's smile is utterly genuine. "I'm happy for you. I really am."

"Thanks, Aeron. You're a good brother."

Abandoning his usual response, he says, "Not in the last few days, I haven't been. That's what I've been trying to say. It's *my* duty to make sure you're safe. So when you told me Lyam rescued you when I was gone, I have to admit I was a little . . . jealous. I blamed myself for what happened to you. If I hadn't left you . . ." he trails off, unable to finish.

"Aeron, you can't blame yourself for that. Just be grateful Lyam was there to intervene."

"That's what I keep telling myself. Still, I don't know how to get rid of that feeling. I've always been there for you, but that night I wasn't. I failed you."

"You could never fail me, you hear me?"

His response is silence.

I crook a brow at him. "So, that's why you've been so undone? You're *jealous*?"

"That's part of it. A small part."

"What's the other part?"

Now he's the one staring at his feet. "I . . . I felt afraid."

"Of what?" I can't recall ever hearing those words on his lips, unless the fear he's shouldering is on my behalf.

To the ground he admits in a sullen voice, "I was afraid you wouldn't need me anymore. You know, Aeron and Aeria till the end."

It breaks my heart to hear that Aeron thinks himself so disposable, as if Lyam could replace him.

"Aeron, how could you say that? I will *always* need you. You're a part of me, regardless of anyone who comes along. Our lives are like this," I say, twisting my fingers together, "just like the A's."

He meets my eyes then, and a small smile escapes him. "Now," he says, "there's something I have to do." All of a sudden he's towing me through the moving throng of people toward the place where Lyam stands alone, after having politely disentangled himself from a giggling Eleaz Lofton and her friend Leivia Daeston. Both cute, but too young to be a real threat. I wonder how many other girls have sought his attention since he arrived. Again, I am reminded of the girls he left behind in Garrison, curious as to how they reacted to Lyam's sudden departure.

I throw a whisper ahead to Aeron. "What are you doing?"

"What I should have done days ago," he says, glancing back at me.

When we reach Lyam, Aeron says to him, "I'm sorry about the way I've treated you. And for not doing this sooner."

"Doing what?" I ask again.

Aeron first takes Lyam's hand and flips it palm side up. "I'm giving you my blessing." Then he lays my hand on top of Lyam's. "One hundred percent this time."

Lyam curls his fingers around my hand.

I'm so choked up by Aeron's gesture that I have to blink to fight back the sheen in my eyes.

"Thank you, Aeron," Lyam says. "This really means a lot to me."

"To us," I barely manage.

"I love you, Aeria," Aeron tells me.

"I love you more."

Aeron laughs. "I doubt that." And he walks away, leaving me and Lyam and his blessing behind.

Lyam watches me as I study my brother. "Has anyone ever told you that you have a way of making happy tears look painfully attractive?"

I shake my head at him. "No, that's a new one." Then I point in the direction of the dais, my usual perch. Lyam nods, and we work our way to a little sanctuary of privacy in the midst of the celebrating.

Sitting with our shoulders touching, Lyam toys with my hand, his fingers drawing figure eights on the inside of my wrist. "What spurred all that on with Aeron and your mother?"

"They wanted to apologize for not being supportive before, and promised to make a more substantial effort."

"Does that mean the end of harsh, icy stares?" asks Lyam humorously. "Or slamming doors? Or right hooks?"

"Yes. Well, conditionally."

"Conditionally? Do I have to maintain a ten-foot distance from you?" Lyam hops to his feet and pulls me into his arms to show how impossible that would be. We whirl around and around and then he sets me back down, and for a second I've almost forgotten his question.

"He, uh . . . he's quite insistent that you not, uh, kiss me in front of him."

Lyam issues this hardy laugh that makes his eyes water, and it's delightfully contagious.

"You should have seen the look on his face," I say. "He was literally going to turn green."

"Is that what's gotten into him?"

It's a good minute before our mirth fades. Then Lyam returns to the dais and sits, suddenly thoughtful. He says, "If you really want to know, the thought doesn't sit well with me, either." I make a face, and he tacks on, "Not about kissing in general. I mean about the audience."

"Does that mean you've thought about it? About kissing me?" I sit, avert my eyes, and stare into my lap. I know he's thought about it, he must have, but I need to hear it for myself.

"Are you kidding? I can't stop thinking about it. Remember the night I came back from Garrison? It took everything I had to restrain myself."

"Why didn't you, then?"

"I wanted to," he says, "don't get me wrong, but it didn't feel right. Not the kiss, but the place. You deserve better than that."

I have to agree that the dark side of a shed isn't the most romantic place for your first kiss. Or any kiss, for that matter. Not that I would have turned it down, be it our first kiss or otherwise.

But the way Lyam stares unblinkingly into the fire ahead causes my chest to tighten. Is all this talk of kissing making him feel uncomfortable, or pressured, or cornered, maybe?

He says, "I need to tell you something. It's been grating at me all week."

Seconds pass like eternities, slow and stretched out.

Lyam sucks in a deep breath, and the exhale is even louder. "In light of all these apologies, I have one to offer."

My thoughts instantly go to all the moments we've spent together, the conversations we've had, but nothing I can call up even remotely suggests the need for an apology. I twist my neck to get a better view of him and tell him as much.

His brows, even darker in this scant light, come low over his strained eyes. "I— I didn't get there in time. I shouldn't have waited so long." He shakes his head as if to dislodge some memory I can't even name.

"What in the world are you talking about?"

He looks at me knowingly, speaking so softly I can hardly hear him. "That night." I make a face of understanding and he goes on. "I hesitated. I should have stopped him before he ever touched you." He's grown rigid, terribly quickly, like Aeron on the edge of his bed, with the intensity of both of them combined.

"Lyam, you did more than anyone else here ever would have considered doing. You saved me. He couldn't hurt me . . . because of *you*."

Lyam's eyes grow smaller, darker, fiercer than any I've seen before. "But I saw him," he says, almost snarling. "I saw the way he held you down, how he forced himself on top of you. The way he was touching you. . . . I knew what was on his mind. I knew what he wanted, and I wasn't fast enough. I tried—"

His head won't stop shaking, and his shoulders shudder as if he's sobbing tearless sobs, and I don't know what to do to help him forget. I feel scared, not of him, but for him, because I know what it's like to let the past pollute everything it touches. But I'm at a loss because my words are not enough for him.

Hard lines of anguish form when Lyam's eyes shut. Then his face is in his hands and I have to incline my ear to catch his words. "I can't get those images out of my head. Aeria, you have no idea how badly it haunts me."

I reach out and gather up his hands, lacing my fingers with his, and when he looks at me I see pain and bondage and oppression and more pain still. But when I say, "We'll just have to make memories of our own," he smiles and wraps his arm around me.

Lyam echoes my desire with a mock laugh. "If we could ever be alone."

TWENTY

plans

I'm not saying anything."

"Come on, Aeron," I beg. "Tell me."

"What are you two arguing about?" Mother asks sleepily, her voice entering the front room before she does. She's still in her night robe, and her feet seem heavier than usual.

"Aeron said he had plans for us today," I explain.

"And she's dying to know," Aeron adds.

"But he won't tell me," I finish.

Mother yawns, slumps onto the divan, and says, "It looks like you're going to have to be patient, Aeria. I know how difficult that can be for you."

I huff and cross my arms, exaggerating my ill-content. Pretending I don't see my mother wink at Aeron, I go to the kitchen to prepare breakfast, which consists of porridge and fresh blueberries.

Over steaming bowls, Mother and Aeron talk of last night's celebration. Lyam and I had been so lost in our own brand of dancing that it's as if Aeron and Mother had gone to another celebration entirely. Even

179

the food, which Mother claims was "better than if the gods had prepared it themselves," had slipped my notice last night. I can remember the act of eating, but the rest of me was so busy enjoying Lyam's company that I didn't have any enjoyment left over for anything else.

I'm filling the empty pot with water to sit overnight when Aeron strolls into the kitchen, whistling merrily, opens his satchel, and stuffs it with food he's brought home from the night before. I watch silently. I have one guess where his plans will lead us.

Aeron tows me to the back door. "The *clearing*?" My tone neatly bespeaks my disappointment.

Unapologetic, he says, "Since when do you, Aeria Morgan, turn down a chance to swim?"

I stroke my arms through the air, swimming in place. I even spit out an imaginary fountain of water at him. "There, I swam."

My mother laughs.

Aeron tries not to.

I stick out my lower lip, an artificial pout. "Can we please go see Lyam? Just for a minute?" Today marks one week since I first learned of Lyam's arrival. It's also Lyam's first day off work, his first Rest Day in Avalon Valley, and his unwillingness to tell me his plans yesterday has left a pit of curiosity in my stomach.

"No point," Aeron says. "He's not there. Now, can we please go take advantage of this amazing day?"

And with that we go. Him smiling, me sulking.

It *is* an amazing day, bright and beautiful and generously warm, but it may as well be dark and dreary and frigid for all the good it does me. I don't care to swim or picnic or do anything but spend the day caught up in Lyam's arms, with the sun smiling down on us both. I hate that I have no idea where he's gone.

What's worse is that somehow Aeron does know. But how? And why can't I know?

I sigh and continue to sulk along as Aeron leads me through the woods. He ignores my moodiness. His cheery tune makes bitterness boil beneath my skin. I imagine what it would have been like if Lyam had shown up at my door this morning and stolen me away. Far, far away.

But then I remember, somewhat potently, Chief Cole's words about not taking our loved ones for granted. I refuse to do that to my brother.

As I cross the boundary of the woods, I determine to change my outlook on the day. I lift my face to the sky, to the great, blue expanse that stretches above me and around me and fills my lungs with fresh air. I can feel the grass wrapping up around my ankles and folding beneath my feet. The sound of frogs croaking in the distance mingles with the cheery songs of robins as they sing from their high perches amongst the conifers, declaring the splendor of nature's artistry.

Aeron looks skyward and makes a declaration of his own. "What an incredible morning!"

I leap ahead of him, jostling him in the process. "First one to the falls wins." And I tear off across the clearing.

Aeron paces behind for quite some time, and I don't have to see him to know he's holding back. He's probably not even out of breath while I'm gasping, calling for more speed than my legs care to give.

For the first time, I reach the water's edge before my brother.

Breathless, I call, "You let me win," and when he finally catches up, hardly at a loss for breath, I give him a playful shove.

"Maybe I did," he says. "Maybe I didn't." He drops his satchel to the ground, tugs it open, and produces two waterskins. I tip mine to the sky with my eyes closed, reveling in the kindness of water in my throat and the sun on my cheeks.

I nearly jump out of my skin when I hear a huge splash behind me. Aeron, who was standing before me, is now bent forward, hands on his knees, laughing hysterically. He can scarcely get his words out: "You should have seen . . . the look . . . on your face!"

I think, at first, that he's thrown a rock into the pool while I was drinking. I turn to where the sound originated, but I can only see the ripples expand outward from the center of whatever hit the water.

There's no way Aeron could have thrown something clear to the other side of the bank. It's hard to see past the sun's reflection that shimmers over the surface of the pool, but the longer I look, the more I believe that something is down there. Or rather, some*one*.

I step away from the bank, the hair on my arms standing on end. Aeron's still bent over, howling with laughter, but this is so far from funny that it makes me sick. I'm stuck in the memory of the night I was attacked, almost in this very spot, and it chills me.

There's a dark figure. The surface flutters with movement. My heart lurches in my chest. Then he breaks the surface and draws in a long breath.

I punch Aeron in the arm. Twice. "You knew all this time!"

This doesn't quiet Aeron's laughter. It makes it worse. Lyam joins in.

"Did she jump?" Lyam asks him, cutting neatly through the water.

"To the sky! Her eyeballs were as big as my fists," Aeron crows, wiping his eyes dry with the back of his hand.

I can't begin to express my exuberance over their newfound amity, even if their prank was at my expense. "So you two are good pals now, huh?"

"I thought he might come in handy one day," Aeron says. "Maybe we'll keep him."

I make a sour face at my brother. "Maybe then we can trade *you* for a goat. Mother always wanted a goat."

"Don't count on it," Lyam says. "You may have to settle for just the tail. Makes a good stock, though, the tail." He sucks in a mouthful of water and spits it in Aeron's direction, though he's too far to reach him.

Lyam comes ashore and slaps Aeron on the shoulder by way of greeting. "Thank you for inviting me here."

"Thank *you*," Aeron says, "for scaring the life out of my sister."

Lyam grins and drips toward me. Aeron takes that as his cue to leave, whistling to himself as he makes his way to an old, hollow log where he usually sketches or plays his flute while I swim myself into a raisin.

Lyam's arms open wide, inviting me in. I slide my arms around his shirtless frame, and water from his spiked hair trickles onto my arms and shoulders. The front of my dress grows wet from our embrace.

"I'm glad you're here." My words pale in comparison to the joy I feel. "Really glad."

"Sorry about scaring you, and about your dress."

I shrug. Being scared is a small price to pay for him being here today. And about the dress, "I'm swimming anyway, right?"

"Absolutely!" With one swoop he snatches me up in his arms, cradling my body as if it takes no effort. Feeling light as a butterfly's exhale, I lace my fingers behind his neck. I'm about to say something, but I come up short when Lyam turns so that his face is just a whisper away from mine. Into my ear he says, "Your brother's here, so let's keep the stripping to a minimum this time."

"You were the one stripping," I counter. "I have the shirt to prove it. Besides, I wasn't undressing for your benefit." I thought before that he hadn't seen me. Now? Now I'm not so sure.

His words are warm against my skin. "Still, it was great."

I cringe. If Lyam weren't carrying me, I'd seek a rock to hide under. A big one.

"Don't be embarrassed. You're," his brows raise at the memory, "well, you're incredible."

I cover my face with the flat of my hand and groan. "It gets worse by the second."

Lyam laughs. "I promise I'm done, but first there's just one more thing. . . ."

We come to a stop and I tear my hand from my face. I hadn't even noticed that Lyam is wading knee-deep. I ask, "What might that be?"

His voice comes low and sultry. "I imagine you every night before I fall asleep." With that, he quickly twists at the waist, unwinds, and tosses me out into the water.

It's not too deep where I land, so I scramble to my feet and push back the hair that covers my eyes. I use my palms to send a wall of water at him and it soaks his bare torso. But that's the end of my retribution, because all I can think about is running my hands over his wet chest, and I can't help but stare.

Lyam, taking notice of my ogling, smiles a playful smile.

Suddenly bashful, I mumble a curt, "Sorry," and force my eyes to the water.

"It doesn't bother me any. I guess that makes us even."

Oh, but it doesn't! I think. I hike up my skirt, stride toward him fiercely now, and press a finger into his chest. "We are not even close, Lyam Trey. Not by a longshot."

"Fair enough," Lyam says in mock surrender.

I gesture to the green and blue and open world around us. "Is this what you talked to my mother about in the garden yesterday? For permission to come here?"

"No. We spoke last night while you danced with Aeron. She agreed that we could spend more time together, but that was also accompanied by an explicit warning that I will be hunted down if there's any *inappropriate* activity."

I roll my eyes. Of course she'd say something like that. "Are those her words or yours?"

"I'm paraphrasing." His smile disappears. "Does she really think I would take that risk? That either of us would?"

Sex outside of marriage is strictly forbidden, punishable by death. Which is the very reason it's such a miracle our mother wasn't executed for conceiving us out of wedlock.

The law, mandated by the gods themselves, has been upheld since the beginning of time. It protects the very essence of the family dynamic, and since the days of the Darkness, abiding by that law has become increasingly important. For in that single, lawless act, you invite the Darkness in. It's like a sickness you can't feel, can't see, can't cure. When we were younger, Mother would compare it to a dam, owing to the way it shuts up the womb. Even the man is stopped up, unable to reproduce.

My mother was eleven when it last happened here, a sharp reminder that this is more than a cautionary tale. The couple held fast to their secret, and they

went on living their lives free from suspicion even after they were married. It wasn't until two childless
years later that the girl fell into a slumber from which
she could not be roused, and finally the truth came
out. The guy didn't even make it through that month.

And so, I think, this is what Lyam was talking
about last night, the thing that haunts him but he refused to say aloud: Had my attacker gotten what he
wanted that night, without killing me afterward, I
would have become a girl in waiting, a walking corpse
until the Darkness came to finish the job.

TWENTY-ONE
the falls

The sun is a rider clothed in white, its mount an infinitely blue sky that yawns above and beyond, as wild and free as the wind and the stars and the sea. And below that sky, beneath a host of unseen stars, with the wind filling my lungs and a sea of hope brimming in my heart, Lyam and I glide through the water, drunk on laughter and playful banter and secret caresses, innocent yet dangerous at the same time—his hand at the small of my back, my palm sliding over his bare bicep, our fingers entwined beneath the surface of the pool.

Overhead, a raven circles, its feathers glossy in the sunshine. It's Lyam who remarks about its size, but I'd noticed it, too. "That must be the biggest raven I've ever seen."

Squinting up at it, I say, "It almost seems like . . . "

"Like what?"

"Like it's watching us," I finish.

"Speaking of being watched." Lyam sends a minute jerk of his chin toward Aeron. "Have you noticed how many times he's looked over here?"

I hadn't, actually.

I steal a glance at Aeron, and he peeks at me at the same time, holding my gaze for a bare moment. He's leaning against the log, knees pulled up near his chest. One arm is a long line that rests on his knee while the other hovers mid-thigh, still as can be.

Aeron stares back at his lap, focused. His hand makes a long downward motion against his thigh. He doesn't seem to notice that the raven now circles above him.

I grin at Lyam, and my seductive voice makes another appearance. "Then let's give him something to look at."

I only half mean it. I want Lyam to kiss me so badly it hurts, but to do that now, with Aeron watching, would put an end to days like this.

For a second the idea seems enticing to Lyam. Then he says, "What would be the fun of that?" Winking, he adds, "Come with me."

I draw out the word "*Where?*" suspiciously when Lyam turns for shore, towing me by the wrist. We follow the bank, Aeron eyeing us as we pass, and I feel smaller with every step toward the falls.

"No way!" I yell over the rushing water.

"I won't let anything happen to you. It'll be fun."

My gaze creeps up, up, up to the highest ledge. I swallow. "Fun?" Already my knees knock together.

Aeron's jumped from the lower ledge many times, but I've always refused to join him. Lyam is harder to deny. It must be the lure. I'm pretty sure I would do anything for him.

I cling to Lyam as he practically hauls me up the side of the falls. My free hand grasps at anything and everything along the way, burying my fingers in the rocky crevices, seizing exposed roots as an anchor, while my feet work to gain purchase in this unfamiliar and uneven terrain.

When we reach the lower ledge, I hunch, bending at the knees to keep my body close to the rock. My hand fans out over the sun-warmed surface of the shelf below me. Water rushes beside at my left, and I can feel my fingernails as they drive into the back of Lyam's hand.

My heart hammers against my breastbone, nearly as loud as the *Shhhhhhhh* that fills my ears. Slowly, slowly, I make myself larger and more vertical, though I'm not entirely upright. I peer ahead at the woods in the distance, but I do not look down.

"Together?"

"Definitely," I reply.

"On three?"

"I'm— I'm not ready."

"You'll never be ready. You think too much. Sometimes you just have to take the leap."

But it's much too similar to those dreams I've had, in which Lyam and I are fleeing from a ferocious bear. Only in my dreams I am much less fearful when it comes time to jump, and I wish now that I could assume that same brave mien. Except I am still just me. And I am afraid.

My voice shakes along with the rest of me. "Please, don't let go."

"Never." Lyam squeezes my hand, a reminder that it still bears mine. Then the countdown begins. "One."

I clamp my eyes. . . .

"Two."

Suck in a bit of courage. . . .

"Three."

And jump.

My stomach climbs into my throat as we soar through the air. Then I pierce the surface like lightning pierces the sky, sudden, and with a rumble of warning. The bubbling water is above us, the deep below, and the whole time my fingers are twisted with Lyam's. When we breach the surface it is as one, unlike my dreams, in which he is gone and my fist is full of blanket, not flesh.

I sweep my hair from my face with my free hand, and together we swim to the bank, where we won't have to shout to be heard.

"That wasn't so bad, now was it?"

I understate my fear. "It was only *slightly* terrifying."

"No, that was fun. Admit it."

I won't, not out loud, but internally I confess that there was something exhilarating about the way we flew, weightless and part of the endless, crystal sky, even if only for a moment.

"I'm guessing that won't be the last time you make me do that."

Lyam regards me with concern. "I'm sorry, I wasn't thinking. I should have asked you first."

"It isn't that," I say quickly. "It's just that I've had these . . . uh, dreams."

Lyam seems not-here for a sliver of a moment. "About the falls?"

I hesitate. "It's a river. We're being chased, so we have to jump, but then we hit the water and I wake up and you're not there."

Lyam touches my cheek. "I wish you would have told me."

"Told you that I have dreams about you?" I scoff. "I don't think so."

"Why? I'm not ashamed to admit that I've dreamed of you."

"Really?"

"Really," he says, one brow arched.

"Good dreams, I hope."

For a time, his eyes are lost in some remembrance. "*Very* good dreams."

"I hate to ask, but would you care to elaborate?"

Lyam's lips curl up on one side, wielding that crooked smile I find so devastating. "I better not. I wouldn't want to embarrass you."

Oh, but he already has, first by revealing that he did see me naked, and now by revealing the fact that he's dreamed dreams that would likely render my face blood red.

"Are you two building a dam over there?" Aeron calls, ending the conversation. "Mind if we eat sometime today?"

"We should go," I say with feigned urgency. "He gets irritable when he's hungry." I can already hear it in his voice. He thinks he's fading into nothingness. And so before that becomes a reality, we slosh ashore, my dress pasted to my body so that it feels more like a second skin. I'm attempting to pull it loose, but I'm too busy dragging Lyam along.

Over my shoulder, I say, "You doing all right?"

"I'm better than all right." Then he mumbles something that I think has to do with the night we met, and my face burns hotter than the sun.

I stop mid-stride and whip around. "Lyam Trey, you are going to get yourself into trouble!"

He throws his hands in the air in surrender, but the smile on his face is nothing if not mischievous. "One day," he says, matter-of-fact and a tad smug, "none of this will bother you."

I press my finger to his lips. "Just hush," I say. But he bites the tip of my finger, so lightly that every inch of me tingles with desire, yearns for more of his touch, more of him.

I give a start at my name coming from my brother's mouth. I'd all but forgotten he was there, not ten yards from us. "Let's go."

We join Aeron at the hollow log, and I situate myself between him and Lyam. Aeron's already dividing up the food, but there are only two waterskins, so Lyam and I will share mine.

Aeron's journal catches my eye. It must have been in his lap earlier, before we jumped the falls. "What is it you've been working on?" I ask, reaching for it.

Aeron snatches it up to his chest, protective as a new mother. "It's private."

I shrink a little at the callousness in his voice. "I— I didn't mean to pry." *He's* never *not shown me his sketches.*

"It's . . . It's not ready yet," he stays, stowing the journal in his satchel for safekeeping.

We eat in relative silence after that. Me because I'm puzzling over Aeron's behavior, Aeron because he's rueful, and Lyam, I think, because he feels slightly out of place.

I'm the first to break the silence. "Aeron, would you mind playing for me?" He hasn't played for me all week. Since before he left for Jesyel Grove, actually.

"I don't know. I, uh . . ."

I wonder if he's uncomfortable because Lyam is here.

Uncomfortable or not, Aeron has snapped at me. I know that will make him more inclined to appease my request. "*Please.*"

I watch Aeron's lips tighten, making a thin line that crinkles at the corners. He meets my eyes, considering, then exhales and acquiesces. "Fine."

I thank him more times than I can count as he re-trieves his flute with practiced care. It's constructed of reed tubes laid side-by-side, seven of them, increasing in size from one side to the other. A colorful band of greens and yellows and reds weaves between them, holding them in place. Next to his journal, it is his most prized possession. Eyeing me one final time, Aeron brings the flute to his lips with hesitation.

I slide closer to Lyam, so that our thighs touch, and without prompting he wraps his arm around my back.

Aeron blows into the pipes across the top, and so begins the familiar tune. It is lulling and magical, hauntingly beautiful. He composed "Aeria's Dream" in secret three years ago, then played it for me as a birthday gift. That birthday has always been my fa-vorite.

Eyes closed, I repose against Lyam, drinking in the melody and the sun overhead and the nearness of Ly-am. I couldn't have asked for a more perfect way to spend my day.

"Aeria's Dream" can be played on a loop so that it is a graceful thing that never ends. Aeron has played many songs for me over the years, but today, "Aeria's Dream" comes to an end, and he starts a high, buoy-ant tune I do not recognize. It calls to memory his behavior this morning: spirited whistling, a silent trance during breakfast, his changed voice, even more cheerful than usual. Not to mention his refusal when I asked to see his sketches.

Something is strange. Different.

Only I don't dare ask what has caused it. Not yet, anyway.

TWENTY-TWO

torture

I wake slowly from my dream, registering details individually. The sun is bright against my closed eyelids. A soft wind carries the scent of pine and grass. Water tumbles and splashes, tumbles and splashes. Birds chirrup, their songs high and buoyant.

Only then do I remember that Aeron had been playing his flute for me. Only then do I realize I'd fallen asleep, my cheek rested against Lyam's shoulder. Only then do I hear their hushed voices.

I remain still, the epitome of a sleeping girl. It's not right of me to listen in like this, but how can I not?

Aeron says, "You care about her a lot, don't you?"

Lyam replies, "More than my life."

Aeron's voice is softer now, wistful. "I want that someday."

"You will have it. I know you will," assures Lyam. "It's the greatest feeling, but it's also torture."

"How so?"

Lyam sighs, low and forlorn, like a lover who's lost the path to his beloved's house. "You want to be with

195

her so badly, every second of every day, but you can't. There are so many things that keep you apart. And being without her is like being trapped in a cold, dark room. The walls are so close it's hard to breathe. It's so dark you can't see past the tip of your nose. All you can think about is escape. *She's* your escape. Then she's there with you, taking your hand. All those walls around you crumble. You can see again, breathe again. But your heart beats so fast for her that it leaves you breathless. She's so stunning that your head spins. And if the entire world faded from existence, you wouldn't notice, because she is all you see. She is all that matters."

There's a long pause. Then, riding on a gusty breath come the words, "I want that."

I feel Lyam's silent laugh. "So go make it happen. Don't be afraid to take a chance. All you have to do is reach out for it. The torture is yours for the taking."

That's when my control begins to slip. It's all I can do to keep from chuckling. I sense their eyes boring into me. So much for my covert operation.

Aeron is first to react. "How much of that did you hear?"

I open my eyes now, craning my head side to side to stretch out my stiff neck. "Not much."

Aeron shakes his head. "You, Aeria Morgan, are a terrible liar."

A retort hangs on my tongue, but I think better of uttering it. My brother is turning out his innermost feelings for someone other than me, to Lyam no less. To misspeak here would only put that in jeopardy. The closer he and Lyam become, the higher the chance that Aeron will put his confidence in him. Which is to say that he will trust Lyam to be alone with me. At least . . . I hope.

I cast a sidelong glance at Lyam, trying to gauge his reaction to my eavesdropping. His eyes hold mine momentarily, and I put my hand to his stubbled cheek. I think he's going to turn away, but he doesn't. I whisper to him, "What you said was really beautiful," and his smile in that moment is the most beautiful thing of all.

Perhaps feeling out of place, Aeron gathers up his satchel and waterskin, and wordlessly starts toward the eastern tree line that leads to our spot. We are expected to follow.

My dress is dry and a bit stiff when I get to my feet. "How long was I sleeping?" I ask Lyam. We start off, a handful of strides behind Aeron, but he still hears me.

Aeron spins around, says, "Depends on how long you *pretended* to be asleep." He shakes his waterskin at me, the drizzle missing me by at least four feet, but it was good-natured enough that I think he's forgiven me for intruding on their private conversation.

I peer up at Lyam, trying to sound reassuring. "It really wasn't that long, I promise."

Lyam smiles again. "Actually, I'm glad you heard. It's good for you to know how I feel."

Aeron waits for us at the mouth of the pool so that he can fill our waterskins. While he does, I point down the trail and explain to Lyam, "This leads to that tree I told you about, the one where Aeron and I go to talk."

He glances ahead at the woods, then back toward the falls. "It's a stunning view, but you should see it at night." He waggles his brows suggestively.

"What do you mean?"

He jerks his chin at Aeron, presses a finger to his lips, and mouths, "Shhhh."

I nod, but the question scratches at my insides.

I thank Aeron with a smile when he hands me my waterskin.

"Shall we?" he says, striking off again.

Soon our brilliant sky, the color of morning glories, is replaced by an enchanting, emerald one, shimmering with delicate beams of sunlight that slant through lofty boughs overhead. Aeron, seizing the opportunity to pass some of his wisdom on to Lyam, is explaining how vital the woods are to our valley. We only pretend to listen, hanging back so that Lyam can offer an explanation of his own.

He gestures to a particular tree, but I can't tell which. His voice is pitched so low that I can scarcely hear him, let alone Aeron. "That's where I was that night."

I almost freeze right then. "And you could see that well?"

"Yes," he whispers. "The moon and the stars, they all shone for you. I didn't miss a thing." This is a fact he is obviously proud of.

I groan. "So you've said."

Aeron's chatty voice continues to lead us along the trail. Even as we take respite under the grand oak, his enthusiasm about the plants and wildlife rolls on. Sometimes I don't know how his head stores so much information: the name of every tree, the usefulness of certain leaves, the ones to watch out for, even the mating seasons of the numerous woodland creatures that call this place home.

"You see those A's?" Aeron says, peering up at them with satisfaction. He tells Lyam about the day he carved them, about the time and care that went into it, and that the interlocking letters symbolize how our lives will be linked together for all eternity. It is a memory I will always cherish, and even now it makes me a little teary-eyed, as if he's just revealing them for the first time.

But the conversation takes an unexpected turn when Aeron begins to describe the amazing barvju trees that grow in Jesyel Grove. That paves the way for talk of Lyam joining Aeron the next time he goes for trades. And that makes me a bit uneasy.

"I probably won't go again until next summer," Aeron says, "unless some emergency arises, but you're welcome to come along. That is, if Aeria doesn't tie you up first."

Again, they mock at my expense, but I play along. "That's why I'll gag him, *then* bind him. That way no one will hear his cries for help."

"You could never overpower him," Aeron points out.

My gaze shifts from Aeron to Lyam's impressive muscles, and there it lingers. "Hmm. That does present a problem."

The shape of his chest, his taut stomach, make my fingertips prick with wonder. His body is a land of undiscovered mountains and valleys begging to be explored.

Lyam grins at my hungry gaze. He taunts, "So what's your plan now?"

I consider for half a second. Casually, I say, "I'll sneak into your room while you're sleeping and—"

"And then," Aeron cuts in, "she'll trip on a shadow and—"

THWACK!

Aeron rubs the side of his head, narrowing his eyes at me but laughing all the same. "You hit like a girl," he teases.

I shrug. "What can I say? I am my brother's sister."

"As much as I enjoy being here," Lyam says after an hour or so, "I should really get back to the Browns'. I told them I'd help with supper tonight."

"We should get back, too," Aeron agrees. "Mother will wonder what's keeping us."

"Best not to push our luck with her, either." Lyam's words are directed at me, at my crestfallen mien. To Aeron he says, "I hope she'll receive a good report."

Aeron ponders Lyam's question for a moment too long, as if he's really struggling to offer his approval. I wonder if he overheard something he shouldn't have and now plans to give our mother a bad report.

Just when I think that things will never truly change, that freedom is too elusive to really grab hold of, Aeron tosses his head back and crows. "I'm just yanking your tails. But really," he adds, "it's nice to have a guy to talk to. Tomorrow we should come up with a plan to question everyone. Now, I've already—"

"Aeron, no," I say, "Leave it alone. It wasn't anyone here, and you know that. If you go poking around asking questions, people are going to get suspicious. Then they'll find out what happened and . . ." I can't finish the thought, because the last thing I want is for Lyam to be forced out of Avalon Valley. They won't care that he was protecting me. All they'll see is the violence. And to them, one display of violence, regardless of its intent, is a promise of more to come. "He doesn't live here, so please, drop it."

Despite my plea, Lyam nods to Aeron. Their matching expressions have "plotting" written all over them. "Tomorrow."

"You two are impossible." I stalk down the trail toward home. Frustration emanates from my face like waves of heat.

Footfalls sound behind me. Being that Lyam is heavier than Aeron, I assume it's him. The hand that swings me around is bigger, mightier. He's holding tightly to my arms and I'm unable to get past his grip.

I never thought I would see the day when I wanted to get away from Lyam.

His expression is twisted into something that looks like the product of sorrow and guilt. "I'm sorry," he says. "You have to know that we have your best interest at heart. It'll only be a few questions, nothing else. Nothing that will raise suspicions, I swear. We only want to make sure you're safe. I worry about you constantly, Aeria. I'd die if . . ." He can't go on. But he doesn't have to. I know what it's like to be eclipsed by that kind of worry.

Lyam pulls me into his arms, his embrace warm and soothing.

It's not their motivation that concerns me. Of the three most important people in my life, two are conspiring to search for answers I'm certain they will not find. I recoil at the possibility that their quest, harmless as they may think, will only jeopardize everything Lyam and I have worked for. I cannot stand by and watch them travel down that road.

That would be my torture.

TWENTY-THREE

euphoria

When Aeron catches up with us, his tone is more pragmatic than repentant. "Look, I'm sure you're right about this guy being an outsider, but what if we could find out where he lives? How could I not try? Maybe someone saw him earlier that day, saw which direction he came from. Or what if someone was expecting a guest and he didn't show? One question could give us the clues we need." He lowers his brows at me, his expression sober now. "You do understand that I have to try, don't you?"

Try as I might, I know there is no dissuading him, so I nod, clinging to Lyam's promise that they'll do all they can to avoid raising suspicion.

We reach the border of the woods all too quickly. The whole day has flown by, and I could kick myself for sleeping through part of it.

We're about to go our separate ways when Aeron begins to hover more than he had earlier in the day. It dawns on me why when Lyam looks at me, looks at him, then looks back at me, holding my gaze as if this moment is incomplete. After spending so much of the morning and afternoon together, the time has come for goodbye. And kisses are synonymous with good-byes, aren't they?

"I had a great time today, Aeria." Lyam opens his mouth to say something else, but he stops. He muses, warring internally, his brows pinched. Then he turns to Aeron, his voice too low for me to make out. Aeron replies with a nod before turning on his heels and heading home.

My forehead scrunches. "What was that about?"

Lyam doesn't answer, not with words. He slips his hands behind my neck, leans down to me, his eyes burning as they did the night at the shed, and presses his firm lips to my . . . cheek. "I'm sorry. I don't want to lose his trust."

I am both pleased and disappointed, but I can see that Lyam's disappointment far surpasses my own. It's written in the corners of his eyes.

I smile. Just a tiny one. "Small steps."

"I'll see you tomorrow," he says, walking reluctant-ly away from me. Our arms stretch to their limit, until our fingers are no longer linked.

"Thank you," I tell Aeron, who waits for me at the front door. "For everything."

We go inside, and Mother appears from the kitchen before the door even closes. She has a tart in one hand and a knife in the other. The house smells wonderful-ly of warm blueberries.

She says, "I was beginning to wonder about you two. Did you kids have a nice time?" She seems to be directing that more at Aeron than me, as if it's her way of covertly requesting the information she desires without having to say it outright.

"We all had a good time," comes Aeron's reply. I suppose that's his way of saying everything went smoothly and to his satisfaction.

Mother turns to me. "Did you have a pleasant swim?"

"Yes, thank you. The water was lovely."

"Aeria jumped the falls," Aeron announces. I sense some pride in his tone that turns up my lips unintentionally.

Mother's expression is both dark with past memories and strained with the present troubles those memories have caused. "From the lower ledge, I hope." I cannot even count how often she's warned us against jumping from the uppermost shelf.

My "Yes" is as reassuring as they come.

I excuse myself to change into something more comfortable. Already, Mother probes Aeron for more answers to her flow of questions, which shift from clear, distinct words to nothing more than murmurs, until finally I shut myself inside my room with the silence.

Pressing my back to the cool plane of the door, I stare ahead, smiling, waiting to wake up, because all of this cannot be real. Yet somehow . . . it is. Somehow, this outcast has found someone to call her own. Someone who looks at her and sees the true person that hides within this hardened shell of rejection, and makes her feel as if the world would crumble to the ground if she did not exist.

After changing into a clean nightdress, I throw on my robe, tying it around my waist. My hair is a tangled mess. I work my brush through it, twist it into a braid, and let it hang over my shoulder.

Aeron's back to his whistling when I return to the kitchen in my nightclothes. He's roasting buttered parsnips over the fire, seemingly entranced by the flames. He works them around the pan slowly, but I'm not sure if he's purposeful or if his hand just moves of its own volition.

I set out three plates, but the instant I relax against the back of my chair, a surge of fatigue crashes into me. My eyelids are heavy with the weight of a full day of sun and water, and it's a strain just to keep them open. Still another side effect is this piercing hunger, and my need for food wins out over my distaste for parsnips and my desire for slumber.

Afterward, I bid Aeron and Mother a groggy goodnight and make my way down the hall, running the pads of my fingers along the walls to steady myself. I stumble into bed, and in a matter of seconds, my consciousness begins to fade. That's when the bedroom door creaks open, sounding more distant than it actually is.

"Aeria?" Aeron's voice is soft as peach fuzz.

"I'm awake. Kind of."

"I was kind of hoping to talk."

Abandoning my quest for sleep, my eyes flash open. I sit bolt upright. "Get that goat tail over here," I demand, patting the bed beside me.

Chuckling, Aeron closes the door and lights the lantern on my bedside table. Beside it lies the necklace he gave me and the wilted remains of Lyam's orchid. Distorted silhouettes dance on the walls of the once-dark room, one of which looks like a prowling feline.

Aeron sits at the edge of my bed, his hands folded in his lap. *He's nervous*, I think, puzzling over what he could want to talk about.

Then I think I understand. "Is this about Satrie?"

Aeron smiles slowly, revealing his perfect white teeth. He nods, as if his smile wasn't telling enough.

He sucks in a breath, and when it comes out it resembles an embarrassed laugh. "I think she might like me."

"I know that! Tell me what happened. I want to know *everything*."

Aeron moves to the center of my bed and crosses his legs, mirroring my pose. He grins as if he's been hiding a secret for ages.

"So, you know how I was put in the same group as Satrie for the funeral preparations?" I say that I do and Aeron goes on. "Well, when I joined my group, I noticed that she went out of her way to ignore me. I thought you were wrong about how she felt about me. I had this whole speech going in my head for how I would tell you so.

"But then, when we were working in the field, she kept smiling at me. It would only be a second, and then she'd look away. But it happened over and over. I knew I should talk to her, but I couldn't think of anything to say." Aeron pauses, covers his face with his hands. His shame is palpable.

"What did you say?"

He takes his hands away from his face and uses them to gesture as he explains. "It started with debating whether to say something funny, or smart, or maybe complimenting her, and it ended with me mumbling something about her dress, that it was pretty and it fit her nicely." He slaps his forehead. "It was *so* stupid. I felt like such an idiot."

I laugh. "I bet she was speechless."

"She was embarrassed is what she was. But somehow that got us talking. She wanted to hear about my trip to Jesyel Grove, and I found out that she likes to draw, too."

"Any flirting?"

Even in the dim light I see Aeron's face go red. "A little," he admits. "Our fingers touched when we reached for the same pair of gloves and we didn't pull them back right away. I felt like Sebaan was standing on my chest!"

"Torture," I murmur.

Aeron groans. "I knew you were lying about how much you heard."

"I only heard the end, I promise."

"Well, in any case, Lyam was right about all of it." Aeron hesitates. "But it's different for me. Worse, maybe."

"How so?"

"You and Lyam have an advantage. You know how he feels, and he knows how you feel. You don't have to tiptoe around the subject. But I don't have that freedom. I can't even put into words what I'm feeling, but somehow I'm supposed to explain it to her? How do you do that?" Raking his fingers through his hair, Aeron grabs a generous tuft of dark locks between his knuckles. He looks deeply disheartened, and there is no more apt word for him than "tortured."

"I don't think you need to have all the answers right away, but if you do feel something, she should know."

Aeron holds my gaze in thoughtful silence. "How?" he asks finally. "How do I tell her without fear of rejection?"

I shake my head at him. "It isn't rejection you're really afraid of, though, is it? Because Satrie adores you, and you know it. So it all comes down to you. Take it one day at a time. Let your actions show her how you feel until you figure out the right words. Just don't keep her waiting too long, and don't be afraid to put your heart on the line. The true torture would be losing her because you never tried."

Aeron stares into his lap for what feels like an awfully long time before looking back at me. "You're absolutely right," he says, seemingly determined now. "If you don't mind me asking, how did Lyam tell you he's in love with you?"

I chew my lip. Sheepishly, I admit, "He hasn't. He's told me bits and pieces, but he's never said it outright."

Aeron makes a face of surprise.

I go on before he can say anything. "He's probably just waiting for the right moment. I mean, we haven't exactly had a whole lot of *privacy*." I give him a light shove.

"Sounds like I'm not the only one who has some talking to do."

"I guess you're right." Suddenly, winged creatures are aflutter in my stomach as I ponder Lyam's feelings for me. I think back to our goodbye, to that unmistakable flame of desire in his eyes. I give a small chuckle. "He actually asked for your permission to kiss my cheek?"

Aeron chuckles back. "That guy is earning some major points in the trustworthy category." Then his forehead crinkles into a field of ridges. "I'm ready to show you my sketches now. Would you like to see them?"

For a second I am tongue-tied. "Absolutely."

Aeron fishes through his satchel on the dark side of the room and returns to his cross-legged position opposite me. Clinging dearly to his journal, he says, utterly serious, "You can never tell anyone what I'm about to show you. Understand?"

I pantomime locking my lips and throwing the imaginary key into an abyss.

I watch eagerly as Aeron thumbs through pages and pages of upside down images. The winding stream, the falls, a flock of birds in flight, the clouds on a stormy day, the black elk we saw last week. He lifts the journal out of my view, examining the page before turning it around and placing it in my lap. "I drew it from memory."

Arrested by the beautiful portrayal that lies before me, my mouth forms an inadvertent O. What's more astonishing is his claim to have drawn if from memory. "It looks exactly like her."

Aeron peers at the image, which is upside down from his perspective now. "You really think so?"

She is a vision. Lying on her stomach in a field of grass, her hands frame her flawless face. Her long locks are tugged by a gentle breeze, her full lips turned up in a small smile that puts her tiny dimples on display. But it's Satrie's eyes, fringed with thick lashes, that are the most prominent attribute. Even on parchment they seem to sparkle. Aeron has depicted her stunningly.

My countenance falls. I feel all at once self-conscious, inadequate, seeing how the graphite version of Satrie surpasses what I could ever hope to be.

Softly, Aeron says, "Aeria, turn the page."

Although his sketch of Satrie's unfailing beauty is a remarkable sight, I do not wish to be reminded of my lack thereof, and so it is with intentional slowness that I turn the page.

But the next page is *not* devoted to Satrie.

Instead, on this one a man carries a woman in his arms. There's no mistaking that the man beside the waterfall is Lyam, but the woman in the picture could not be me. She's far too exquisite. Her face is delicate and captivating, her body shapely and very alluring. An enchanting smile tugs on her lips, her eyes penetrating.

I am at a loss for words.

I look up, finding a less than confident Aeron staring back. He says, "Don't you like it?"

"Lyam looks, well, phenomenal. I see someone was a little stingy in the muscle department."

Aeron lets out a guilty laugh. "I figured it best to underestimate rather than overestimate."

Demure, I say, "But this doesn't look like me. Is this how you see me?"

He shakes his head in disbelief. "Aeria, this is how everyone sees you. From Avalon Valley to the far side of the earth and back again. Not one person can match your beauty. And I'm not just saying that as your brother."

I squint at the graphite me in wonderment. Is this really how people see me? How Lyam sees me? How could that be? How could the reflection that's been staring back at me all my life be so different from this girl that Aeron drew?

TWENTY-FOUR

stolen

Lyam is waiting for me beside the stream the next morning. Arms crossed at his chest, he wears a smile that is seductive and inviting. It's the kind of smile that can make a girl forget her name.

Meeting me halfway, Lyam takes the load from me, not only this morning's breakfast dishes, but those from yesterday's meals as well.

"Did you sleep well?" he asks, heading toward the water.

"I did. And you?"

"I did, thank you. Of course, it's nothing you'd want to hear about."

I blush, regretting now that I asked. "There's something I want to talk to you about."

My hesitation is plain. Without my pot full of dishes, my hands absently worry the skirt of my dress. "So Aeron and I were talking last night and—"

I stop at the sound of dirt shifting nearby.

213

"Good morning," says Naasvyth Daeston, unaware that she is presently endorsing fate's design to unravel even the most tenuous thread of privacy Lyam and I manage to weave.

Lyam acknowledges the woman kindly. My words hang around us, suddenly silent.

I say nothing. I can't help but feel Naasvyth's greeting was not meant for me. She sets a basket of clothing on the bank to start her wash.

Lyam and I clean the dishes in relative silence. He frequently meets my eyes. I wonder if what I wanted to say is written there, but even more so I wonder what would have become of our conversation had it not ended before it could begin. All the while, Naasvyth is chattering idly about the weather, the temperature of the stream, the morning bird songs. There are no question marks attached. Lyam's attempting to hold his manners and my gaze at the same time, but it's easy to see which one is winning out when his replies come out curt and mechanical.

Soon I begin to believe that Naasvyth has brought a basket with no bottom. I am even more undone by her thoroughness. And her nearness. Does she really have to stand five feet from us?

We finish before Naasvyth. Lyam hefts the pot laden with dishes to waist level and carries it back home for me. "Look," he says when we're out of earshot of Naasvyth, "I have an idea about what you were going to say, and I have something to say as well. But I can't just throw it out there in the open. It's . . ."

"Private," I finish.

"I was going to say important, but private works, too."

Already my heart's knocking on my chest as if the moment's here, hoping with all hope that he means to say those three little words I've been longing for.

Three little words that, when spoken apart from one another, have little value. But string them together and they bespeak something so magical. They solidify feelings, chase away doubt and insecurity, unleash the freedom to express true emotions without fear of rejection. They are the catalyst to a lifetime of romance and intimacy.

"Then I guess it will have to wait," I say, my shoulders sagging. I hadn't fully realized how desperately I wanted to hear the words *I love you* until now.

We reach the front door with too much left unsaid, and I'm clinging to the fantasy of promises blooming into reality. But that all feels painfully far away.

"I have to get back to the shop," Lyam says, his expression regretful.

I open my arms to receive the pot. "We'll talk later."

But my later involves Aeron and me striking off for the barn, each with a produce crate. We set the crates side by side in the bottom of the wheelbarrow. Aeron offers to push it to the orchard.

I watch with hungry eyes as we approach Saeth's workshop. Lyam is measuring and cutting long planks into shorter pieces, which he casts into a pile near a chopping block a few paces away. I can't help but stare at the way he moves, at the way his bicep flexes as he saws back and forth, back and forth. It is pure brawn in action. Mesmerizing. Intoxicating.

Under his breath, Aeron mutters, "Showoff."

I roll my eyes, just as Lyam looks up. He smiles instantly, wiping his brow with the back of his gloved hand. I cast one last glance over my shoulder after we've passed, only to find that Lyam has yet to look away.

Before I know it, the rest of the village is behind us and we've come upon the Mercers' shop. I fight the familiar shudder that threatens to sprint through my veins, turning my blood to ice. *He's not there*, I remind myself. *He's not there.*

Daveed stands outside his shop, collecting pelts from the line one by one. Four grayish-brown hares, six squirrels, and one sleek-coated skunk, all stiff as boards. Turning to go back inside, carrying his pelts with a nurturing sort of care, Daveed spots us. He tips his head in greeting, letting his gaze linger approvingly at the barrow for a bare moment. Then he goes inside.

In the orchard, Aeron sets up the stepladder beneath one of the more top-heavy peach trees, not wanting to thin the lower boughs so much that the youngsters can't reach the fruit without aid.

Mounting the ladder, he says, "So Lyam and I did some talking to people this morning." He twists a peach off the branch and lowers it to me.

I take it and place it in the crate, I try to keep my voice even when I say, "I know. And you didn't learn anything, did you?"

Aeron goes still for a moment, then lowers another peach. "In short, no. No one saw anyone coming or going, nothing out of the ordinary happened by any stretch of the imagination. The only thing I found out was that Jas twisted his ankle playing a game of Fox and Hens with Ilora." Jas Eland is Emay Brown's father, and Ilora is Emay's daughter. At only two years old, Ilora apparently makes one cunning little hen.

"I told you." Now I sound haughty, but worry is quick to take over. "So is everyone in the village wondering why you two were asking so many questions?"

"No," he starts, handing me the final peach. But then he missteps and crashes down the ladder, landing with a grimace. He holds tightly to the rung, though he's on solid ground. "I'm all right. I'm all right."

After taking a few moments to collect himself, Aeron continues as if nothing had happened. "Lyam came up with the story that he saw a stranger when he was on his way back from Garrison, which coincides with what he told Reed last week. It was the perfect cover."

The relief is as abrupt as Aeron's fall; it crashes through me, and in the end I'm all right. I am perfectly all right.

"Let's move on," Aeron says, steering the barrow while I drag the ladder beside him.

Next up, apples. An undertone of relief fills the reticence as I pile golden apples into the second crate.

When we finish, Aeron dismounts the ladder, exercising more care this time.

I ask, "Do you mind if Lyam eats lunch with us? I was thinking about surprising him."

Jerking the wheelbarrow into motion, Aeron replies, "I don't mind." I was hoping he would remove himself from the picture, giving Lyam and me a chance to talk. Alone.

"*Or*," I suggest, "you could surprise Satrie with lunch. Show her you hope to get to know each other better."

Aeron lets out a mock laugh. "I think a semi-romantic gesture like that requires more talking first. Like you said, one day at a time."

I return the ladder to the lean-to, shut the gate behind us, and Aeron works to keep the momentum going where the grass meets the dirt path. "In the very least," I say, "you should say hi if we see her. That way she'll know you're interested."

"You're probably right," he agrees with a sigh. Nerves have crept into his expression.

It's not so much a matter of *if* we see her, but *when*.

As we draw near the enclosure where the children play, we spot Satrie perched atop the uppermost rail of the fence, attentively overseeing four youngsters. Aeron becomes the one to watch from under his lashes, furtively eyeing her every move, so weightless and beautiful. He makes a shape with his mouth, a soundless whistle, as she gathers her hair to the side to let the sun kiss her neck and exposed shoulder blades.

The sound of the barrow moving over dirt catches her ear and she turns in our direction. Aeron wasn't expecting her to look, and Satrie wasn't expecting to find Aeron at the other end of her gaze.

It's one of those things you wish you were never a part of. There's an intimacy in the moment their eyes meet that doesn't feel right for me to have witnessed.

I whisper, "Go talk to her. I can manage this." My palm covers his shaking hand.

"I— I don't know what to say."

I give him the best advice I know. "Be yourself."

Aeron's steps are hesitant, but when he joins Satrie on the fence, it's as if he belonged there beside her all along.

Getting the wheelbarrow going is a task in and of itself, but keeping it from toppling to the side, spilling its contents in the dirt, is another story. The weight of it surprises me, but more so is how Aeron made it look easy.

Somehow, the fruit makes it home unscathed. I abandon the barrow in a shady spot beside our house and go inside. I throw together a quick lunch, including enough for Lyam.

But the last thing I want to have to do is knock on Saeth and Emay's door to ask Lyam to eat with us. I'd rather not face them, knowing how concerned they are about Lyam's involvement with me.

I go to check the shop first to see if Lyam's there. Peering through the open window, I see that he is, and that he's alone. Standing in the threshold, I tap on the open door.

The sound startles Lyam and he whips around. The surprise on his face makes me smile. His eyes flit to the basket in my hand.

Raising it a little, I say, "I hope you're hungry."

He sets down a sanding stone and pulls at his gloves from the fingertips, placing them beside the stone. "Starved."

I extend my arms to embrace him, wanting nothing more than his touch right now, but his embrace is so far away that a whole person could stand between us. When I frown, Lyam explains, "Sorry, I must smell terrible."

I don't tell him he's wrong. Even drenched in sweat, he still smells intoxicating. Still has that woodsy sort of aroma about him. "You haven't eaten yet?"

"No." A handkerchief makes a brief appearance from his pocket, and Lyam wipes his brow. "Will it just be the two of us, then?"

"Aeron will be here soon to resume guard duty. He stopped to talk to Satrie."

The smile on Lyam's face is proud, the kind the male species reserves for other males they've mentored when things like women are involved. "Good for him."

We go outside and settle in the grass, and not even a minute later Saeth comes stalking toward the shop. When he goes inside, the workshop door slams shut.

"Just ignore him," Lyam says, but his expression tells me that even he finds this difficult.

"What's his problem?" I ask, probably too loud.

Saeth emerges from the shop a few seconds later, seemingly undone. He shoots an answering scowl at me, fierce as he is intimidating. My mouth forms the word "Oh" with no sound. He storms off as if the ground is on fire, glowering once more at me as if I were the cause of it.

"He *really* doesn't like me," I murmur when he's out of sight.

Lyam takes my hand, rubbing the top of it with his thumb. "It's me he's mad at. He's upset that I'm ignoring his advice." The word *advice* is a marriage of sarcasm and annoyance.

"Why does *he* care so much?" I say, sharing his annoyance.

"He says he thinks I would be better received around here if I didn't associate with you."

"That still doesn't tell me why. Why is he making it *his* personal mission to keep us apart?"

"Because he doesn't have a son. He puts a lot of trust in me, and he's dead set on me taking over the shop one day, but . . ."

"But what?"

Lyam pinches his lips together. Finally he says, "He thinks my being with you will have a negative impact on my future."

My heart plummets. Could Saeth be right? What if my only chance at gaining a future costs Lyam the one he so richly deserves?

I assume an unaffected mien, though my heart dies inside. "Well, he's right. You didn't come here to be counted among the outcasts. Your life could be so much better, and there are plenty of pretty girls."

Lyam, on his knees now, cradles my cheeks between his hands, framing my face to direct my attention. Still, I look away. "Aeria, do you hear yourself? Why, how, could I ever turn my back on you?" I meet his gaze, holding it. "There is no one else. You're everything to me. I—"

I think, for a moment so brief that I don't even have time to hold my breath, that I'm finally going to hear those three words I've been longing for. But as fate's design goes, the moment is stolen by the *boom-boom, boom-boom-boom* of nearby drums.

TWENTY-FIVE

homecoming

*B*oom-boom. Boom-boom-boom.

Lyam, wide-eyed and still, arrested by the beat of the drums, wears the same terror-filled expression as the night Debayah passed. "Again?"

My attempt to not laugh fails. "Can't you tell the difference? That's triumphant drumming. Everyone's to go to the plaza. Chief has a message of good news for us."

Aeron rounds the corner then. The word "urgent" doesn't even begin to describe his gait. I rise, sensing something is terribly wrong. He works to catch his breath and speak at the same time. "They're . . . back."

Lyam shifts his weight to see Aeron better. "Who's back?" he asks.

Aeron pants out, "The fishing . . . party. There's to be . . . a feast." With a grand smile, he tacks on, "Tonight."

"Already?" I blurt. "They weren't supposed to come back until tomorrow." My stomach does this little lurch, as if I'm falling from someplace I shouldn't have been. I grab hold of Lyam's shoulder to combat the sinking feeling. I'd thought I had another day before Iverett returned, and the news that he's here now, and so, so close without me knowing it, makes me feel dangerously exposed, like a girl in a lighting storm with nowhere to run for cover.

"They got back twenty minutes ago," Aeron explains, breathing closer to normal now. "But it's only Reed, Saiah, and Zede. Iverett and Elancian stayed behind to do some trapping."

I let out a relieved breath, then clap my hand over my mouth, wishing I could undo the sound.

Lyam and Aeron fix me with identical stares. Drawn brows. Ridged foreheads. Slits for eyes. The weight of their gazes combined almost has me wishing Iverett had just come back with the rest of his group. Now, after years of silently enduring his piercing glares, I have to explain to Aeron why I never told him how I felt. How my fear of Iverett chases the blood from my veins. How not one person has ever made me feel so small, so loathed, as Iverett has. Not even Saeth, whose anger toward me stings like a bee, while Iverett's is a dagger to the heart.

I've never understood it, how he could hate me so, because our mothers are best friends and his family has always supported us, which is a large part of why I never said anything. I've never wronged him, never hurt him in any way. Never did anything that warrants such venom, apart from simply existing.

"I—" I begin, struggling to keep my voice even. "I just know he doesn't like me."

"Who?" Aeron and Lyam say, almost simultaneously.

"Iverett," I mouth, because I hate to say his name aloud.

"Which one is he?" Lyam asks. He's talking to Aeron.

Aeron goes about describing Iverett in a very Aeron-ly fashion, all hands and exaggerations. "He's as tall as a tree. His head is this big. His hand is longer than my foot."

This goes on for some time, until it's decided that, yes, Lyam does recall seeing Iverett before he left for the fishing trip last Monday.

The distraction is enough that when the focus returns to me, Mother appears beside me, slipping her arm around my waist. "All ready?" she says, delivering a smile to each of us.

We leave our uneaten lunch behind and when we reach Central Plaza, it seems everyone else has already arrived. We stand at the back, and Lyam joins us, holding my hand in his.

At the head of the plaza, Chief Cole scans the crowd. Beside him stands the tired and unkempt group, sans Iverett and Elancian. Chief's son, Zede, stands closest to him, a trimmer, younger version of his father.

At first, Chief Cole's mouth shapes words we don't hear but the threesome does, then he begins to project his voice over the crowd. "Today we have been blessed with the safe return of Reed, Saiah, and Zede. The great Aandorn River proved their fishing trip quite successful, bestowing upon us a multitude of fish that will provide our families with many days' sustenance. Let us thank the gods for the plentiful supply, and thank these three for their sacrifice and hard work. May they be blessed a hundredfold for their goodwill and charity.

"Let us, however, be mindful of the two whose journey is not yet over. Until they are safely returned to our bosom, may we lift them up in our thoughts and prayers." Chief Cole tucks his chin to his chest, offering a silent petition.

When he finishes, he extends his arms in a grandiose gesture that makes his paunch lurch forward. "Tonight," he declares, "we will celebrate this joyous event with the Homecoming Feast. At sundown we will gather together to dine on nature's bounty, with solidarity and gratitude in our hearts."

There's a swell of applause, punctuated here and there by hoots and whistles and an almost drunk-sounding "Bring out the wine!" which elicits more hoots and applause.

With tonight's feast soon upon us, the plaza empties at a rapid pace. A dozen or so stay behind to discuss the fate of the fish. Salmon, it seems. Talk of seasonings stirs up a spirited debate.

Chief Cole steps down from the dais before the rest of the men. Reed, Saiah, and Zede huddle around for a quick conversation, utterly normal, but there's something about it that I find strange. Familiar almost. As if I've lived this moment before.

I hear Aeron cough, and when I turn I see that Mother has already left for home. His expression is apologetic, for he knows I hate these abrupt ends with Lyam, but there's also something anticipatory in it. A flame that dances in his eyes. He's looking forward to tonight's feast, and there's only one reason why.

"I'll see you tonight," Lyam says, and I can see by his expression that he, too, is excited for the feast.

Returning home, Aeron pushes for answers regarding Iverett. "Did he say something to you?"

"Yes," I tell him in a mocking voice. "He told me my dress was pretty and that it fit me nicely."

Aeron hides his blush behind his palms and nothing more is said about Iverett or the fact that I've hidden my aversion to him for so many years.

Inside, the kitchen is brimming with bowls and mixing spoons, burlap sacks of flour and sugar, eggs to be cracked and milk to be measured, and more apples and peaches than one would care to count.

"Is this why you sent us to the orchard?" Aeron asks Mother. "Did you know they were coming back early?"

Mother waves a knife as she speaks. "Not exactly, but a day early is better than a day late. It's all Tavine's been able to talk about. Although she must be rather puzzled that Iverett didn't return. But I'm sure he and Elancian will be fine. Iverett is as responsible as they come."

We slice peaches and apples until the crates are empty, mix and roll dough until our hands hurt, all to the symphony of the crackling hearth, the air colored by the warm scent of spices and the bubbling insides of pies and turnovers.

I'm picking sticky dough from between my fingers when Aeron starts up on how everyone's going to be sweating fish scent for the next week after the feast we'll have tonight, and how so many fish were brought back that there couldn't possibly be any left for the animals to catch. That's when it hits me. That strange I-seem-to-have-lived-this-before feeling I had earlier. I dreamed it. Last night.

I almost laugh at the absurdity of it all.

Gathered in a half circle stood a donkey, a badger, and a rooster. Their mouths spilled over with fish, so many that they waded in a sea of them. A noonday sun shone overhead, and in the distance, an arching line of suns crossed the sky like a fiery rainbow. In the dream I counted the suns. Seven. And below the seven suns, embraced by a shadowy wood, were two sets of eyes, animal eyes, so far off and so cloaked in darkness that the bodies of the creatures could not be seen.

When I tell Aeron of my dream, he stops rolling his crust and says, "So you had a dream they'd come back early?" I shrug and he adds, "Weird."

A minute passes and Aeron chuckles. "Mind dreaming up Satrie dancing with me tonight?"

Returning from the stream with a pot of clean bowls, Mother tosses me one of her glorious smiles before putting the dishes away. "I saw a certain gentleman on my way back. How are you and Lyam doing, anyway?"

Last week, her voice would have sounded hopeful that I'd say that things weren't going well. Now, her concern is clear and her smile is caring.

"Good," I say automatically. I don't mean to be so vague.

"Well, you know I'm good at listening," she says, "if you ever want to talk about it."

I don't know if it's the disappointment in her eyes or the set of her lips or the way her shoulders sag. I say, "Actually, there is one thing."

Mother heaves a sigh of relief. "Oh, good. I was afraid you were hiding something from me. What is it? What's bothering you?"

"It's Saeth," I say.

Aeron makes a puzzled face; I haven't mentioned this to him.

"He eventually wants Lyam to take over his shop, and Saeth worries that if Lyam's involved with me, it will reflect negatively on his family and the future of his shop. So he's been warning Lyam about spending time with me. What should we do?"

Mother taps on her lips. "It sounds as if Lyam has a choice to make. There is a dividing line between us and everyone else, and he has to decide what side of the line he wants to be on. I don't think he can continue to straddle it as he has been. Unfortunately, consequences come with the territory. Being on our side presents its own set of disadvantages."

The topic is quick to put me in a bad mood, and my mother's words don't help in the slightest. They only confirm my belief that I am doing Lyam more harm than good. I am conflicted, as if I'm the one straddling two lines. I know Lyam's future is better without me, but I also know that my future without him is not.

The mood at the Homecoming Feast, however, is jovial. Musicians deliver feet-moving rhythms of celebration. Torchlight ripples and blinks across the plaza, fending off the dark. Long tables boast delectable dishes bearing more food than we can possibly consume in one night. Fish and smoke scents the air, swelling with the tang of lemon and the sweetness of honey and the bite of pepper.

Aeron stands at my elbow while I scan the crowd. He says, "You should have told me about Saeth."

I shrug. Aeron nods his understanding.

My searching goes on for several agonizing minutes, and though I'm still on the outside, worry drives like gale-force winds within me, tightening my already-gripped chest, recalling those early days when Lyam was nowhere to be found.

When a hand brushes against my side, I spin on the balls of my feet and my heart crashes back to life. "Lyam!" I screech. "Don't do that!"

Lyam grins. "I love the effect I have on you."

I shake my head. "If you only knew."

Aeron takes this opportunity to flee the scene lest something vomit-inducing comes next.

What comes next is actually this: Lyam says, "Would you mind if we eat now? I haven't had salmon in weeks."

Lyam loads our plates with roasted potatoes, salads topped with fresh berries, and when it we reach the platters of fish, he chooses the honey-glazed salmon. Mine is seasoned with lemon and pepper, and when we sit down at the dais to eat, each bite melts in my mouth, an explosion of fire and zest and mouth-watering goodness.

While Lyam goes back for seconds, I stay where I am, skimming the crowd for Aeron and Mother. Mother is easy to spot. All it takes is searching for Tavine's crown of red hair and there she is. It works every time.

To find my brother, I employ the help of a certain dimpled smile and long, flaxen hair. Sure enough, Aeron and Satrie are walking toward the food tables, Aeron talking, Satrie listening and nodding and smiling along.

Lyam returns with a proud grin, asks, "Did you see your brother with Satrie?" and when he's finished with his fish, he sets his plate on mine, takes my hand, and whisks me off to dance.

The feel of him so close is intoxicating. My skin prickles with want. With need. A need so strong that no degree of nearness is enough. Snaking my arms around his waist, I eliminate what little distance remains between us and gaze unflinchingly at him. As his breaths become my breaths, mutiny rises within me. His lips are so close, yet so far. So close, yet so painfully unattainable.

In a highly seductive voice, I say, "Want to be alone? We could go to the stream. No one will notice that we're gone."

Lyam tosses his head back and groans softly. "You know I want to, but it's a terrible idea. Your mother could find out, and I'd hate to—"

"Lose her trust, I know. Maybe I don't care any-more."

Lyam regards me with a weighty, thoughtful kind of consideration, searching my eyes as a war rages within him. "All right," he finally surrenders, enlisting in my mutiny. He takes my hand and we skirt the plaza, avoiding the crush of bodies.

My heart takes flight, like a caged bird set free. *Is this really happening?*

It comes as no surprise that everyone else is too involved in their own celebration to notice our escape.

All but one.

My brother's voice trills his joy while draining mine. "Aeria! Lyam!"

I decide right then that Aeron has turned interruption into an eerily precise art form. He jerks to a stop, but there's an intensity about him that keeps him far from still. He speaks in a rush. "Where are you going? Never mind. Let's head back before Mother notices you're gone. I have something to tell you."

I can't imagine what Aeron could have to say that warrants such urgency, and such untimely interference, but before I can tell him so, he goes on. "I did it. I actually did it." His crooked smile is so wide, so telling, that I need no explanation.

He offers one anyway. Or at least, he begins to. Suddenly I can't hear his voice. The world goes dark, as if light itself has ceased to exist. It feels like a living thing, this darkness, heavy and oppressive. It snakes around my limbs, crushes my lungs, weighs my feet. My body refuses to move. A whisper crawls up my skin—"You can't stop me"—and I shiver as with fever.

Peeling laughter explodes from the plaza nearby, but in this darkness it feels thoroughly out of place, as if it mocks me. "You think you're so special," it taunts wickedly.

Somehow I lose Lyam's hand. My body lurches forward on its own accord, my throat swelling as if I've swallowed the night and all the secrets it contains. My guts are snarled up inside me, convulsing and stealing each breath so that I'm gasping for air. But the night has hidden that away, too.

What's left is a girl crumpled in the dirt, her elbows locked to keep her from falling into her own vomit. Her throat burns and a bad taste stains her mouth, but she still can't breathe. Salty tears slip past her lips. She wipes her eyes, her mouth, unable to stop the onslaught of tears.

She can't see her onlookers, but she hears one of them say, "It must be something she ate," but the voice sounds distant, as if the night has stolen yet another thing, and its desire is the girl and all that she is, all that she will ever be.

"Leave me alone," she says, unable to recognize her own voice. But the darkness won't leave her. She can't shut it out. It's always there, lurking, waiting. There is no escaping it.

A strong hand cups her shoulder and the touch feels familiar, but at the same time she's too unsure about anything in her life to know if it will be around long enough to *stay* familiar.

"Let's get her home."

The voices grow more distant as the girl is scooped up and cradled. She knows somewhere in her consciousness that she is cared for, but part of her tells her that that matters little. There are formidable forces with their mark set on destroying all that is left of the girl named Aeria Morgan.

TWENTY-SIX

prisoner

A gentle nudge rouses me from dreamless sleep. My eyelids are heavy and difficult to manage, and my body wants nothing to do with wakefulness. I feel like an animal drawn out of hibernation too early.

Aeron whispers my name, but even that makes my head throb and my ears ring. Aeron's voice sounds as if it's been thrown and returned in a second. Then I hear my mother's voice, thrown and returned, saying, "Can you sit up? We brought lunch."

Lunch? How long have I been sleeping? I labor to sort my memories of last night, trying to remember how I wound up in my bed. All I can call up is a most undignified spectacle that involved me hunched on all fours, staring at what used to be dry dirt.

I peel my eyelids apart, squinting at the bold light that pounds through the open window. The room spins. I don't bother trying to sit up.

"You. Look. Terrible." This comes from Aeron, of course. Mother swats his arm.

"Thanks." After a pause, I say, "What happened?"

Aeron replies, "You mean before or after you tossed your supper?"

I hide my face in my hands. "After."

"Lyam and I brought you home, and you've been out ever since."

Mother touches the back of her tiny hand to my forehead. "Are you feeling any better?"

"Not really." At least the ringing has subsided, and the room is working on being as still as it should be.

Aeron says, "Do you think you can hold anything down? I made soup."

I crane my neck. On my bedside table, next to my necklace and sad orchid, sits a bowl of translucent liquid. "What kind?"

His lips quirk into an almost-grimace. "Technically, it's broth. But you know what Mother says about chicken broth."

"'There's no better medicine for a weary body or a troubled mind than chicken broth,'" he and I say in unison, which makes Mother smile proudly.

She cups my cheek. "I'll give you two a few minutes. I'll be back to check on you later."

"So," Aeron says after she's gone. He's wearing a smile that suggests he knows something he possibly shouldn't. "Does Lyam always meet you at the stream in the morning, or did he just miss my striking conversation and good looks?"

I chuckle. "Poor guy. I should go talk to him."

But Aeron pushes me back down. "You're not going anywhere. I won't allow it."

I don't argue, only because I feel so weak, then realization dawns. "Oh, Aeron, I'm so sorry. You've had to pick up my slack today, haven't you?"

Aeron sits on the edge of my bed. "You need your rest. I'm handling things just fine on my own."

"You're a good brother, Aeron."

"The best," he declares with a spirited grin. "Because I am the one and only."

A rumble emanates from deep within my stomach. "I think I'm ready for that soup now."

With a little help I come to a sitting position, resting my back against my pillow. Aeron carefully hands me the bowl of broth. "I let it cool for you."

I let out a gusty exhale. "Bet I could have slept another ten hours."

Aeron regards me, his reply quicker than I'd like. "Another ten hours may do you some good."

I peer down at my broth, at the hazy, ever-moving surface, but the picture it paints leaves much to be desired.

"Go ahead," Aeron urges, as if my scrutiny has something to do with his ability to prepare a quality chicken broth.

I bring the bowl to my lips. The broth is warm and it feels wonderful as it careers down my throat.

"Slow down. Slow down. It's not going anywhere, except maybe back up. Give it time to settle."

"You never finished," I take a small sip, "telling me what happened," and another, "with Satrie." Then another sip. Tipping the bowl back, I drain the last of the broth and add, "Last night" to clarify.

Aeron grins his crooked grin. "I asked her to dance with me, and she said yes! I was so afraid I'd step on her feet, but I didn't. And I didn't say anything stupid, either. It was kind of . . . perfect."

"Must be nice." My words are laced with sourness, which is not my intent.

"What do you mean by that?"

"Remember when you ran up behind us last night?"

Aeron nods, his brows gathered as if he's trying to find the end of his nose.

"Lyam and I were going to the stream. To talk. Alone." I do my best to say it without heat, but still it sounds like the kindling of a flame.

"What if Mother had caught you?"

This fans the flame. "So what if she did? Maybe I'm beyond caring. She says she'll give us more freedom, but I feel like that's never going to happen. Not without my brother following along as my chaperone."

Aeron speaks into his lap. "Do you need anything else before I go?"

"I'm sorry. I shouldn't have said anything. It's not your fault."

Coming to his feet, he says, "Try to get some sleep."

"I'm sorry," I say again.

"Don't worry about it." He takes the bowl from my hands and ducks down to kiss the top of my head. "That's from Lyam." Aeron draws the curtains. Then he closes the door behind him.

When I dream, I dream of a place where time seems to stand still. Where dazzling stars roam the face of this alien planet, not the heavens. I can't see the sun or the moon in the orange-and-midnight streaked sky, nor do I see that they even exist beyond my own memories of them.

The land is uncultivated, a painted wilderness with thick tangles of deep, purple vines that stretch from the boughs of vibrantly-colored trees to the autumn-colored underbrush below. Emerald and fire-red grass whips at my calves, and I sense that no other human has stepped foot here for some time. If ever.

Despite its rich, untamed beauty, I am over-whelmed and undone by what I can't see. Something dark and dangerous reigns here, evidenced by chills rather than sight. It's the *knowledge* of it, whatever *it* may be, that pricks at my spirit and shakes me to the core. I want to flee, to wake, but I'm prisoner to this resounding sense of emptiness, which almost feels worse than the unseen presence itself. I'm lost and sad and frightened, with no hope of salvation.

Until a voice speaks to me . . .

"Aeria, wake up."

I'm still nuzzled in my blanket, more cocoon-like than anything, with a fistful of Lyam's shirt, and the sunlight beyond my still-heavy eyelids. I sigh, content that the sun and the moon and I are right where we belong. I wipe my eyes with the palms of my hands and look up at Aeron. When he finally comes into focus, I say, "I can't believe I've slept all day."

"How do you feel now?" he asks.

"Better." Though there's a remembrance of my headache that threatens a full-fledged return if I make any sudden moves. Guilt still eats at me that Aeron's had to pull double weight on account of me. "Tell me about your day."

"Sebaan sends his love." Something about his quick and vague response stirs my curiosity.

"And?" I draw out the word, long and reaching as evening shadows.

"And," he says, blushing, "I picked some plums for Tavine."

I study him with an expectant look.

"And I went to help out Doctor Solmon."

Now we've gotten to the root of it, I think. "Of course, you were there to see Satrie."

"Naturally," he admits, cheeks growing pinker by the second.

I roll to my side as he takes a seat beside me. "Did you talk to her?"

"Well, I didn't serve up my heart on a plate, if that's what you're asking. I've decided to give it more time. I want everything to be perfect."

"Good luck with that. So did you happen to mention the gorgeous sketch you drew of her?"

Now his face flushes. "I don't think I could ever tell her about *that*. She'd probably peg me as," he searches for the word, "*obsessed*."

"Maybe a little. But if things work out, I'm sure she'd love to see it one day."

"I'll wait until after the wedding, how about that?" he jokes, but I can't help noting a touch of hope in his voice.

Aeron stays a few minutes longer, offering water and the promise of food in the near future. I offer to help with supper, but my body warns that isn't such a well-thought-out notion. So I stay in bed, trusting that *food* is not synonymous with *broth*.

Time creeps by slowly. Thumbing over the buttons of Lyam's shirt, staring up at the exposed ceiling beams, my mind wanders back to that strange land with the drifting stars, to the hollow sense that sat deep in my chest as if I were the only human in existence, to the something, somewhere, that found that one human to be one too many.

Then comes a series of dainty knocks. They sound more like: *Ar-i-a?*

When the door opens, just a sliver, my gaze follows the vertical crack until I find an even smaller sliver of my mother. She sends her words through the crack in a way that suggests her mere breath will push the door wide. "May I come in?"

"Yes."

In her hands is a tray of food. "Do you feel well enough to eat?"

I sit up slowly, and scoot back, positioning my pillow against the wall. I pull up my blanket and smooth out the wrinkles.

Mother sets the tray on my lap and settles into the spot Aeron's been keeping warm today. This version of *food* is not what I had in mind, but the small bits of chicken, rice, and onion are welcome additions to the broth. Beside the bowl is a thick slice of still-warm bread, the butter melting around the edges.

"Thank you," I say, then swallow down a hearty spoonful.

Mother lifts the back of her hand to my forehead again. "You're looking much better. I came to see you earlier, but you were sleeping like a newborn." Her endearing, reminiscent smile tugs at my heart. *How you've grown,* her eyes say.

"I'm sorry about this." I gesture to me, here in this bed, useless.

"Hush now. You just focus on getting well. You leave the rest to us." Mother tucks an unruly lock of hair behind my ear. Then she pats me on the cheek. "I just miss your smiling face. So does a certain gentleman I know of."

After she leaves, after I've emptied my bowl down to the last drop, I get out of bed, swaying for a moment as the floor moves beneath me. Pinpricks assault the soles of my feet as I make my way around the end of my bed, narrowly avoid kicking my clothes trunk squatting there, and push my palms to the window frame to steady myself.

World righted and feet tingle-free, I stare longingly into the near-twilight sky. Too many hours I've spent under this roof, too many hours prisoner to heavy eyelids.

Still, I am compelled to sleep, and so I shut out the dwindling daylight and return to bed. I settle into my cocoon and let my need for slumber prevail.

TWENTY-SEVEN

I wake feeling refreshed and much more like myself, ready to greet the day. Ready to leave my bed
and put a proper meal in my stomach. I am especially ready to shed this skin of inactivity and use-
lessness. I long for the sun on my skin and fresh air in
my lungs and Lyam's hand in mine.

I sit up to stretch, surprised at the fact that Aeron
didn't wake me, when I spy something out of the corner of my eye. On my bedside table is a plate of fried
eggs, still steaming, and beside it lies something
wrapped in cloth, a note tucked under the twine. I
come to my elbow to reach for the gift, eager to see
what's written on the parchment.

Leaving the twine intact, I slip the note from its
place. As I read, I feel curiosity weigh my brows.

Aeria,
Here's something to pass the time. Do me a favor
and stay in bed. I told Mother you're still not feeling
well, so please listen to me for once. I hate lying, but I

feel I owe you. I've got some chores to get done, but I'll be back soon. Promise.

Why would Aeron lie to Mother? And why does he think he owes me? Owes me for what?

My hands explore the mysterious shape of the cloth-wrapped item. Thin and rectangular, flat on top, save for a long, narrow protrusion that runs down the center.

It's not until I loosen the bow of twine and pull back the cloth that I discover what caused the strange ridge, a stick of graphite encased in pale wood. Beneath it lies a leather-bound journal similar to Aeron's, but only in shape and color.

I trace the beautiful, embroidered exterior with the tip of my index finger. Elaborate stitching showcases flowers in full bloom, with lavish petals that overlap one another. At the top is my name in elegant script.

I open the ornate cover and find this inscription penned inside:

My dearest sister,
Now you have somewhere to write down your thoughts and feelings. You may want to share them with someone special one day.
Love,
Aeron

I polish off the plate of eggs with marked eagerness. Flipping through the empty pages, my hand revels in the freedom waiting to be spelled between them. Here I can turn out the secrets of my heart with abandon. Here there is no condemnation. No noose to tie, no stone to throw, no past to hide from. I can be exactly who I am, no holds barred.

Maybe, I decide, I'll even have a go at sketching, though I could never hold a light to Aeron's talent.

I begin with the obvious, the night Lyam and I met. I write about how a terrifying event was turned into something so extraordinary, by a newcomer with golden-ochre eyes and the most captivating of gazes. My skin feels his touch even now, describing his warmth and tenderness, the intoxicating scent of his embrace.

I shut the journal and press it close to my chest.

I don't realize I've fallen asleep with it until Aeron brings me lunch, and urgent instructions to wash up and change out of the dress I've been wearing for two days now. He rushes out of the room before I can thank him or ask what all this deception is about. *Please listen to me for once*, his note had said. I do, my curiosity raging like a wildfire.

"Are you ready?" he asks through the door a few minutes later.

I open it. I'm ready, but for what?

He reminds me, "You're sick, remember?" Then we go to the front room, where Mother is finishing her lunch. I feign a sick appearance as best I can.

Mother's eyes travel up and down the length of my body. When she meets my eyes, I wonder if she can see through the façade. Instead she says, "You don't look so well. Are you sure you're up for this?"

"I'll be fine." Being that I've no inkling of what *this* is, I hope it's an apropos response.

"Then have a good time." She shakes a finger at Aeron. "But you bring her home immediately if it's too much for her. Even if you have to carry her back."

Shouldering his satchel, Aeron delivers a reassuring smile, but his voice carries a subtle undertone that I can't decipher. "She'll be in good hands."

I wait until we enter the woods to ask, "Will you explain what's going on? I think I deserve some answers."

Our brisk clip has me struggling to keep up with Aeron's long, purposeful strides. "You can use the fresh air. That's all I can tell you."

I don't push him for information, knowing that to do so would be futile. So I keep quiet as a noonday shadow as I rush along behind him.

Then we're striking across the clearing under a bold, blue sky exploding with sunshine. The air swirls with life and purity and the warm promise of a beautiful summer day. Looking skyward, I draw in an easy breath, letting it out a little at a time. Even if Aeron's plans were not as surreptitious as they seem, this alone would be enough for me. Save for that one harrowing incident, all my best memories were born in this place.

I drop my gaze for the first time since emerging from the woods, and the smile that would have adorned my face is stolen. Lyam paces the bank of the stream nervously, his expression sharp.

Trepidation rakes through me. It trips my pulse and drives me onward. Now the struggle to keep pace belongs to Aeron.

Lyam's expression is hard to read. *Have things gotten worse with Saeth?* I wonder. *Or has someone discovered why Lyam and Aeron were asking so many questions?* I feel I'll be sick again. "What's wrong? What happened?"

Lyam dons an expression of surrender and collects me into his arms. "Nothing. Everything's perfect . . . now."

"When is someone going to tell me what's going on?"

Neither of them says a thing. I glance up as Lyam jerks his chin at Aeron, leaving the explanations in Aeron's hands. But Aeron only passes by us as if I hadn't said a word. My head turns like an owl's, watching in bemusement as Aeron sets course for the eastern wood line.

Without pausing, Aeron spins, his feet still carrying him farther, not nearer. "I'm being a good brother," he calls to me. "You can thank me later."

When he's gone, I look back at Lyam with ever-increasing confusion. Lyam lets out a small laugh. He sweeps me up in his arms, fast and deliberate, which inspires a gasp of surprise from my lips. Then I think I may need to wake up because this cannot be real. "Why are you carrying me across the stream?"

He holds me close, his steps through the water guarded and calculated. "Well," he says, "for one, you can't go back home with your pretty dress all soaked. Two, Aeron is giving us our time alone. Which brings me to three. Time is not something we have a whole lot of."

My heart's about to leap right out of my chest. "You're kidding. How did this come about?"

"Like he said, you can thank him later."

We reach the far shore, and Lyam sets me on my feet. His pants are dark up to his knees, but my dress is dry.

I've never broached this side of the stream before. Never stepped foot on this unexplored terrain. And I can't come up with a proper reason why. I just never have. There's a newness to it, to entering the unknown, though these trees have been with me all my life, watching from a nearby distance.

Lyam leads the way, winding and weaving with purpose, following a stubborn trail I don't see. We pass the group of poplars that Aeron's elk had used as cover just before darting into the secret places that don't dare be revealed. We pass a moss-covered rock that points upward as if it's grown up out of this foreign soil, striving for daylight amongst shadows. We pass evidence that a human has been here recently, an abandoned branch that seems more *placed* than *fallen*, as if it were an in-the-way sort of thing amongst all this nature.

Lyam stops, and when he looks into my eyes his hypnotic gaze renders me completely, absolutely, and utterly speechless. I can barely breathe. I definitely cannot move.

"There's something I want to show you," he says. Something akin to vulnerability softens his voice. "Will you close your eyes for me?"

All I can do is nod. I worry my lip as Lyam guides me carefully, until all of a sudden the sun is on my skin, warm and welcoming.

"What do you think?" he asks. "Now we have a place of our own."

My eyes open with marked slowness. I turn full circle, once, twice, at a loss for words. Haloed by a dozen or more trees, we stand sheltered, concealed, in the hollow of this wood. A miniature meadow for two, with tender grass that reaches for the uneven ring of sun-filled sky directly overhead. A small, open space nearly *too* perfect, as if it were cultivated for this very purpose, a secret place for lovers to meet.

I spin in another slow circle, rapt with the beauty, the refuge, the aloneness. A tendril of empowerment curls in my belly. *Now we have a place of our own.* No Mother, with her lofty promises not fully kept. No Aeron, with his hawk-like gaze and his *no kissing*. No Saeth, with his glaring disapproval.

Then something catches my eye. I point to an elm where the grass greets the tree line. There, encased in a generous-sized heart, two letters have been carved into the trunk. The image is not as sharp as I imagine it to have been long ago when Zeccion Morgan carved it for his beloved Jautrith, but their timeless love has protected the precious *J* and *Z* over generations.

"I love it. It's so beautiful. It's . . . perfect."

Lyam's voice becomes sultry. "Only because you're here."

I feel my face flush. "Exaggerate much?"

Lyam takes a small step toward me, his expression intense. "Aeria, without you, this world has no beauty." Lyam tips my chin. "I wish you could see yourself as I see you."

We stay that way, me gazing at him and him gazing at me, locked in a moment that feels both unmoving and fleeting at the same time. Lyam traces my bottom lip with his thumb, seemingly testing the waters, and my heart lopes frantically at the touch, at the wanting. At the waiting.

Then there is a long, perfect second where Lyam's lips brush mine, firm and sweet and controlled. But the way he draws back has my eyes flashing open for fear that I've done something wrong. Maybe it was that I simply *received* the kiss, rather than actively *participated* in it.

The expression of satisfaction on Lyam's face says that it went as planned, another testing of the waters, so to speak.

I need his lips on mine once more, and Lyam acquiesces with a smile and another tender kiss born of our cautious movements. Then his lips part mine and his sweet breath fills my mouth. I breathe him in as if I'm starved for air and he is the one true source.

I can feel the intensity building between us. Raw emotions trigger a stronger tug of our bodies to one another. My fingers twist up in his hair, his are at the nape of my neck, and all sense of control has fled, for its presence here is undesired. Our breathing escalates, hard and labored and audible to match the pace of our racing hearts. Mine sounds like the song of a thousand drums. There's an ecstasy in the way our lips dance in unison, but there's also a hunger in them that cannot be satiated.

Lyam withdraws again, eyes ablaze with a passion unquenchable, as if he could never get enough of this. Of me.

Wickedly I think, *And this is only kissing.* It takes a great deal of effort to keep my mind from traveling to loftier things.

Heavy breaths and mere inches separate our mouths, though it feels as if an ocean exists between them. With intentional slowness and restored restraint, Lyam comes nearer, slowly, slowly, slowly.

Head tilted and inviting, I let my eyelids slide closed, leaving my body my main sensory avenue. Palms glide down the long sides of my torso, gathering at the small of my back. Gentle lips press against my chin, traveling down the slender column of my neck to the hollow between my collarbones. I bite my lip to fight back small utterances of pleasure, my skin prickling with a craving I've never known before.

Then Lyam's breath, fast and hot, plays in my ear. He struggles to regain it, whispering a heavy but velvety, "I love you." His lips hasten back to mine. "I love you, Aeria Morgan."

My "I love you" is equally breathy as I tease him with a seductive kiss.

Holding my face as if the whole of the universe rests in his palms, Lyam regards me in a way that only he can. In a way that only he ever could. His voice is still smooth as velvet. "I don't want another day to go by without telling you how I feel. Never have I been moved the way you move me, or touched the way you touch me. I've never laughed so hard that I almost cried, or cried so hard that I couldn't breathe. I've never spent countless hours in bed, imagining one look, one touch, one moment . . . until you.

"I love you with every breath I breathe, with every thought I think. Every moment of every day, you're on my mind and I can't imagine a life without you. The mere thought of us being apart stops my heart. Then I envision your beautiful, smiling face, and that gives my heart a reason to keep beating. It beats for you, because without you, there is no me. There's no reason to go on. What I'm saying is that I am in love with you. As long as there is breath in my body, I want us to be together, in every way two people are meant to be together . . . if you'll have me."

A tear swims in my eye and when I blink it away, it dives down my cheek, skating beneath Lyam's fingertips. I come up on my toes to reach Lyam's ear, to offer my eternal vow.

"I'm yours," I whisper. "Always."

TWENTY-EIGHT

reasons

Those three little words are the ray of sunshine that scatters darkness. An ever-present light that drives away fear.

Lyam's "I love you" has somehow turned our future together into something irrefutable, no longer a thing of fantasy. It's something tangible that I can draw close to my chest or tuck under my head at night. Something overflowing with power. Something that transforms the impossible into the possible. With Lyam's love, the horizons are boundless.

Lyam appears happier than I've ever seen him before. His eyes are still fixed on me, still burning with passion, still reaching from someplace deep within with words of their own. "You have no idea how badly I've wanted to do that."

"Yes, I do," I say under my breath. Because my own want has matched his.

The backs of his fingers brush my jawline. His exhale is loud. "Would you think less of me if I told you how nervous I was?"

"You . . . nervous? I can't imagine that. You're always so confident."

Lyam chuckles, gives his head a good shake. "The only thing I'm confident about is this: *Us*." Another kiss, long and lasting, sends my heart soaring, my pulse racing.

Then Lyam lowers himself to the grass, holding my hand in the process, guiding me to fill the space in front of him. I sit with my back against his chest, giving him ample access to my bared neck. My eyes flutter shut as parted lips explore the crook of my neck. Next it's the slender column of flesh which leads, most dizzying of all, to tender nibbles on my earlobe.

"How much time do we have?" I ask, dreading that I will not like his answer.

Lyam says, "Just a little while. Why?" But it comes like this: *Kiss*. Words. *Kiss*. Words *Kiss*. Words. Ending with a kiss.

"I wish this day could last forever."

Lyam's reply is a kiss planted just behind my ear. Circling his arms around me, he says, "I missed you yesterday, but I'm glad you're feeling better. You had me worried."

"I missed you, too, and I really am fine now, but don't tell my mother that. You wouldn't believe how long I slept! I had the strangest dream, too."

Lyam rests his stubbled chin on my shoulder. "Would you tell it to me?"

"I was in some other world where there was no sun, no moon. Stars were everywhere but the sky. Everything was so beautiful, the trees, the grass, the horizon, all painted in colors like you've never seen. But there was something so cold about it, as if love itself had died and the whole world mourned its loss. And I felt like I wasn't the only one there, as if some *thing* was living in the shadows. All I wanted was to leave and I was afraid I'd never get away."

I wait for some kind of response, but Lyam only goes silent. When still more silence comes, I turn, squaring myself to him. Face to face now, his eyes are intense and focused, but not on me.

"What is it?" I say.

Finally he blinks, meeting my gaze with narrowed eyes. Then he laughs a dead and humorless laugh and says, "I think you just described my life before I came here." More silence. "There's something about myself that I haven't told you." He sounds anxious, or ashamed. I can't tell which. "I wanted to tell you earlier. But I was afraid you would think I'm not . . . strong enough. That I'm weak."

Lyam leans back, extending his arms out behind him. His brows are low over his eyes, and suddenly I'm sinking into the depths of his silence. His lips purse. My heart falters. Then he reveals his secret. "I was attacked before I left Garrison."

An icy wave shivers through me as my mind relives my own ordeal with a piercing kind of *nowness*, as if no time has passed at all and my attacker's breath still warms my face. I shake my head in disbelief. I can't imagine my strong and brave Lyam in the hands of an assailant, under duress and in need of rescue. "How? Why? Who?"

Then his story begins, brutally honest. "I was out riding my father's horse, trying to escape from the day the only way I knew how. When dusk fell, we worked our way back to the barn. I put up the horse's tack and brushed him down, and by then the sky was black. The side of the barn was even more so, but that was the fastest route back to the house. There were footsteps behind me, but I didn't give them any thought. All I wanted to do was fall in bed and pretend sleep could fix my life.

"Then I heard my name. The acid in his tone was unsettling, but I had no enemies, so I stopped.

"I recognized the man as the father of a young lady I'd been introduced to three days prior. She was the first of four refusals I'd had to dole out in that short time, hence the need for *escape*," he says with an exasperated tone. "They had come from Crowellhaven, which is what we call a two stones' throw from Garrison, not exactly *near*, but near enough that they should have been long gone and forgotten by then.

"But there he was. And there I was, a fool thinking, 'How many times do I have to tell you I'm not interested?' I was ready to offer yet another round of explanations, but then . . ." Lyam trails off.

When he starts again, he speaks as if he's been insulted. "Then he told me that I wasn't good enough for his daughter, that my parents would live the remainder of their days in shame, and I would die young and alone. I couldn't see how any of that was his concern, though, even if what he said was true. It just didn't make sense. I tried to walk away, but all that did was make him angrier."

His posture becomes rigid, bracing against a storm of which the rest of the world has no knowledge. His expression is saturated with pain and suffering and everything in between. Seeing him this way is chilling at best, and haunting at worst.

"Then he told me she died," Lyam continues, despite his one-man storm. "She was only eighteen, and she died. Because I refused her. He told me this with tears streaming down his face, and then he started shoving me—and this guy was huge, just *monstrous*—but honestly I couldn't feel a thing. The last thing he said was that I wasn't even worth his spit on my face. Then he punched me. Knocked me out cold."

Lyam takes a moment to collect himself. "It was still black outside when I woke up in a pool of my own blood. I felt like I'd been kicked by a horse. I realized then that his first blow had not been his last, and I actually laughed out loud because I would have rather been kicked by the horse. That was a mistake, let me tell you."

He laughs now at the memory of it, which sheds a bit of his brokenness. "Needless to say, sleep and I were not on the best of terms that night. And with that night came the first of many bad dreams."

I work to keep my voice calm, but really I am torn to pieces inside. "It's not your fault, you know. You couldn't have known, and even if you had, was it really your responsibility to marry her?"

"I suppose not, but still it's a hard thing to swallow."

"What about your parents?" I ask. "Didn't they wonder what had happened to you?"

He laughs. "Told them I was thrown off the horse and hit a tree. It was a far-fetched story, though. For one, I have *never* been thrown by that horse. And two, the likelihood of a tree causing that kind of injury was ludicrous."

"But they believed you?"

"I'd never given them a reason not to."

"That's why you left," I say, understanding now. "Because of what he did to you."

"It had already been heavy on me, but that pushed me over the edge. Once I was all healed up, I left and I didn't look back. My parents had nothing to assume but that the marriage pressure had been too much for me. That's how I wanted it."

My heart feels as broken as the boy left unconscious in the bloodstained dirt. "Lyam, I'm so sorry. I had no idea."

"Well," he says coolly, "at least there are no scars. Not physical ones, anyway." The last part is toneless and much, much quieter.

I wish there were something I could do, something I could say to lessen his pain. But I know all too well that I am powerless to help. Still I say, "If there's ever anything I can do . . ."

Lyam leans forward to take my hand. "Just keep making me smile. Keep being you. That's all I need." Then he pauses. His expression turns penitent. "Oh, Aeria! This was supposed to be special. I didn't mean to—"

I press a kiss to his lips to smother the words I can't bear to hear. It lasts longer than I expected. "Lyam, I cherish every moment we've spent together. I'm just glad you felt comfortable enough to tell me. But, honestly, if you hadn't come . . ."

I stop myself, a grimace on my face. This is one of those things better left unsaid because it screams loud enough on its own.

Lyam says, "I've gone over that night a hundred times, and I know how it would've ended if I hadn't been there." He clamps his eyes shut. Rakes his fingers through his hair. Finally, he chuckles. "You know, it's amazing how the timing worked out so perfectly. My injuries hadn't healed until the day before I left, and it was the night after my arrival here that you were followed."

Lyam goes silent. His forehead furrows.

The abrupt reticence causes me to wonder . . .

Is this the faceless outsider I've been pointing a finger at all along? Could this mourning father have gotten his first taste of blood and was now unable to control himself, waging his own war against helpless victims from village to village? If so, would he return for more?

"You don't think . . .?"

Lyam's internal dialogue must match mine, for he takes my cheek in his hand, the way one would shelter a nestling from the cold. "I won't let anything happen to you, Aeria. I swear."

We sit quietly for several minutes. I'm still working to piece together this image of victim-Lyam, but all I see is impervious-Lyam. Protective-Lyam. The I-will-always-keep-you-safe-Lyam.

Then, with startling clarity, I recall the Lyam who simply slipped his hands up in surrender when Aeron, flaming mad, shot toward him, all fists and fury. Aeron's intent was evident, yet Lyam resigned himself to Aeron's will as if there were no other option.

"What happened to you in Garrison, is that why you wouldn't defend yourself against Aeron?"

Lyam toys with tufts of grass between his legs, pluck-lift-release, pluck-lift-release. The green rain starts and stops. He nods the tiniest nod. Speaks with the tiniest voice. "I froze up. I knew it was coming, but I couldn't move."

Now he looks at me, releasing an entire handful of grass-rain. His expression is a mask darker than night. "That's why I didn't get to you sooner. I froze that night, too. I should have been braver. You deserved me to be braver. I can't explain it, I just—"

"Lyam, it's not a matter of *when* you acted, it's *that* you acted. No one else would have risked themselves for me. But you did. You are the bravest, most self-sacrificing person I have ever met."

That coaxes a smile out of him, but it's more the suggestion of a smile. He says, "Have I ever told you how much I love you?"

Cocking my head to the side, I raise my eyes, arch one brow, as if struggling to pull up the memory. "Hmm." I tap my lip for effect. "Maybe, but it was so long ago . . ."

This earns me a real smile. "Then I'll say it again so you're sure. I love you." He kisses me. "And I'm sorry," he kisses me again, "but time's up."

"Already?" I groan. I tug the collar of his shirt to draw his lips back to mine. "Do we have to go so soon?"

"I'm afraid so, my love."

"*My love* . . . I like that." I mouth the words a second time. A third. Already, I can't get enough of them.

The words continue to play in my mind. It's almost as if, after sixteen years of life, I've discovered how to say my name in a language as ancient as it is foreign.

My love. My love.

We pick our way back toward the stream, sheltered beneath the glorious green canopy and miniature sunbursts that filter through the boughs. A red-breasted blackbird hops along a downed trunk, then amiably flits to a nearby shoulder-level branch, watching with interest as we pass.

I remember what Aeron has taught me about red-breasted blackbirds, how to discern their gender. This one is a glossy, true black, with a bright, red apple-shape on its belly, which means that it's male. Females are dull brown, so as not to attract predators to their nests of eggs.

The bird takes flight, making no sound.

Lyam carries me across the stream and sets me on my feet on the other side of the bank. "What was your excuse for getting out of work?" I wonder.

"I told Saeth I was meeting up with Aeron to discuss the construction of a drawing room. A job is a job, after all."

"A drawing room," I echo. "Why does that sound more like a real thing than an excuse?"

Lyam smirks. "It has been discussed, just not today. But Saeth doesn't have to know that, and with him thinking you're still sick, he won't suspect a thing. Besides, it's not technically lying, I did meet Aeron."

"What about this?" I say, yanking at his dripping pant leg.

"Aeron's proposed location is across the stream," he says with a sly grin. "Honestly, I doubt Saeth will even ask. That would require a conversation."

"It's that bad, huh?"

"Oh, no. Things are great. Saeth gives my work assignments to Emay, who passes them along to me. I actually prefer the silent treatment, you know. It makes for a very interesting living situation," Lyam adds with little humor.

He goes silent then, and I am the red-breasted blackbird, watching with keen interest as Lyam takes my hand, sets his chin, and continues on toward the place he calls home, knowing full well what waits for him there.

Hauntingly, I imagine we haven't seen the worst of it.

TWENTY-NINE

adversity

Because I am supposed to be sick and bedridden, Aeron and I don't take our usual route home, for that would only betray my sick and bedridden pretense. We cut through the trees instead, picking out a path where there is none. Naked branches, fallen needles, the disintegrated remains of cones, and leaves abandoned by another season make a bed at our feet, complete with the scent of decay.

"You know," Aeron says, "you have to get rid of that look before we get home."

"What look?"

His brows shoot up to meet his hairline. "That 'I've just been kissed' look."

I can't imagine that my face could burn brighter than it does right now. *Is it really that obvious?*

A massive rock sits adjacent to our imaginary trail. Instinctively, Aeron darts to my side as I mount the impossibly large rock, green and cool with moss, gray and hard with design.

"I'm fine," I declare, brushing away his out-stretched hand.

"Be careful, Aeria. You don't have wings, remember?"

From my perch, his head is level with my calves. "If I had wings, Aeron Morgan, I'd smack you with them."

Aeron attempts a wounded expression, then gives up and laughs.

I leap down from the rock, landing gracefully, and tell Aeron about the tree with our ancestors' initials.

"I wonder how long ours will last," he muses.

Waving a hand in grand fashion, I say loftily, "They will endure forevermore, along with the legacy of Aeron and Aeria Morgan, the only Dviinu ever born."

Aeron smiles wistfully. "You really think so?"

"Aeron," I say softly. "Why did you do it?"

He stops, shifts the strap of his satchel. "Do what?"

"Lie to Mother. Plan this whole thing."

"Because, after all these years of being rejected, you've found someone who loves you. I didn't feel right standing in the way of that. You and I deserve some happiness of our own."

I hook my arm around his waist. "You, Aeron Morgan, are the very best brother in the world."

Aeron issues a crooked grin. "That's a given, I'm the *only* brother in the world."

We both laugh.

Nearly home, we can see Mother waiting for us at the back door. She waves us onward, calling, "Come inside. It's getting a bit nippy out."

It most certainly is *not* getting a bit nippy. But if Aeron and Mother could share only one trait, it would be their protective natures.

"We're coming," Aeron and I call in unison.

When Mother disappears into the house, Aeron playfully rubs his upper arms against the imaginary cold. I roll my eyes.

We enter to the aroma of bread baking, warm and inviting. Mother gestures to the divan. "You should rest," she says. "You expended a lot of energy today."

Because Mother can't see him, Aeron makes kissing faces behind her back, but really he looks like a fish gaping for air and I am forced to stifle a laugh. Because Mother *can* see me.

Then she and Aeron head to the kitchen to fix supper, and soon the sounds of productivity fill the house. A pot clamors. Water empties from one vessel, filling another. Something heavy *plop-plop-plop*s into the water. It sounds like the beginnings of a hearty vegetable medley. But these are Aeron's hands, not Mother's, that produce such exaggerated noises when it comes meal preparation.

Supper is a relaxing, far less noisy affair than the *making* of supper was. Even more quiet than usual, which leads me to think Aeron has some thoughts he wanted to drown out with all the racket. When we finish, Mother clears the table, despite me telling her I can do it, and Aeron takes the dishes and his noisy pot to the stream for washing.

Because Mother has noise of her own to make.

She joins me on the divan, taking my feet in her lap. "I'm glad you had a good day with your brother, Aeria. I hope you realize that you don't have to be with Lyam all the time to enjoy yourself."

"I still enjoy my time with Aeron," I assure her, "but it's different now. I love Lyam, and it's natural for me to want to spend time with him, too."

Mother sets her gaze, her voice changing ever so subtly. "Aeria, I'm afraid you're growing too . . . dependent on him." She's chosen her words carefully, but they sting all the same.

"Isn't that what family is, being able to depend on one another? I need Lyam in my life just as much as I need you, and just as much as I need Aeron."

She rubs a hand over my shin, picks at the hem of my dress like this is any ordinary conversation. "Lyam isn't family, dear."

I bite my tongue, knowing she didn't mean to be cruel in pointing out the misnomer. "Maybe not officially," I say, "but you may as well get used to the idea, because one day he will be."

Mother shifts her eyes to her crowded lap. "I've been trying to prepare myself for that eventuality. Although I had hoped for . . . more time."

She should have known better than to hope for that. "*Mother*," I say, with a delicate potency, "*time* is the one thing none of us has."

A gusty exhale follows. "I know. And I want to be around to see that day, I do."

I sit upright, taking hold of her hand. It's small and weathered, but it has that *I'll always be here* kind of feel. But I know better. "So do I, Mother. So do I."

Then comes a *knock-knock-knock* at the door, but in my mind it's more like KNOCK! KNOCK! KNOCK! It thunders urgency.

Mother and I spare each other the briefest look before turning to the door. "Stay right there," she orders, her brow wrinkled at our unseen visitor.

Mother is more puzzled than anything. I, on the other hand, am overcome with a sense of dread. It pins me in place like a winged creature on display, and all I can think is, *Something is wrong*.

Mother opens the door just a crack, peering out through the long slit. "Oh!" she says. It's a flustered sort of "Oh," more air than word the way it catches in her throat. She pulls the door open with a hospitable "Hello," but I still can't see the knocker. Probably Tavine. It's too soon to be Aeron and his noisy dishes.

"Good evening, Nira," I hear Lyam say. My heart doubles its frantic pace.

"Would you care to come in?" Mother's question is framed with hesitation. She hadn't been expecting company, much less him.

Lyam is polite as usual. "Yes, thank you." I stand as he crosses the threshold.

My heart rate triples. Though it has no form, something insidious follows him inside. It pulses throughout the house, silent and loud all at once, as living and present as the rest of us. Suddenly this room feels darker, the walls closer, the breathing space shallower than a teardrop of air.

Mother gestures to the oversized chair, the same spot Lyam occupied when he came for dessert. I can't decide if he looks ashamed or distraught, but his expression is sharp as a dagger's edge. My throat squeezes shut, seeing it.

Resting a hand on his shoulder, Mother says, "Lyam, you look upset. Is something the matter?"

"Actually, there is." Lyam draws in a deep breath that makes his chest rise quickly, but fall slowly. "I didn't want to come here." He stops. Elbows on his knees, he rakes his fingers through his hair.

His expression is killing me.

Lyam meets my mother's eyes, holding her gaze for a fistful of over-long seconds. "I'm sorry, but I didn't know what to do. I've got no one else to turn to."

I hear rattling from the other side of the door. I watch the handle turn slowly. Then Aeron's face pales. He closes the door behind him with uncertainty. Dishes clatter against the inner walls of the pot. In his pot-free hand is an unfamiliar pack. Lyam must have left it outside the door.

It's the pack that's the most damning thing of all. Aeron stares at Lyam. "You're not leaving. Are you?"

Lyam's already on his feet. Looking from Aeron to my mother, his words are directed at both of them. "I've come here tonight . . . to make a plea for your hospitality."

"What happened?" It's what we're all thinking, but Aeron actually says it.

"I mentioned to Aeria the other day that Saeth has been warning me to stay away from her," Lyam begins. "For the past few days he's been keeping his distance, but tonight was his breaking point. I don't know what set him off, but long story short, I am no longer welcome to stay with him." Lyam drops his gaze, his voice humble. "I have nowhere to go. No friends. No family."

Few things can render Aeron speechless, but here we are, Mother, Aeron, and me, all at a loss for words. Surprising, for we know Lyam's plight. He's taken a big gamble in crossing to our side of the fence, and now Saeth's making him pay for it in a big way. Where will he live? Work? Who else in the village will be influenced by Saeth? Will Chief Cole, under Saeth's encouragement, force Lyam to leave?

My eyes travel from Lyam, dejected in the worst kind of way, to Aeron and Mother.

Aeron, the first to find his voice, shoots back, "Of course you can stay. What kind of family would we be if we turned you away, too?"

Then Mother is whispering in Aeron's ear and my insides clench as she drags Aeron into the kitchen, their voices hushed and mysterious.

I rush over to Lyam and fall into his arms, pressing my cheek to his chest.

He smooths a hand over my hair. "We'll figure something out."

"Garrison," I whisper, a sliver south of audible.

Lyam draws back, unsure that he's heard me correctly. Eyes trained on mine, his mouth works, pursing up. There's an answer there, but it's not the one I want.

He breaks our embrace and takes my hand as Mother and Aeron return. There's a solidarity about them that suggests they've reached a decision. Aeron lets Mother speak.

"Lyam," she says, "we would be honored if you stayed here tonight. However, given your relationship with my daughter, I hope that you can understand that it is just for one night."

Reaching forward to shake her hand, Lyam says, "I completely understand. I won't be any trouble; you have my word." He shakes Aeron's hand, which is a longer, more studious affair. The unspoken language of men. Of friends.

"I'll go with you to the Solmons' tomorrow," Aeron says. "I know the doc will open his home to you. He's a good man." He claps Lyam's shoulder, the timbre of his voice fluid and resolute. "You are not alone in this."

Lyam looks ten shades, maybe a hundred, more at ease. He can't stop saying how much this means to him, how he'll find a way to repay our kindness, and how happy his parents would be to know that their son was being treated as part of our *family*.

Mother, of course, blanches a little at that part, regret sinking her brows.

"But," Lyam goes on, "if this is the price I have to pay to be with your daughter, I will gladly pay it."

Something about the comment strikes my mother in an uncomfortable way. She rushes out of the room, seemingly aimless at first, but then she returns, more composed, with a pillow, a fresh pillowslip, and a blanket. "I trust you understand that you'll have to sleep out here." She's already changing out the pillowslips, her gaze locked on me. Which is to say that her word is nonnegotiable. "Say goodnight, Aeria."

I consider telling her I'm not tired, which is a partial lie, or that I'm still hungry, which is a full-fledged one. Anything to buy more time with Lyam.

But my mother's gaze convinces me otherwise.

"Good night," I say sweetly, though a touch of disappointment slips into my voice.

In a whisper, Lyam says, "Sleep well, daughter of light."

In the last sixteen years, I have been called a number of names. Daughter of light has never been one of them, but the way Lyam says it, with *admiration*, makes me feel for once that my unorthodox conception is nothing to be ashamed of.

A smile accompanies me to my room. After I've changed into my nightdress, I move one curtain aside, revealing a rainbow-colored sky. The sun is gone, but the memory of daylight remains deep on the horizon. Golden yellow turns to rich orange turns to dusky red turns to all shades of blue, from powder blue all the way to a cloudy purple-blue. The air is pregnant with seduction. It's the kind of sky that begs to be kissed under.

I let out a forlorn sigh. *How on earth am I supposed to sleep with Lyam less than thirty feet from me?*

Curtain drawn, I light my lantern, dig my journal out from its hiding place at the bottom of my cedar trunk, and settle into bed. The words flow like a steady stream, almost poetic in the story they tell of the brother who offered his sister the most precious gift imaginable, time.

As the girl's story continues, it feels quite surreal that the girl is me. And it feels quite impossible that anyone could have had a more perfect first kiss.

I've nearly finished when Aeron enters the room, not quietly, considering I should have been asleep. I eye him as he sprawls on his bed, one arm bent against the wall, the other dangling. A bare foot dangles over the edge, too. Staring at the exposed beams above, he says, "Mother's asleep. She's been out for a good forty minutes."

I reply, "Good for her."

Aeron shakes his head at me, or at the ceiling. "Aeria, sometimes I wonder about you."

"What did I do this time?"

"Aeria, Mother's asleep," he repeats with emphasis. When my response is still lacking, he adds, "You have twenty minutes."

This is when my eyes pop out of their sockets. "Seriously?"

"Twenty," he presses.

Unwilling to waste even one second, I abandon my journal, cast aside my blanket, and rush for the door. As my fingers grip the handle, Aeron calls my name.

I pause. "Yes?"

"Grab your robe. Please."

THIRTY

the voice

Voice burning with unease, Aeron pleads, "And be good."

I mumble a quick, "Yes, of course," as I fumble at my robe with rushed fingers. Finally, sleeves right-side out, I tie a questionable knot and steal from the room.

I return two seconds later. Aeron says nothing as I blindly burrow through the chest at the end of my bed, relying solely on touch to guide me.

When I find something suitable, I leave again, as silently as the first time. I let the door hang open, nearly touching the wall behind it. This allows Aeron an ample view in the event that Mother isn't as "out" as he claims her to be. The hall is softly lit at both ends, from the lantern in my room to the square of moonlight sneaking through the window ahead.

Soft footfalls carry me toward the front room, but my breath comes heavy and uneven. I peek around the corner to the divan, begging my heart to still, but it grows louder when I take in Lyam's slumbering form.

I spare a glance down the hall. Empty.

Sending up a prayer that it remains that way, I pad around the oversized chair, running my palm across the top of the worn leather.

I feel a funny tickle in my stomach as I approach this new version of Lyam. I've never seen him so at peace, so immune from Saeth's rebuke and his parents' pressure and the burdens of loving an outcast. For a moment I am content to just watch the gentle rise and fall of his shoulder as he breathes, the way he tucks a single hand beneath his pillow.

I clutch the offering in my fist.

Lying on his left side, Lyam faces the center of the room, his back pressed against the divan cushion. The space that remains is just enough to accommodate me, so I climb onto the divan with measured care, fitting myself against the curve of his body. I tuck my hair out of the way before resting my head on his crooked arm. Lying here with him like this is more than enough.

Lyam stirs, then lets out a soft "Mmmm" as his hand slides from his hip to mine. His touch burns like coal through my robe, and I can understand now why Aeron was so insistent about the addition to my wardrobe.

I keep my voice pitched low. "Sorry to wake you."

Lyam's voice takes on a new level of seduction when reduced to a whisper in the dark. He could say, "I need to gut the fish," or "How do you take your tea?" and my knees would buckle and my heart would take flight. What's worse is that instead of something ordinary he says, "Have you come to tie me up?"

I think I may just melt with how hot the room has suddenly gotten, but remembering that my time is short, I announce, "I have something for you."

"What?"

"You know how you gave me your shirt the night we met?"

"You came to give it back?" His tone is playful, unconcerned that I've held his shirt hostage all this time.

"Absolutely not. It's under my pillow. I've slept with it every night since then. It brings me comfort. So I thought that if you had something of mine . . . well, maybe you'll sleep better."

Lyam touches my hair, my shoulder. "You don't have to give me anything. You are all I need."

"It's for when we're not together," I explain, rolling onto my back. I hand him an ivory veil I used to wear when I was younger, utterly plain save for the scalloped hem. Using the kind of voice that can't be refused, I say, "I know it's not much, but I want you to take it."

Lyam does, bringing it to his nose as if I've handed him a flower. "It smells like you. And *cedar*," he adds with a quiet chuckle, tucking the token from view. His breath warms my ear, then he kisses my cheek. "Thank you, my love."

"Lyam?"

"Yes?"

"After what happened tonight . . ." I trail off, afraid his desire won't echo my own.

Lyam's arm snakes around me, urging me to face him. I follow his lead, coming to my side, meeting his eyes for the first time. "Aeria," he says solemnly, "I can't take you away from your family. They need you more than you realize, and the same goes for you.

273

Taking you from them would be the most selfish thing I ever did."

"Lyam, please." With startling clarity I can see this future we have worked so hard to nurture being torn from our grasp. I'm holding on and holding on, but it continues to dangle by an ever-weakening thread.

"Can you imagine your wedding day without your mother to help you with your dress?" He pauses to let that sink in. "Or what about the day Aeron welcomes a child into the world, but his sister isn't there to celebrate with him?"

His words cut like a blade, but so does the fact that Chief Cole might not even consent to marry us. Garrison is our only true hope.

Lyam wipes away a tear that hangs at the corner of my eye, then reaches for my hand, centering it over his heart. "Do you feel that? Aeria, my heart beats for you. We're in this together. Our love is strong enough to get us through any adversity. You have to put your faith in that. Please believe me. You have to let our love be enough."

I don't know how, but I manage a small smile as I place Lyam's hand on my chest, on the V made by my robe, flesh to flesh. His fingers fan out, the tips brushing against the base of my neck. I doubt my heart has ever pounded so fiercely.

"And mine beats for you," I say. "Always. Don't you wish for more, though? Is this really the life you hoped for when you left Garrison?"

"You forget that I came with no expectations," he says. "I only hoped for work. Everything else fell into place the moment I saw you."

"What if things get worse?" I ask, my words trapped in a timorous whisper.

"The only way things could get worse is if I lost you." Lyam comes up on his elbow, hovering over me so that he can kiss the tip of my nose.

Desire has me tilting my chin upward, wetting my lips against my will. His breath dances across my face, warm as summer. I have to remind myself that this is my mother's divan, that there's no ring around my finger. That he's not wholly *mine*. Not yet.

I run my hand over his cheek, feeling the tiny hairs bend beneath my touch. My fingers trace the shape of his lip before curling around his neck to pull him closer. In my mind, Aeron reminds me to "Be good." But it's too late for that. My lips part without hesitation. Shifting his weight, Lyam braces his arms on either side of me.

Then, breaking away, he says, voice thick, "I told your mother I wouldn't be any trouble."

The look I give him is nothing if not sultry. "But *I* didn't." I crush my lips to his, my fingers tangling up in his shirt, desiring but refraining from slipping beneath it to caress the sides of his waist, to trail down the contour of his spine, to explore every inch of his trimmed chest and taut stomach.

The kiss deepens, becomes more wanting, more hungry, and then Lyam draws back completely, tugging the hem of his shirt down. His words come out breathy, and almost uncomfortable. "We should stop." Then he collapses beside me and rests his hand over his heart. "You are going to get me into so much trouble, Aeria Morgan."

I bring my lips to his, gently but quickly, reveling once more in the aloneness, because who knows when another day like this will come?

"Time to scoot back to bed, my love."

I grumble something about time, how it seems to skid to a halt when Lyam and I are apart, then it's as fleeting as a forgotten childhood dream when we're together.

Lyam comes back to his elbow beside me and turns my chin toward him. "One day it won't be this way. We can spend an entire day in bed, if that's what you want."

I let out a breathless, "Yes!" I've visualized days like that more times than I can count. But unlike our love, the future is growing more and more uncertain, and I still have this deep-seated fear that Avalon Valley won't grant us the kind of future we desire. The kind Lyam deserves.

"Then that's what I'll give you. I promise. But for now, you better go before I wind up homeless twice in one night."

My lips form a puerile pout, but this gets me nowhere. Lyam settles back against his pillow, the void beside him larger somehow now that I'm not there. "Sweet dreams, my Lyam."

Smiling, Lyam stuffs his hand beneath his head, and suddenly my veil is dancing in the scant moonlight. "That shouldn't be a problem."

I steal back to my room, closing the door as slowly as possible so as not to inspire a betraying creak.

My lantern still burns. I can't tell if Aeron is awake or asleep. He remains still and silent, betraying as much as the door. *Some lookout*, I think as I make my way to my bed.

Cradled in a nest of blanket is my journal, the result of my speedy exit when Aeron announced his approval of my moonlit rendezvous with Lyam. Which is yet another story to tell.

After I finish, I return the journal to its hiding spot and send the room into darkness. Aeron still hasn't made any indication of his state of awareness, causing me to assume he is sleeping. Thumbing over the buttons of Lyam's shirt, I imagine him telling me in the morning that he slept better than he has in weeks because of my offering. As I drift off, I too am looking forward to sweet dreams of my beloved.

But I do not dream of Lyam. Nor are my dreams sweet.

Instead, I find myself returning to that strange, colorful land inhabited by brilliant, roaming stars. This time is different, though, for the stars attempt to communicate with me. But their language is as strange and foreign as this place. Their messages swathe me in harsh, urgent tones. Warnings. I am on the verge of tears, trying and failing to understand. As their urgency continues to mount, their sounds become so bloodcurdling that I feel sick.

Then, perhaps because they realize that all the warning in the world can't fix my inability to understand, the stars fall silent. As if no time has passed since my last visit, the sky displays the same orange and midnight streaks. The absence of the moon and the sun is as unsettling as the stars with their warnings. Painted trees tower over me, their long shadows abounding with unseen dangers.

The stars have left me, taking with them their light, so that the dark is even fiercer. I cover my arms with my hands, but my chills are deeper than skin-surface. The loneliness and sorrow of this place kindles a burning in my chest. It stings like the pain of a thousand heartaches and a thousand years of loss. As my fear intensifies, I succumb to the emptiness, once again a prisoner to the insidious presence that remains unseen. My face is wet with tears. I loathe this place.

I seek escape, trudging through the jewel-tone grass, crying unrelenting tears. Then a voice calls to me, speaking my name in a way I've never heard before. The voice is deep, clearly male, and it thunders authority. I find it powerful yet gentle, fatherly almost. And I find myself drawn to it, unafraid. I wait for it to call again, unsure where it came from.

"Aeria." It calls from the north. "Come to me."

Fearless strides through the vast wilderness bring me to a small pond. I stop to quench my thirst, the unpleasant result of both my chase and the thick air. I fall to my knees to draw the crystal water to my mouth, balking at the reflection that stares back at me. The surface ripples and waves, though it should be still, the figure blurry and indistinguishable. But it has *my* eyes. My green eyes.

The voice calls again, and this time it seems to come from everywhere. My attention is his.

"Aeria, you must listen to me. What I have to say is of utmost importance. You were brought here to be warned."

Hunched over the water in a motionless stupor, the distorted image looks back at me with my questioning eyes. Who is it that speaks to me with such power and authority, and why have *I* been chosen to hear this urgent warning?

"I have been watching you," the voice tells me. "You, your mother, and your brother."

At that, creatures appear before my eyes, one, then another, the *nowness* of them mirroring my remembrances of them: a stallion dark as obsidian racing through a moonlit clearing, racing through my dreams with a voice like a friend; an elk, black as pitch, silently observing from afar, his eyes alight with pride; a raven, bigger than any I've ever seen, circling overhead, gaze keen and intentional.

He's been watching us. Even before we were a flutter in our mother's belly, he was with her. Autors, god of humanity.

Voice bright as a smile, Autors says, "You remember our rides together."

"I do," I say. My voice is a trembling thing.

"You, Aeria, are the light to shatter darkness. Tell me, child, will you still race with me anywhere?"

When I nod, tears spill past my cheeks.

"Then you must heed my warning."

What comes next is a punch to the gut.

"Lyam will die in your embrace if you do not release him."

Then I'm torn from the dreamland. I shoot up in bed, drenched in a cold sweat. My hair is damp and my shoulders quake. My ghastly shrills travel to the ends of the earth.

I don't fully wake until I feel my body being shaken violently. "Aeria! I'm here. You're safe." Aeron's voice, and I'm glad. His grip is firm. "Aeria," he says again.

My response is a blank stare.

The door slams open, striking the wall behind it. Mother enters, flying to my side as quickly as the door was thrown wide. Lyam emerges a heartbeat later, eyes wider than the room. He, too, rushes to my side.

Three sets of eyes bore into me, all pleading for an explanation.

I meet their gazes silently. What is there to say? How can I explain what I've seen? It all seemed so real, the strangely colored sky, the screaming stars, the power-filled voice, as I looked into my own eyes set in the face of another, as if it hadn't been a dream at all.

Though it breaks my heart, I know I have to heed this warning. I can't chance that it was meaningless. The price is far too great.

It is a price I cannot bear to pay.

THIRTY-ONE

broken

Aeron's patience is the first to break. "Aeria, are you hurt? What's wrong?"

"Please speak to us, dear," Mother implores. Ghosts of worry dance on her face in the faint light of early morning.

"I . . . I . . . Can I be left alone? I need . . . time." Finding my voice is far easier than finding words. They are indefinite things my mind can't process.

I fix Aeron with a glance. Quick to act, he drives Mother and Lyam toward the door. "You heard the girl. Give her some space."

I watch as they go, Mother, then Lyam, both reluctant. Aeron, gripping the handle, gives me a departing look as he begins to close the door.

"Wait," I call, my hand stretched in front of me, a branch striving for the sun. "Stay."

Aeron nods to me, then to the two standing outside the door. He shrugs in response to something I don't hear before closing the others out. He lights my lantern, but its glow is not enough against my dark spirits. He sits facing me and gathers up my hands. Mine are balled, empty, yet full of hopelessness.

Aeron can be good at waiting, a quality I have been unable to cultivate. He recognizes that this is one of those occasions when time has to do the coaxing. But all the time since the invention of time can't make it easier for me to say what I am about to say.

The air feels sharp as I draw in a fortifying breath. My voice is listless, as if my dream has sucked the life out of me. "Things are . . . they're . . . really bad. What's happening to Lyam is only going to get worse."

"What do you mean?"

"I was given a message. A warning, really."

"From who?"

I sigh, a soft sound forged from my splintered insides. I'm afraid he won't believe me. "It was Autors."

"Aeria, the gods haven't spoken to mankind since the Darkness began. It was only a dr—"

I stop him, my gaze insistent as I look up. "It wasn't only a dream, Aeron. I know I sound mad. Believe me, I'd prefer that! But he spoke to me! It was as real as you and I."

Aeron asks with no trace of mockery in his voice, "What's the warning, and why were you screaming?" His eyes narrow.

A chill slithers up the backs of my legs, up my spine to the nape of my neck, where it lingers like a wintry shadow. I shudder, remembering the sounds of my own screams. "It hurt." This comes in the tiniest of whispers. Aeron has to incline his ear to catch it.

Grip tightening, he says, "What hurt?"

Tears fall like January rain, harsh and unfriendly. "The warning," I say to our hands, mine heavy and his heavy around them. So much weight Aeron's carried on my behalf, always wanting to protect me, but not knowing how, or if such a thing is even possible any-more.

"I'm here for you," he says.

I shut my eyes, hiding there in the darkness for a time, searching for words to speak, the composure to not break down.

Then I tell him.

Aeron's voice becomes a trembling, unruly thing. His hands are flittering leaves that cover mine. "That can't happen. I won't let it. It was just a dream."

As far-reaching as Aeron's protective instincts are, this is one thing from which he can't save me. I regard him somberly, watching as understanding dawns. Aeron bows his head. His grip slackens. Eyes shining, he says, "You can't do this."

I fight back a sob. "I can't *not* do it."

"You deserve to be happy."

"He deserves to *live*. I can't risk him."

Looking back at me, Aeron speaks with finality. "And I can't risk you."

I only wish Aeron's sentiment was strong enough to prevail over the words which were so urgently pressed upon me.

"Aeria, you don't have to go through with this," Aeron says, serious.

But he's wrong.

My lips draw a straight line, thin and resolute. "I don't have a choice."

Something plays over Aeron's face, acceptance per-haps, knowing he doesn't have the final say after all. "What are you going to do?"

It takes me long, painful moments to form the words. "I have to let him go."

With that, I have sealed my fate.

Aeron's silence is brutal. His expression more so.

I say, "He's going to need you."

Voice hushed in defeat, he replies, "I know." Then, "It's going to feel like hell."

"It already does." My chest feels empty and my throat is closed up and one thought plagues me:

This is only the beginning.

One steeling breath follows another, granting a sliver of collectedness, if my grasp is firm enough to maintain it. I stare off, but I see nothing. Which is to say, I see my future. So with effort I ask, "Will you get him for me?"

I draw back, setting a mask to hide the anguish. Lyam cannot see me distraught. He has to think this is an easy decision.

Aeron makes a study of my expression, his eyebrows gathered in the center, eyes tight. "Are you sure about this? Don't you think Lyam should be able to decide his own fate? He loves you, Aeria."

"Look where loving me has gotten him." I sound cross, but I don't mean to. "And look where that leads. I cannot willingly take him down that road. Aeron, he'll die because of me."

Different scenarios play in my mind, possible ways Lyam could meet his end. The images are ghastly. I see his body taken captive by a forceful undertow, the air squeezed out of his lungs in panicked breaths; a deadly illness feasting on his insides until he's nothing but flesh hanging on bones; a venomous snake leaving him numb and helpless until his heart beats no more.

The lump in my throat threatens to choke me. It takes every fiber of my being to reset my thoughts and remind myself that this is what must be done. That Garrison isn't the answer. That I must continue on with my life, whatever is left of it, independent of him.

Aeron leaves the room. Time becomes immeasurable, spans as long as the day, vanishes as quick as a blink, and as I sit alone with my heartache, tragedy draws nearer.

This is only the beginning.

Footsteps reach the door, but the owner lingers beyond it. In that space, it seems there is a decision to be made. Enter? Or retreat? For some reason, I can imagine him *not* wanting to know what lies behind my door.

But then the handle moves so imperceptibly that I think I didn't really see it. Lyam enters the room and the door is shut and my heart is a flighty thing that doesn't want to go through with this.

Breathe, Aeria. The first thing I notice is the redness in his face, the luster in his eyes. *Breathe, Aeria.* He stands motionless after his sudden entrance.

Breathe, Aeria.

I catalog this moment for many reasons. First, I have never seen Lyam cry, and the thought of him spilling tears in the presence of my mother, worrying for me without even much of a reason to worry, is strangely endearing. Second, the fact that Lyam's the kind of guy who would cry over *this*—what if it *had* only been a bad dream?—goes to prove that he deserves much more than I can offer.

But these things pale in comparison to the fact that I am acutely aware, as Lyam turns his eyes downward, that this will likely be the last time I ever see him.

I watch everything, from the intensified recklessness of his always-reckless hair to the dejected slope of his shoulders, all the while not making eye contact. Aeron promised not to tell him anything about the dream, so how is it that he almost seems to know what's coming?

And how am I to convince him that what we share, what I feel for him, is meaningless?

Lyam sits, gaze cast toward his lap, right leg bent over my bed, left leg hanging over the edge, his foot planted firmly on the floor. *Halfway here, halfway gone*, I lie to myself, trying to make it easier. Then I tell myself I'm a terrible liar, and readjust my expression in case it's too emotional to satisfy my feinting.

Breathe, Aeria.

The sheen of his eyes reflects back at me, identical pools of grief, as Lyam lifts his face. It's ironic how hard we're working to keep ourselves together, both trying to be strong, but for different reasons.

"Are you all right?" he says, voice as broken as he looks.

I forge the bravest of miens, summoning everything I have to speak in the most unaffected of tones. "I didn't mean to worry you. I've just been doing a lot of thinking, and—"

"Please, don't say any more. If this is about what Saeth did, about what kind of future you can or can't see us having because of where we live, then let's go. Let's pack up and leave and never look back. I can do that, if that's what it takes to—"

"Lyam, stop. I don't want to go to Garrison."

"Then name the place. I'll go wherever you like, so long as we're together."

This stings, and I force myself not to wince at the words that come too little too late. As long as we're together, death will find him no matter where his head rests at night.

What I want to say is, "Let's go!"

I turn my voice into a callous creature that feeds off the misery of others. "I don't want to go anywhere. We can't do this anymore. We can't pretend we live in a world that doesn't exist."

"What are you saying? You don't want to be with me?"

I set my jaw, but I can't meet his eyes. "I don't want to be with you," I say. Inside, something screams, begging me to stop grinding our hearts to dust.

"I— I don't know how you could say that. What we have can overcome anything."

"Not death," I breathe.

Then I do what I said I wouldn't. I tell him about the dream. Certainly a god's promise of his impending death will persuade him if I cannot.

Before he can plead his case, I add, "Lyam, let me go. Go home to your family." The words are poison on my tongue, Lyam's expression a fatal aftertaste.

Coming slowly to his feet, Lyam drags his gaze from the floor to me. Brows low and knotted, eyes narrow, he says, "You're making a mistake, whether you think so or not. Know this, Aeria Morgan, I am not going anywhere. So when you change your mind, you know where to find me. I'll be here, and I will not stop loving you." He covers the center of his chest with the flat of his hand. "My heart still belongs to you. It always will." Before turning for the door, he regards me with a look of conviction. "I love you, Aeria. Remember that."

Then he's gone. Really gone.

"I love you," I say under my breath, listening as Lyam's retreating strides carry with them all that I am. My future grows dimmer, until it fades into nothing at all. For a bare moment, it's all I can do to not run after him.

"Goodbye, Lyam."

THIRTY-TWO

pieces of me

ere's the thing about time: It is its own master. It trickles by, unhurried, like water between rocks. Or it dashes past, diving headlong over the edge of a waterfall with no regard for those in its wake. It does as it pleases, and there's not a damn thing any of us can do about it.

Time with Lyam was the latter, swift and cunningly fleeting. It was not even a breath. It was the suggestion of a breath not taken.

Now time has reassumed its former state. All the chores in the world will not make it budge. I work in the vineyard. I fill feed and water troughs. I help Tavine in the garden. I tidy up the storage shed, the tack room, the house. I wash dishes, do the laundry, shelve plates and cups and bowls, and hang clothes to dry. I even bathe Sebaan, who is uncharacteristically cooperative.

Then I'm fighting with Aeron.

And still it's not even noon.

I'd just gone home to change. Despite Sebaan's rare dose of cooperation, I managed to walk away from the affair looking as though I had been bathed instead. Soaked to my ribs. Hair dappled and matted. A trail of water behind me.

Aeron was already home, for reasons unknown to me, and it was the first time I'd seen him since my dream. I wasn't even fully inside the house when he said, "You should get some rest."

That was all it took.

"I don't need rest, and I don't need you telling me what I need or what I don't need, or what I should or shouldn't believe, and I am so tired of, of . . ." It's not that I can't think of an *of*. It's that there are too many. *Of feeling smothered. Of feeling vulnerable. Of being reminded of what I've lost.*

Of being afraid.

Aeron makes a pained expression, and I swallow down all the things I could have said.

"I've got to go." It's a whisper, told more to myself than him.

"Let me get us some lun—"

"No." My anger is dead, my voice is dead. "No. I'm going alone."

I walk out the back door, send it slamming behind me, and head toward the tree line. The door stays shut long enough that I think my escape will go un-contested. Until: "Wait! Aeria, wait!"

I spin on my heels, the sweep of the grass cool against my bare feet. I don't yell, but my words are as poisonous as they come. "I don't need a chaperone, and I don't need your permission."

"Now wait a second," Aeron says, wounded, but not fatally. "What if—"

Tossing my arms out at my sides, I repeat, "What if, Aeron?" Because if you allow them to, the *what-if*s play over and over and over. If you allow them to, they feel like shadowy, crippling things that hide beneath your mattress and lurk in corners that are nearer than they are far, all with the intent of turning the most innocent of thoughts into something that renders you motionless and much less fearless than you ought to be.

"What if," I say again, "I go to the clearing like a normal girl with a normal desire to clear her head and I come home when I'm through and I'm still just a normal girl who can now live with herself and the choices she's made?"

I give him a minute to let that sink in before adding for good measure, "I'm going alone, and you're going to have to find a way to be all right with that."

Then I go.

Aeron doesn't follow.

I love the smell of the woods. The rich scent of earth and moss and pine. Of green leaves and green undergrowth and a false green sky. Of living things, and of growing things.

I could live here, I think. *Deep, deep in the woods. Away from everyone and everything. No one but a tiny neglected cottage to mourn me when I'm gone.*

When I step beyond the emerald canopy of the trees, the sun feels warmer than before, a forceful reminder that no matter how broken and empty I feel the sun will continue to rise and fall, the moon taking its place in due course, and until my body breathes its last, there will be another day.

My intention was to swim, but as I near the falls, I realize that's not what I came here for. My eyes travel up, up, up the length of the waterfall, from the foamy pool to the lowest of the two ledges, then down and up again to the highest. *Shhhhhhhh,* she says. *Shhhhhhhh.*

She is the great keeper of secrets, Eliysha Falls. Always watching, never revealing.

Shhhhhhhhh

I begin my ascent. My fingers reach for branches, for rocks, for roots, one, then another, and another, as my feet search for footholds along the way. Moss-covered rocks jut from the dirt, some flat as steps, some round as eggs, some sharp as blades. Those I avoid. I slip once. Twice. A root comes free, rotted, and I slip a third time, scraping my wrist on a broken branch.

I make it to the lowest shelf, which towers thirteen feet above the pool. I pause there, keeping myself small. Water races by my knees, loud and fast. Faithfully purposeful. My heart crashes inside my chest, loud and fast. Faithfully afraid.

I cross the icy water, gaze up at the steeper, higher ledge, and continue climbing.

Here's the thing about fear: Once you conquer it, you are its master. It cannot control you unless you let it.

I reach the summit without further injuries to my person—the scratch on my wrist is so insignificant that it doesn't even bleed—and slowly, slowly I make myself upright. Feet wide, I stand with the cliff I just climbed to my right and the water to my left. The ledge is before me, dangerous as it is breathtaking. The crystalline pool below mirrors a yawning blue sky.

And beyond that, barely breaching the wood line, stands the black stallion. His hide gleams. His eyes watch. All but his neck, chest, and front legs are lost in the shadows, but I can just make out what looks to be a pair of tucked wings on either side of his belly, as if a massive bird roosts on his back.

In my dreams he said, "You, Aeria, are the light to shatter darkness." And, "Shall we race against the darkness, you and I?"

But what if what he said was *Darkness*, not darkness? A light to shatter the Darkness.

The stallion nickers to me, soft and encouraging, though I should not hear it from this distance. And though I came here to be alone, I know that, in a way, I really never am. He will always be watching me.

So to the heights and to the Darkness, to my attacker and to the future, to bad dreams and to dying young, I say, "I'm not afraid anymore."

And I jump.

This time, I do not scream.

The stallion is gone when I come ashore.

Aeron is gone when I get home.

At least, I thought he was. Shut inside my room, the curtains drawn but the shutters open, I hear him outside the window. He's grunting, and my only guess is that he's finally gotten around to pulling the weeds that have been dominating the small flowerbed beneath the window. Another grunt is accompanied by a mild curse, and I cross the room to say something about weeds being partial to niceties, imagining what his retort will be. Instead, I balk at the familiar voice that drifts in.

"Where's Aeria?" The question comes in a whisper that barely reaches my ears.

The pull of my heart and the need to hear his voice more clearly gets me inching toward the window. I envision Lyam's knotted brows and narrowed eyes just before he walked out of my room.

Aeron doesn't bother with whispers. "She's off being Aeria." He sounds as if he's working hard to not sound irritated. I wonder if Lyam will pick up on it.

"I wouldn't expect anything less," Lyam says, both amused and oblivious to the inflection in Aeron's tone. "Look, I need a plan. Having a place to stay is great, and I really appreciate you going to the Solmons' with me, but I need to find work. I can't sit around doing nothing. My mind just . . ." He doesn't finish.

"Isn't there something you can do for Doctor Solmon?" Lyam must make some kind of silent, negating gesture because Aeron suggests, "What about the Loftons?"

Lyam chuckles despite himself. "Getting things to grow isn't exactly my strong suit. I was actually thinking of talking to Daveed, but I wondered what you would think."

"Think about what?" Aeron pauses, grunts, then says, "Sounds like a great fit to me. How do you feel about dead skunk?"

Lyam lets out a breath that resembles a laugh.

"I'll go with if you want. I'm sure Daveed's had his hands full with Iverett gone."

"That's what I was thinking," Lyam agrees. "And I'd hoped that, based on your mother's friendship with Tavine, they would be open to hiring me. I feel I don't have many options, but I have to find a way to make a living here. For Aeria." Silence falls. It spans so long that I wonder what expression is written on his face. On Aeron's. When Lyam speaks again, his voice carries an unmistakable edge of certainty. He says, "She'll take me back, you know."

His words tear open the part of me that is trying to let him go.

"I hope you're right," Aeron replies.

Lyam begs, "Just make sure to keep an eye on her. Don't let her out of your sight."

Aeron doesn't answer right away. When he does, something like guilt colors his words. "You can count on me."

THIRTY-THREE

pieces of him

I stand at the window, shivering in my wet dress, long after the space beyond it goes quiet.

When Aeron returns, he finds me in the kitchen kneading dough for bread. Mother is in the field gathering zucchini, which gives us a chance to talk in private.

I'd considered apologizing to him for earlier, for leaving the way I did, but I decide in the end that I won't. Instead I confess, "I thought he'd leave."

Aeron grins with satisfaction. "Well, he's not."

"Maybe he will," I say, to convince myself more than anything, "after some time."

He doesn't suppress his frown. "Do you *want* him to leave?"

"How could I not?" There's heat in my voice and I have to collect myself before going on. "If he stays, is he really going to give up trying to win me back?"

"No," Aeron says automatically. "Absolutely not."

"Exactly. So if he stays, all this," I make an all-encompassing gesture, "all this was for nothing. Because he's going to die anyway."

"So," Aeron says slowly. "He'll die if you're together and he'll die if you're apart? What's the difference, then? Why not just be together? Why go through all *this*?" He makes an all-encompassing gesture.

I punch my dough for a long while before responding. "I will not watch him die in my arms."

After supper, Mother sends Aeron to do the dishes. All I'd told her this morning was that Lyam and I couldn't be together because of what's happening with Saeth. She knows nothing of the dream, of the warning, of the truth about her black stallion. As far as I can tell, she doesn't know about me stealing away to the falls today, either.

"Come," Mother says, waving to the divan. "Sit. Let me do your hair." With a pat to my cheek, she's off to retrieve a brush.

I sit on the floor with my back to the divan, listening as she opens her bedroom door and shuts it a moment later. Then another door opens. Something falls to the floor.

I jump to my feet. Start down the hall. "Are you all ri—" And stop. Everything stops.

Mother glares at me from the doorway of my bedroom. In one hand is my pillow, and I barely have time to register that she likely got it for me to sit on before I see what's in her the other hand. Lyam's shirt.

I swallow. My mother stares down at the shirt. Her lip quivers, her eyes turn glossy.

"I can explain."

"When?" she says, and it takes me a moment to realize what she means: When did we have sex? Mother is furious, and so many shades of betrayed that her voice breaks. "Is that why you broke up? To cover up what you've done?"

"We didn't. I swear. I— He gave it to me. You have to believe me . . . We didn't . . ."

That's when Aeron walks in. "I forgot," he begins to announce, then he narrows his eyes at the scene before him. At my mother's murderous expression. At my tense one.

"What's going on?"

"Go," Mother orders him, but she does this with a hand gesture that brings Lyam's shirt into view.

Aeron breathes, "Oh." He meets my eyes, but I find no condemnation there. He blurts, "He gave that to her last weekend. I was there. It's a token, nothing more."

"Go!" she demands, low and vehement.

Aeron looks back at me, and it isn't until I nod that he finally obeys.

Seconds wear the skin of minutes. Minutes wear the skin of hours. The weight of her gaze is crushing, as if someone's stacked Eliysha Falls on top of Eliysha Falls and added one more for good measure.

Voice hoarse, she says, "Is that the truth?"

I nod, thankful she found the shirt and not my journal. "It was a token. Nothing more."

"And what am I to do with it now?" She raises the shirt, and my chest constricts. Because I know what must be done.

Per my request, my mother promises to stay out of the kitchen, but only after warning me to be careful. "I'm here if you need me," she adds, setting a bucket of water beside the hearth. Sympathy has replaced her anger. Her eyes shine with tears she won't let fall. Not for me to see, anyway.

Then I set Lyam's shirt aflame.

Watch as the fabric goes from white to gray to black, edges curling in the fire's orange embrace.

Swallow back tears I won't let fall.

Goodbye, Lyam.

I wake Monday morning to Aeron bouncing on my bed. Retribution for not going to the clearing with him yesterday. Instead, Mother and I baked tarts and sweet loaves and fine cakes until our noses, cheeks, and aprons were dusted with flour and our feet were a powdery white. The wooden floor was nowhere to be seen.

The house smelled so delectable that Aeron couldn't bring himself to go to the clearing after all.

I adjust my pillow; it feels flatter now that my secret doesn't hide beneath. "This is some way to repay me for all those treats I made you."

"Maybe," he says, still bouncing, "it's *because* of all those treats you made."

"Maybe," I retort, "I should have baked you instead. Maybe I still will if you don't get off my bed." Then I launch my pillow at him.

Aeron rushes through breakfast. Mother regards him with one brow spiked, but says nothing. "It's our turn to muck out the barn," he reminds me. Or Mother. Or both of us. I'm about to tell him that I haven't forgotten when he tacks on, "I'll get you when I'm ready," and starts toward the door.

"Wait," I call, coming to my feet. "Where are you going? Shouldn't we get started?"

"I'll be back."

As Aeron and I approach the barn over an hour after his speedy exodus, I notice that something is different about it, but fail to place the change. I appraise the weathered structure one feature at a time. The thatched roof looks no different since undergoing maintenance the spring before last. The horizontal planks that clothe the outside are still sun bleached and lichen-covered, and the large, rectangular windows with their sturdy shutters also appear unchanged.

I realize the change the same moment that Aeron points it out. "Saeth put up the new doors. Lyam did all the work, though. All but the final installation. The hinges don't groan anymore, and the doors are really solid."

"They look . . ."

"Good, I know. There's a new door for the shed, too, but Saeth hasn't gotten around to that yet."

The memory of Lyam almost kissing me there . . .

I shake myself free of the thought and pull open one of the new barn doors, then the other, allowing in a broad shaft of sunlight. Neither door moans in protest; they open smoothly and effortlessly.

Aeron retrieves a wheelbarrow from the backside of the barn.

I go in after him, drawing in the distinct fragrance of horses. Aeron sets the barrow down outside the entrance to the first stall and gathers our equipment from the small tack room. We each don a pair of tall, leather boots. Mine are too large. Heavy, too. We slide on leather gloves that reach our elbows. Then Aeron arms us with the two pitchforks that lean against the wall beside the tack room.

The barn, mainly used to house stallions or foaling mares, consists of twelve stalls and four small pens. Occasionally, sick or injured livestock are brought here for isolation purposes. It was our job to take the horses to the paddock, but someone's already done it, and the stall doors have been latched open.

I ask, "Where are the horses?"

"Oh," Aeron says. "I took care of it." He suppresses a grin, an expression that can only be defined as "guilty." He points. "I'll start here. Why don't you take that one?"

Brows furrowed, I shuffle to the adjoining stall, leaving parallel lines of exposed dirt floor in my wake. I peek inside, half expecting something, or someone, to be waiting for me, but the stall is empty. I roll my eyes and start at the back of the stall, pushing the soiled straw to the front. Then I scoop up heaping piles, relinquishing them to the barrow.

"There's no rush," Aeron says through the partition when I grunt at a particularly heavy forkful. "No sense in killing yourself over there."

A snappy retort comes to mind, but instead I say, "It's just that the more I concentrate on what I'm doing . . ." I end it there and wipe my brow with the ungloved part of my arm.

"The easier it is to . . ."

Forget.

Neither of us needs to say it.

We work on in silence. In a small way, it feels as if things are back to how they used to be, with life falling back into its natural rhythm, in which Aeron and I are joined at the hip and we know exactly what the other is thinking and feeling. No condemnation lives between us, only whole-hearted understanding and acceptance. It's simpler this way, with no third-party interference.

Save for Satrie, comes the mental reminder. Aeron will continue to pursue a relationship with her, but I refuse to begrudge him that.

I'm halfway through my third stall when we hear the drums. *Boom-boom. Boom-boom-boom.*

Aeron props his pitchfork against the wall and stretches his arms overhead. "Shall . . . we?" he says, his question punctuated by a yawn.

We abandon our gear, and when we join our mother at the plaza, she hands us each a waterskin. "I was just bringing these when I heard the drums," she explains in an unnecessary whisper.

"What do you think this is about?" is what I mean to say, but all I get out is, "What do . . ." For the answer stands before me. Clothes dirty and tattered. Hair disheveled. Two-week-old stubble. Eyes heavy with exhaustion.

Iverett.

In my mind, I'm on the uppermost ledge of Eliysha Falls, my fear behind me, a new world before me. I square my shoulders. Set my chin. Fix my gaze. It declares, "I am not afraid of you."

But for the first time, Iverett avoids my eyes.

THIRTY-FOUR

unveiled

eside Iverett, swathed in his ceremonial robe, Chief Cole prepares to make his address, motioning for an end to the ever-increasing whispers. I expect Elancian to skip up the dais steps any second, grinning his boyish grin, but he doesn't. I survey the crowd for his parents, but Reed and Aarzay aren't here either. Neither is Lyam.

Chief says, "I will not take much of your time. I felt it necessary to welcome this young one back and thank him for his sacrifice. Before I go on, let me first dispel your worries. Elancian is in good care, and Doctor Solmon has assured me that he will make a full recovery.

"I will not get into great detail, but Elancian was burned early this morning. Thanks be to Iverett for bringing him home speedily to ensure he received the care he needed." A blend of murmurs and applause weaves through the crowd. "May our prayers be with Elancian and his family. Thank you."

Chief Cole steps down. Iverett steps down.

Mother leaves us to speak with Tavine, and as Aeron and I head back to the barn, I throw two glances over my shoulder, wondering if Iverett will be on the other end of them, glaring at me like he usually does, but he's already gone.

We're working all of fifteen minutes when I hear, "Aeron! Aeron!" and my heart triples its pace at the sound of Lyam's voice. The stall I'm in is opposite the barn doors, so I see his hurried approach. See the surprise on his face when he says, "Oh," and skids to a halt just inside the threshold. His eyes are trained on me and he can't seem to tell them to look away. "I'm sorry, I thought you were alone."

Aeron claps his gloved hands. *Thud-thud.* "Over here."

Slowly, Lyam drags his gaze from me to my brother. "Can we talk?"

Aeron steps out of his stall, removes his gloves, and scrubs at the sweat that seeps past his brows. "I'll be right outside," he tells me. "Take a break if you want."

After putting some distance between himself and the barn, Aeron turns, keeping me in his line of sight. Lyam stands before him, his back to me.

After three days of doing everything within my power to avoid him, I find that too much of me is elated to see him. I make a note to chastise myself later.

I swallow hard, then force my attention to Aeron's lips as they shape words I can't hear. Then he nods and claps Lyam's shoulder. A smile and a handshake end the conversation. Aeron doubles back to the barn.

Lyam goes the opposite direction. But then he turns, sends a burning stare in my direction. And burn it does.

Aeron's eyes are wide and bright, as exuberant as his gait. He walks on clouds until he reaches me.

Beyond him, I dare one last glance as Lyam goes, though I know I shouldn't. Everything about him, the confident way he holds his shoulders, the purpose in his steps, even the untidiness of his hair, screams a sense of hopefulness. *She'll take me back, you know.*

Aeron, grinning through rows of perfect white teeth, stands before me.

I grimace. "Do I even want to ask?"

"You don't have to because I'm going to tell you because you are *not* going to believe this!" Aeron pauses for dramatic effect, continuing only when my expression is cold enough to freeze time itself. "Well you know how Elancian was brought to Doctor Solmon this morning? And you know Lyam's staying there? Well, Lyam was there when Iverett brought Elancian in, so he overheard Iverett going on and on about how Elancian burned his hand and asking if he'll be all right, but then he started talking about the guy they found in the woods last night."

He stops there. Lets his words hang between us.

I open my mouth, but nothing comes out.

"He was dead, Aeria. He was dressed in black, and he was dead."

Something happens to my heart in that moment. It's in my feet, in my stomach, in my throat, solid as a boulder but lighter than a rose petal. My body feels as far away as the past but here at the same time.

Is it really over? I tell myself that it is, that I'm free, but my mind is still trying to process everything.

"Lyam mentioned someone . . ." I bite my tongue, hoping there's a way to explain this without revealing Lyam's tender secret.

Aeron drops his gaze for a second. "I know about that." By *that* I know he means the grieving father who left Lyam bloodied and bruised.

"He told you?"

307

"We've . . . we've grown very close, Aeria."

"So was it *him*? Is that who they found in the woods?"

Aeron shrugs. "Lyam tried to ask Iverett more about it, but Chief Cole showed up and Iverett explained the whole thing to him. But this time he pulled a black mask from his pocket. Said he found it next to the body. Then Elancian's parents came and they were in near hysterics, so Chief Cole and Iverett left to speak in private before they announced his return."

"Did they say where they found the body?"

"As in a specific location?" When I nod, Aeron's eyes narrow. "Why?"

"I want . . . I want to see it."

Aeron laughs, just once, and at first I think he's mocking me, until he says, "You know, I don't blame you." With a wicked smile, he adds, "What I wouldn't give to . . ." and completes the thought with a colorful assemblage of verbs and curses and verbs modified as curses. The images are both ghastly and amusing.

"All right, hero. I get the point. So did he say where they found him or not?"

Aeron shakes his head. "Too late. They already burned the body. He's gone."

He's gone. He's faceless and nameless and yet another mystery to add to the well of mysteries that surrounds our lives. But he's gone.

The relief is so pure that my lungs feel like they're pulling in breath for the first time.

I say, "Would you pass my thanks on to Lyam?"

The way his name rolls off my tongue makes my mouth water for him, the taste of kissing him rushing into the foreground of my thoughts. *No!* I tell myself, and turn back to my abandoned pitchfork to hide my heated face.

"You could tell him yourself, you know."

I look over my shoulder, meeting his gaze. "Please."

Aeron purses his lips, set with the intent of saying no, only to end up yielding with a sigh. "Fine. I'll tell him this once. But you should try to get back on speaking terms. Real or not, the dream never said you couldn't be friends."

Crossing my arms, I stare at the unclean stall ahead. "It doesn't matter. I can't continue to put myself in his path because then I'll be in his thoughts, which will only give him hope that I'll change my mind. How will he ever move on if I'm a constant distraction?"

"Aeria."

I whip back around at the humor that laces my name. Aeron wears a smirk. "Nothing, and I repeat, *nothing* will get you out of his thoughts. That guy can't stop talking about you even to catch his breath. It's kind of sickening, actually." He makes a face worthy of a toddler.

I roll my eyes. "I doubt you're any better. Do you expect me to believe you keep all your *Satrie* thoughts under lock and key all the time? . . . I didn't think so," I add when his response is a flushed face. "I'm sure Lyam's heard more than his fair share."

Aeron sighs noncommittally. "Let's get back to work."

We return to our chore, me dreaming of clean clothes and Aeron dreaming of Satrie. His humming fills the barn, reverberating off walls accustomed to the whickers of horses.

By the time we finish, my skin is tacky and straw has somehow rooted itself deep inside my boots and I want nothing more than to spend the rest of the day with the summer sky above me, my body cupped in the water's loyal embrace.

Back home, Aeron says, "How about heading to the falls to wash up?" Then he bats away the imagined stench that radiates from my direction.

I lift my nose at him, scenting the air. "You're one to talk."

Aeron's "I'll get the towels!" comes out distorted by his rolling laughter. When he comes back, his bulging satchel is slung over his shoulder. "Ready?"

Stepping out of the sunlight and into the shade of the trees, Aeron asks slowly, "Can I tell you something?"

"Is there an option?"

A mock laugh follows, then, "No, seriously."

I cast a sidelong glance at him, noting his terse demeanor. "Aeron, you know you can tell me anything."

Aeron struggles to say something, but an unseen force hinders him. Finally he says, "I think I'm going to ask Satrie if she'll come to the clearing with us. Next weekend."

"Oh, Aeron, that's great. Why didn't you just come out and say that?"

He shrugs under the weight of his satchel. "It's just that, with what's going on between you and Lyam . . . I just didn't want to upset you."

I wave a hand, shooing off his nonsense. "Don't worry about that. This has nothing to do with Lyam and me. I'm really happy for you."

He peers at me from the corner of his eye, as if weighing my words against my expression. Seemingly pleased that the scales are balanced, he says, "Thank you. I really hope she'll come."

Suddenly Aeron's face is a window of trouble. "What? Do you think she'll say no?"

"No, no, of course not. Sorry. I was just . . . thinking."

We walk in quiet after that. But the quiet can be too loud sometimes.

Everything reminds me of Lyam.

The woods taunt me with his rustic, earthy scent. The brush of air against my cheek lingers like the touch of his hand, like the sweet whisper of "I love you" in my ear. The kiss of the sun prickles over my body, the body that will never be given to him.

I reorder my thoughts. "Beat you to the falls," I call out to Aeron, already ahead of him.

Aeron laughs out a hearty, "You wish."

I have no chance at winning. It's the rush of it that excites me. It's the grass folding beneath my feet. It's the wind tossing my hair. It's the breathlessness of my body giving me all it's got.

The Avalon Valley Series continues with

better shade

JENNIFER PARR set to work writing the Avalon Valley trilogy in 2010 after a long, sleepless night. She lives in California with her husband, four children, and an English bulldog named Zen. Jennifer is an avid reader of YA with an ever-growing TBR pile. Her favorite author is Maggie Stiefvater.

Connect with Jennifer Online:

Facebook:
https://www.facebook.com/Treacherous-Shadows-220739911322041/?fref=ts

Goodreads: Jennifer Parr

Wattpad: Author_JenniferParr

Instagram @Author_JenniferParr